Aventurine at Sea

Also by Anne Britting Oleson

The Springs

Aventurine and the Reckoning

Aventurine on the Bailgate

Aventurine on the Border

Aventurine at Sea

AN AVENTURINE MORROW THRILLER

Anne Britting Oleson

Encircle Publications
Farmington, Maine, U.S.A.

Aventurine at Sea Copyright © 2025 Anne Britting Oleson

Paperback ISBN-13: 978-1-64599-587-6
Hardcover ISBN-13: 978-1-64599-588-3
E-book ISBN-13: 9978-1-64599-589-0

This book is a work of fiction. All names, characters, places and events are either products of the author's imagination or are used fictitiously.

Encircle editor: Cynthia Brackett-Vincent

Cover and book design: Deirdre Wait

Author photo by Rosalie S. C. Bowman

Published by:

Encircle Publications
PO Box 187
Farmington, ME 04938

info@encirclepub.com
http://encirclepub.com

This book is for Ian,
my urban exploration partner,
who is always up for
research and small adventures.

Prologue

"Wait," Aventurine instructed the cab driver. *"Por favor, espere por mim."*

She climbed out slowly into the midday street, her gaze traveling upwards: behind one of those windows in the four-storied hotel, Micheline might be waiting. Despite the surprisingly warm air, Aventurine shivered. She was *this close* to her sister. She waited for a car to pass, then crossed the street to the steps and the door. There was a buzzer and a notice card in Portuguese above it, but the door was unlocked. She let herself in.

A man was being served at the desk, so Aventurine looked through the brochures next to a pair of chairs while she waited. Her Portuguese was even more abysmal than her Welsh, so she mainly looked at the pictures: museums, the Cathedral, the Tour de Belem. Jammed into the lower corner was a single brochure advertising a music festival, and she picked it up just as the woman behind the desk called to her in greeting.

Aventurine smiled. "I'm here for my sister? *Minha irmã?*"

She realized as soon as the woman frowned that there was a problem. In the receptionist's expression, there was no sign of recognition, nothing that indicated that she had seen a face identical to Aventurine's recently.

"You have a reservation?" the clerk asked.

"No," Aventurine stumbled. "But my sister is staying here. Micheline Genthner? *Minha irmã? Aqui?*"

Still the frown. The young woman pushed her dark hair away from her forehead and peered at the computer screen to her right. "Genthner?"

Aventurine took a deep breath. "Yes. Micheline Genthner."

The woman's lips twisted, and her eyes narrowed. She tapped a key or two, leaned forward toward the screen as though that might help. It apparently didn't. She sat back and shook her head. "No. No Genthner."

Aventurine's fingers fumbled with her purse. She drew out the picture of Micheline and slid it across the counter. "This woman?"

The clerk drew back as though Aventurine had set a scorpion between them. "*Polícia?*"

Quickly, Aventurine snatched up the photo and held it up to her own face. "No, no. Sister. *Irmã. Gêmea.*"

The woman pursed her lips, shook her head again, more vigorously this time. "No. Not here."

With a sigh, Aventurine thanked her and stepped toward the door. A dead end, obviously. The address from the package she had found in Genevieve's upstairs closet had been a false trail, a red herring. Something pointless. Then she stopped, and, pulling out the author photo from the back of Nicola's bodice ripper on impulse, tried again.

"My other sister?" she asked, holding it out. "Nicola Hallsey?"

But the receptionist held up both hands this time. "No. Not here. *Aqui não.*"

When Aventurine asked if there was a room available for herself, desperately realizing that to wait here was as good an idea as any, the woman continued to shake her head. Avi gave her one of her cards, adding her phone number in case Micheline should appear, knowing she'd hear nothing.

The cab was still idling in the street. Aventurine gave him the address of the hotel in which she actually had a reservation and slumped back. She had come all the way to Lisbon, to no avail. There were no other leads. She pulled out her phone and checked compulsively, but there was nothing. No contact from Micheline, from Paul or Lance, or from Genevieve. It was as though she were alone in the world: alone in the middle of the wide, cold ocean, with no land in sight. She was completely at sea.

In her hotel room, she tossed her bag onto the luggage rack in the corner, dropped her key and purse onto the dresser, and threw herself across the wide bed. Aventurine felt empty, discouraged. She closed her eyes against the pointless afternoon. She should just pack everything up and go back to Boston. Forget this summer and fall ever happened. If her sister was intent on not being found, maybe Aventurine should just return to her own life and let Micheline appear in her own time. Paul and Lance, too.

But to do what, once she was back in her overcrowded, book-strewn apartment? She threw her arm over her eyes. The story of Genevieve was unfinished, the threads dangling, catching. And that woman: to go home and leave her, an old woman by her own admission, when there was more to learn in order to write the definitive biography? What if she—? Now Aventurine swallowed hard. Old women died. Avi remembered the tide of preemptive grief that had washed over her as she knelt before the box in the guest room on Scarcroft Road. *Old women died.* She had not known Genevieve for long, but the thought of a world without her was still enormously painful. She was mad as hell at Genevieve, but to end up with that anger unresolved, should she return to the US, and should the old woman die—it was too much to bear.

Slowly, she rolled over and sat up. She'd reserved the hotel room for a week. It was warmer in Lisbon than it would be in Back Bay, and there was more sun; the beach was just down the street. She might as well stay; it made as much sense as to go. There was nothing holding her anywhere: no Micheline, Paul, Lance, Genevieve, Shep—or even Dominic Burroughs. At that thought, she laughed roughly. There was nothing between them, except a hesitant sort of friendship that he had rejected, out on East Pier, because *he couldn't trust her.* Fine, then. She was better off without him in her life. Still, it stung. A little.

Aventurine rubbed her face with her hands and reached for her purse: there was still a packet of Panadol in there, and she was starting to get a headache. When she unzipped the front pocket, though, she found the brochure she'd picked up in the other hotel: the one for the music festival. Idly, after swallowing the pills dry, she unfolded the crumpled pages and glanced over the garish paper, trying to decode the Portuguese. When she flipped to the inside, the name, in bold yellow, caught her attention.

Mobius.

Now. There was a group of people who had yet to reject her. There were some friends. The thought of Linny's grinning, freckled face made her smile.

She flicked on the bedside lamp and studied the brochure in earnest. She drew out her computer, and, putting in the Wi-Fi password she'd gleaned from the desk, went to the festival's website. She opted to click on the tab for *ingles,* impatient with herself. The entire weekend schedule was available there, a list of indoor venues. Mobius was scheduled on Friday night, as well as on Saturday evening, early. There was a button for the purchase of weekend tickets, so she quickly entered her credit card information and had the passes sent to her phone. Then she opened Google Maps and, tapping in the festival address, tried to figure out the best way to get to the site. The weekend was coming. She could at least do this much.

<u>*Part I:*</u>

Low Tide

One

She followed the sound of the singing.

The familiar voice made Avi flush with unadulterated pleasure. Here would be someone who was not entangled in the mess her recent life had become, someone whom she didn't have to view with suspicion. Someone with whom she didn't have to pretend. Listening to the bouncing lines from "Mr. Blue Sky," Aventurine found herself smiling, and her step quickened toward the open door of the artists' entrance.

Habit had made her decide on the black jeans and the black Mobius tee-shirt; now she walked purposely down the alley toward the door, hoping the volunteers in their Day-Glo yellow would simply take her for another member of the road crew and not demand her all-festival pass. It seemed to work because, with the exception of one puzzled frown and a bit of a double-take, neither woman moved to stop her.

Aventurine hitched her pack further up onto her shoulder and made her way through the dim backstage area toward the sound of Linny Breedlove's voice. The band members were seated in a large room at the end of the hallway, not far from the door to the stage wings. As she entered, Linny glanced up and smiled, continuing her song, while the others merely nodded. Comforting, in its normality, but somehow somewhat of a let-down as well.

Ruth, their irascible manager, appeared at the door behind her.

"There you are," she said. Impatiently, but Ruth was always impatient. "Did you manage to find Isabel?"

Aventurine turned. "Who the hell is Isabel?"

"God, Aventurine, what is wrong with you today? You've been missing for half an hour, and you haven't managed to find her? Did you look in the office?" Ruth crossed her arms and glared from under her backwards cap.

"Maybe she had other things to think about." Brian sidled up, grinning wolfishly, and rested a possessive arm around Avi's shoulders.

Aventurine stepped away quickly. "Shut it, Brian."

There was a long, awkward pause. Peter Breedlove took a step forward.

Slowly, Linny set aside her fiddle and crossed the few steps toward her, examining her face with a frown.

"Aventurine?" she asked, her voice barely above a whisper.

The import of the question slowly dawned on Avi. "Yes," she said.

"The real you."

"The real me."

Linny opened her mouth, then snapped it shut again. Surprise, shock, and dismay flitted over her wide, freckled face. "Christ on a cracker, Avi," she breathed. Her eyes darted to the door and the dim hallway beyond, and then back, as though she were seeing a ghost. *Or a doppelganger.* Her gaze searched Aventurine's face again, in disbelief. "Then who the hell was that?"

To her right, Brian had his hands on his hips, a thunderous glare on his face. "What the hell is going on, Avi? What's with the cold shoulder? After last night?"

"Shut it, Brian," Linny hissed, still studying Avi's face. "No," she said at last. "She was younger. She looked less tired."

Aventurine ran a hand over her cheeks, then looked around at the others. *Younger.* Her heart had leapt, but now it sank. "I think," she said slowly, "that you've all met my half-sister. Nicola."

The pause stretched.

"We thought she was you," Alan said at last, standing.

"I thought she was you." Brian's confusion would have been funny, had it not been so—cringeworthy.

Aventurine looked around at her friends. Peter held a guitar slackly in his hand, as though he'd forgotten it. Only Ruth managed not to look confused, but Ruth only ever looked impatient. "Now *I've* got to go find Isabel," she spat, and whirled away.

"You'd better tell me about it," Aventurine said.

"You'd better come sit down." Linny's mouth was pursed now. "This might take a while."

That explained why the two women at the rear entrance had evinced so little interest in her, Aventurine realized in dismay: they'd seen her before. They'd seen *Nicola* before—and what the hell was she doing?—and had assumed Avi was her. She took the bottle Alan handed her and then traded it for the mug of tea Linny provided instead.

"We need to keep a clear head for this, I think." Linny glared at Brian. "Even you. Especially you—you're probably hung over anyway."

Brian threw up his hands. "Hey, I didn't drink very much last night at all. I was too busy." He still stared at Aventurine, tipping his head much as a puzzled mutt might.

"I didn't know you had a half-sister," Peter said, resting his chin in the curve of his guitar body, his cheek against the fretboard. "I knew you had a twin—"

Linny waved him to silence, frowning. "But this person was a bit younger. You can see it now, can't you? Now the real Avi is here with us." She patted Aventurine on the arm. "Not that you look old or anything." She returned her glare to Brian. "And we all know that the *real* Aventurine would never sleep with you."

This, at least, was true.

"Did she ever actually say she was me?" Aventurine asked. "Did she ever actually call herself by my name?"

Peter ran his fingers absently over the frets. "Now that I think of it, not really. We just called her by your name, and she answered. We asked her to do things, and she did them."

Ruth reappeared, holding several rolls of gaffer tape and with a black cord coiled over her shoulder. She made a face. "She needed a lot of explanation, that one, about stuff she should have known. I just figured you'd become a flaming idiot on me." She poked a finger at Avi. "Everyone else here already has."

Aventurine flipped her off, but it was rote; her heart really wasn't in the teasing. She took a sip from the mug of tea, finding it black and bitter, and reassuring. Linny always remembered.

"But why?" Alan asked. He dragged an empty silver keg forward and settled on it. It rocked slightly beneath him. "Why would your sister play a trick like that on us?" He leaned forward. "Did you put her up to it?"

"Don't be an ass, Alan. Of course she didn't." Linny's defense, as always, was stout. She shoved her brother lightly.

Aventurine shook her head, taking another sip of tea. "I don't really know why she'd be doing this." She let her gaze travel around this group, these people she'd known for years, perhaps some of the people she trusted most in her life. "Look. I've only known of her existence for a little while, and it came as a shock, if you must know. And—" she made a face—"I really don't trust her."

"Why not?"

"Because she pulls stuff like this." Aventurine shrugged. "But I never have trusted her, even before this. She's secretive. It seems somehow as though she's trying to live my life, do the things I do, insinuate herself into my relationships."

"Your relationships?"

Brian looked stricken. And then enraged. He grabbed a bottle of Sagres and looked around for an opener, his expression darker than the beer.

Aventurine shrugged again, not wanting to broach the subject of Gio Constantine. Instead, she undid the zipper of her pack and took out the copy of *Passion in Portugal*, which she handed to Linny. For her part, the other woman widened her eyes at the cover, with its Fabio-wannabe, and flipped the book over to look at the all-too-familiar author photo. Peter leaned forward to peer over her shoulder, then let out a whistle.

"She writes books?" Alan asked.

"Yes. *Not* the same kind I do."

Brian took the book as it was handed around. He flipped randomly to a page and scanned it, then leaned in more closely, his mouth a surprised 'o.' With everyone's eyes on him, he slapped the book shut quickly, his face reddening to his ears. "I think—she must do—different research."

They all laughed, though the laughter was a bit sharp-edged.

"Obviously *not* the same kind I do," Aventurine agreed.

"Maybe she'll name you in the acknowledgments of her next book, Brian." Ruth's laugh was a bit mean. She swung the cord at Aventurine. "Meanwhile, we've got work to do here. Out on the stage."

Brian threw aside the book and took a long drink from his bottle. Avi took the proffered cord and followed Ruth out into the corridor, where they turned left. After strumming a chord absently, Peter set his guitar aside to join them. He seemed to be trying to formulate his thoughts. "I don't think I'd trust anyone, even my sister, who tried to pass herself off as me. But I can't imagine what she's trying to gain from it."

"I haven't a clue." Aventurine shook her head, wishing she hadn't abandoned the tea mug in the green room. "But I will tell you it's pissing the hell out of me."

At the stage door, Ruth paused, a toothpick in the corner of her mouth much as she would have had a cigarette, had this not been a non-smoking area. "You might ask her," she ground out, jerking her chin towards the front of the stage.

Aventurine pushed past Ruth quickly. Wearing all black as she was, and with her hands jammed into her jeans pockets, Nicola was even now talking to another man in a day-glow vest. She tipped her head back, laughing, and her gold hair swung in the light. Then she lifted a hand and sauntered toward the stage door.

Aventurine froze, fury squeezing her chest.

"Nicola."

The other woman's head shot up. She paused for only a moment before turning on her heel.

"Nicola!" Aventurine shouted again, starting after her. She heard someone call her name from the stage door.

Now Nicola was running, dodging a surprised couple of women with a harmonium, tipping a few chairs to try to trip Aventurine up in her pursuit. She pushed out into the lobby, and by the time Avi, with Linny and Alan behind her, reached it, Nicola had disappeared into the milling crowds in the street.

Two

Mobius took the stage at eight-thirty. Hoping that keeping busy might help stop her shaking—and why was she shaking?—Aventurine helped with the set-up during the dinner break, falling into the same old groove of wiring, taping, checking. Handing Peter first a guitar, then a bouzouki, then a banjo, as he checked levels on each. All the while, she kept an eye on the doors, but the ebb and flow was small, only people in suits or vests who crossed purposefully from one door to another. Chairs scraped; the bar opened. All the time, she kept thinking: Nicola was out there somewhere, with an agenda known only to herself. She'd gone to ground, but that didn't mean she wouldn't be lurking somewhere along the edges of the crowd once the doors opened, once there was more cover, more people amongst whom to hide.

No. Aventurine didn't trust Nicola. Now less than ever, with her half-sister first impersonating her, and then fleeing when caught out. Had it just been a joke, or a game, Nicola would have braved it out, or laughed it off, upon being discovered. *Oh, you caught me!* She was up to something, and had no interest in answering any mundane questions Aventurine might have, like: *What the hell are you doing here? Why do you keep turning up like this? What is it that you want?*

Avi taped a copy of the playlist to the stage in front of Alan's mic stand, and straightened, stretching out her back. The doors had opened. One last look out over the growing audience—the first act was on at seven—and she caught Lance's eye.

He and Paul both leaned against the rail, Paul with a near-empty plastic cup in his hand. She moved toward them slowly; she didn't know whether Paul had noticed her up on stage. She felt rather like a cat, stalking the mice.

"Aventurine," Lance greeted her warily. She had last seen him in Norfolk Gardens, when he'd kissed her cheek and run off toward Paddington and Paul.

"Lance," she said. "Paul." She made no move to touch either of them; she couldn't decide whether she wanted to hug them or throttle them. She kept her hands in her pockets. "It's good to see you both." She hated herself for the formality, hated the situation that dictated it.

Paul turned slowly and leaned over the rail to set the cup on the shelf on her side of the barrier. "Avi." His voice was cool, but tense. His glance took in her black clothing. "You working?"

She shrugged. "Helping out. Keeps me busy."

Paul nodded. "I was hoping I might run into your friend. Peter? Talk to him some more about playing."

"I'll take you back around after the show. I'm sure he'd love to talk to you." The noise of the crowd was swelling as the concierge took the stage behind them. She glanced over her shoulder and then at her; it was nearly showtime. "Listen, can I get you two another drink? I know you can't get out without losing your spot."

"That would be awesome," Lance said quickly, before Paul could have a chance to turn her down. He dug in his pocket for his wallet, but she waved his money away.

"This one's on me," she said. She wondered, not for the first time, where Lance's money came from—he hadn't, to the best of her knowledge, worked since the end of the summer, when they'd come across him in an Italian restaurant in Southampton. Perhaps he had savings? Paul, because of his father, had no money worries whatsoever.

"Thanks, Avi," Lance said.

"Hey," Paul said as she turned away; Aventurine turned back quickly. "That sister—half-sister. Nicola. Is she here with you, too?"

"You've seen her?" Avi's intake of breath was sharp.

The two glanced between them. "Earlier," Paul said. "In the street. She was wearing black, too, so I wondered."

Aventurine looked around the crowd warily and then leaned in close as the concierge's voice boomed over the sound system. There was a high squeal, and the requisite groan from the audience. "She's here," she said. "Be careful of her."

"Duas cervejas e uma agua, por favor," she ordered, then gathered the cups and bottle to herself, to edge her way back out onto the crowded floor. A full house, she estimated, though there was no way of knowing how many had come for Mobius, or for the headline act which followed. Again she scanned, looking for the form, the blonde hair, the skulking in the shadows. A movement in the dimness to her left, and she paused, unsuccessfully trying to make out anything beyond the milling audience. It didn't help, did it, that Nicola was wearing black clothing; throw a cap over that hair, and she could easily blend into the shadows. Hell, she could have followed Aventurine to the bar and never have been noticed.

Paul and Lance had seen Nicola, though. Seen, but had not spoken to. Right? Or perhaps Aventurine had just assumed that. She needed to talk to them further, find out what they had seen. What they had done. Had Nicola seen them? The sense that Nicola had got to Paul in London rushed back in on her, the sense that she had fed his suspicions about Avi and Shep.

Before that, they had seen each other in Milan.

Avi slipped along between the crowd and the wall, holding the drinks protectively. No, that wasn't right, was it? Lance had seen Nicola. Paul had not. But had Nicola seen them? She had not overtly made her presence known to them. Why not? Maybe, just maybe,

Nicola had not known which of the two was family. Or maybe she hadn't seen them at all; maybe her being in Milan was entirely coincidence; maybe her passing the same cafe in which Paul and Lance were sitting was just luck. Coincidences happened, didn't they?

There are no coincidences. Genevieve had impressed that upon Aventurine, and now she heard the words in the old spy's voice. Avi didn't believe that Nicola had accidentally shown up in the same street in the same Italian city where her half-sister's son had gone to escape his demons. The more Aventurine thought about it, the more certain she became that Nicola had gone to Milan intentionally, had followed Lance and Paul. But for what reason?

And now she was here, at the Festival do Fim da Estrada. *For what reason?*

It was enough to make a person look over her shoulder. *Keep looking* over her shoulder.

Except. It wasn't about Aventurine, was it? Possibly not about Micheline, either. Nicola had been in Milan when Paul and Lance were in Milan. Now she was here outside of Oeiras, when Paul and Lance were here. Nicola had—hadn't she?—got to Paul in London.

Paul and Lance were the common denominator. Avi pulled gently at the thread of her thoughts, knowing that at the end would be something she did not wish to consider. But had to.

Nicola wanted something with Aventurine's nephew and his friend.

Aventurine found herself hurrying back toward the barrier, sloshing the beers, and not particularly caring.

Three

Ruth had retreated to the rental van with snarled imprecations and an unlit cigarette dangling from her lips; Brian, sulking, had wandered off in search of a drink. The rest of them, Peter carrying a guitar—when was he ever without one?—followed the alley along to the busy crossing, then through a tunnel down to the darkened *praia.* The music faded behind them, and the stars overhead grew brighter. At mid-tide, they could hear the wash of the waves on the sand; far out in the Tagus, a cargo ship of some sort eased by, a silhouette marked by red and green lights. They passed very few people; one group of seven or eight were drinking around a firepit they had dug out.

"Good idea," Alan said.

"Illegal," Peter said. "Keep walking. The last thing we need is to bail you out in Portugal."

Further along, though, they found a pair of water-bleached logs. Peter handed the guitar off to his wife, and then he, Lance, and Paul dragged the logs around to face each other. Bottles appeared from packs and pockets. Aventurine stuck stubbornly to her water.

Now Paul had the guitar cradled in his arms and was quietly strumming. After a moment, Avi realized that Peter was leaning close to her nephew and humming. Paul's frown gradually eased away and was replaced by a look of intense concentration.

"Let it go, lad," Peter murmured, so low that Avi had difficulty hearing him. "Don't think it. Feel it in your hands."

Paul took a breath and bent to the frets again.

On the other side of her, Lance was looking on with an expression so unguarded that it took her breath away. It made her envious, made her wish that there was someone, out there, who would look upon her like that. It was the same way Shep had always looked upon Micheline, from the very first time Avi had seen them together. The same way her father had looked upon her mother. She bit her lip.

"Lance," she said swiftly. "Come talk to me."

Reluctantly he tore himself away from the music lesson and clambered to his feet in the sand. Aventurine walked down to the water's edge, and he followed. When she turned, the others formed a sort of idyllic tableau, shadowy forms against the moving lights of Oeiras above the beach. She pulled out her phone quickly and snapped a picture; she wanted to remember this moment—and if it turned out well, Mobius could use it for an album cover. She smirked.

"What is it?" Lance, too, turned to look back up the sand, but his eyes, she could tell, were searching out Paul.

"Do you love him?"

She hadn't meant to ask that question. Embarrassed, she tucked the phone back into her pocket. Then she busied herself, kicking off her sand-filled sneakers, and taking a few steps to allow the tide to wash around her ankles. The water was cold, but not as cold as the North Sea. And she hadn't been hurled in bodily.

"Yes." In the darkness, only his eyes showed, glittering in his face. "I didn't intend to. But I do. Yes." He turned a fleeting smile upon her, one of ineffable sweetness. "I want to be near him all the time. I want to comfort him. I want to protect him." His gaze returned to the group on the logs.

Aventurine laid a hand on his arm, then quickly pulled it back again. "That's it, isn't it? What we want for those we love."

Lance nodded. "You want that for him, too. I know. And you want it for Micheline."

His understanding made her choke up for a moment.

"And for you, too," she offered.

This time his smile was slow. "That means a lot," he said.

They stood silently for a moment as the waves washed around their feet. The tide was coming in, the cold water making her ankles ache. Finally Aventurine drew in a deep breath. "About wanting to protect Paul—" she began.

Lance turned expectantly. "Yes?"

"Nicola is here. You know that. You've seen her."

The air between them changed immediately.

"I have."

Avi nodded. "When you're at the festival—I need you two to be careful. I meant what I said before. I don't trust her. Now, even less than before. I think she could be—dangerous." She took a hurried drink from her water bottle and sputtered when it went down the wrong way.

"Isn't that—sort of—melodramatic?"

Aventurine capped the bottle and jammed it into her back pocket. "Don't blow me off on this, Lance. Listen. Please."

He held up his hands.

A couple passed, holding hands, their hair shimmering in the dimness. Aventurine waited until they had moved further along the beach.

"I don't believe in coincidence. Genevieve taught me that much. Nicola followed you to Milan. She followed you back to London." Avi paused, frowning: something was wrong with that timeline, something that niggled at the back of her mind. She pushed on despite it. "Now she's followed you two to Lisbon. I don't know what she wants. I don't know what she's doing. But she's got some sort of agenda, and I can't help worrying. Has she tried to contact you? Or Paul?"

Again with the defensive hands. "Can't she just want to know more about us? If she's discovered Paul—and you two—are family?"

"Then she'd speak to us, wouldn't she? Ask questions. And has she?"

Lance shook his head, backing down. "I've never spoken to her, not before this, not here, either. Maybe she just likes music."

"And art, and Italy. No, the common denominator is you. We know she's Mick's and my half-sister. We know the man I was introduced to as her father *isn't* her father, but that Mick's and my father *is.*"

"The DNA test. I'm following you. But why does she have to have an ulterior motive? Why can't she just be a woman in shock, as you are a woman in shock, at finding out something she didn't know about her own life?"

Aventurine found her frustration rising. Why couldn't Lance see? Why did he insist on being so damned rational? "Because she came to this festival, and almost immediately began to impersonate me with my friends who didn't know any better."

Lance stilled. His eyes widened, glinting in the dark. He waved a hand over his shoulder toward the others. "Those friends."

"Those friends. They didn't know about Nicola, and when she showed up—presumably looking for you—they assumed she was me. Only their manager was vaguely suspicious, because Nicola didn't know anything about stage set-up. But people see what they expect to see."

"But—"

"You saw her in Milan, Lance. You immediately contacted me—*because you thought it was me.*"

"Or Micheline," he protested.

Aventurine dug in the sand with her toe in her frustration. "But the point is that she's here. There's no reason for her to be here at all, unless it has to do with us. Unless it has to do with you."

This time, Lance had nothing to offer.

Aventurine grabbed both his arms. "Lance, you've got to make sure that you and Paul avoid her at any cost. If she approaches you, anything. Until we know for sure what she's up to." When he didn't immediately respond, she shook him, a tiny bit. "Please. Promise me."

Lance let out an enormous breath. "Okay. I'll try. Because you feel so strongly about it." He crossed his arms over his chest, covering her hands with his own. "But I don't know what we should do *if* she approaches. Run? Call you?"

"I don't know." Aventurine dropped her hands. The ache, in her ankles, from the water, was growing to be too much, and she took a few steps up the sand to collect her Chucks. "I really don't know. Try not to be alone with her? Make sure there's always someone close by? A witness?" She opted not to put her sneakers back on, but tipped the sand out of them, and attempted, futilely, to brush the sand off her feet. "We'll try to figure out what she's after, and we'll try to counteract it. I'm not sure how, though."

"Ask Genevieve?" Lance suggested. He gathered up his own huaraches and clapped them together.

Aventurine licked her lips.

"Lance," she said slowly. "Genevieve's disappeared."

This staggered him.

"When? How?"

Swiftly Aventurine told Lance about the afternoon on Scarcroft Road, when she had found the old woman so strangely listless. When she had found Nicola's book in a box in the upstairs closet, addressed to Micheline in Genevieve's distinctive handwriting.

"I just saw her," he protested, then looked up guiltily.

"When?"

"A week ago. Tuesday."

Aventurine did a hurried calculation. Three days after the old spy had disappeared from the house, leaving the French door open to the storm. Aventurine had watched the house carefully for a couple of days, looking for any sign of her return: lights on, Else letting herself in and out, and movement. There had been nothing. On the Monday morning she'd returned to London and booked herself a flight to Lisbon to look for Micheline.

"Where did you see her?"

"At the house. In York." Lance shifted uneasily. "She called me, asked me to come. To help her with a—medical problem."

Aventurine spun back to him, her heart suddenly expanding in her chest and making breathing difficult. "Medical problem?" Specters of grave illnesses arose before her eyes: cancer in all its forms. Dementia. Congestive heart failure. Things that women in their nineties were subject to. *I'm an old woman, Aventurine.*

"She had broken her wrist."

Aventurine didn't know whether to be relieved or further distressed. "How did she do that?"

"She told her GP that she had fallen." There was something evasive in his tone, in his words.

Distressed. Old women fell; even now, when Aventurine herself went to the doctor for her yearly check-up, the medical assistant always asked if she'd had any recent falls, and she was nowhere near ninety-four.

"She *said* she had fallen. And had she?"

Again the uncomfortable shift. "I—am not really sure."

Of course he wasn't. Probably Genevieve had been pulling another one of her Mary Wentworth capers, breaking into cathedrals, breaking into houses like she had broken into Nicola's, into Henry Hallsey's.

Genevieve had disappeared for several days, had outwitted Aventurine's surveillance, and had returned home with a broken wrist and a need for Lance.

"She suggested Paul and I visit another music festival, to get our minds off things."

Of course she had.

"She wouldn't have suggested this one, would she have? '*Oh, why don't you just go to the* Festival do Fim da Estrada?' In that all-too-innocent voice she uses when she's trying to manipulate people? Maybe she gave you a brochure or something?"

Lance had the grace to look abashed. "Well—"

"So, yes, she did." Aventurine threw up her hands. "For God's sake, Lance, don't you have the sense to know when you're being manipulated? Moved around like a pawn on the chessboard?"

Lance put his hands on his hips. In the dimness, his expression seemed harder, as though she had hit a nerve. "I like to think I'm not that cynical, Aventurine. I like to think I trust people."

Not like you.

Though he didn't say the words, they stung anyway.

Cynical.

She hadn't always been this way. Had she? Neil's theft and betrayal, all those years ago—that was enough to make anyone inherently distrustful, but she thought she'd worked her way past that. She'd thought.

Until she'd met Genevieve.

Until she'd become Mary Wentworth.

We're all Mary Wentworth.

Aventurine laughed bitterly, following Lance back up the *praia* to the others.

"Where are you staying?" Aventurine asked Paul as she stood up and stretched some hours later. Somewhere to the east the sky was turning to a strange grey that hinted at the coming dawn, and her water bottle had been empty for some time.

"We're in a hotel on the Rua do Garué," Paul said. He too yawned; he had long since abandoned the guitar to Peter, who still strummed gently. The air was cold just before daybreak, and Paul had one hand tucked into the pocket of his hoodie, and the other in Lance's.

"Call me around noontime," she suggested. "We can do coffee. Or breakfast. Or lunch. Something."

He nodded and clambered to his feet from his seat on the log. Then, hesitantly, he put his arms around her. The hug was brief, but it was an embrace. He stepped back. "I'll do that."

Aventurine wanted to tell him she loved him—there had been a time, ages past, when she would do just that before leaving him. Automatically. She wondered whether those days would ever return.

Four

Aventurine took her time crossing the Avenue Marginal. She was early to meet Paul and Lance at the brunch restaurant they had suggested, down at the water. She had not slept well, dreaming again of her father.

No car crashes this time. The dream itself was timeless, and for the most part, only made up of wispy impressions. Her father's hands, clumsily combing the sleep-tangles out of her hair while her mother tended to Micheline. Those same hands, tying her shoes in the time before she'd pull away impatiently to do it herself. Daniel Morrow holding her first published article, looking down on the college newspaper with an expression so proud she thought she might cry.

Kind hands. Her father had been a kind man, in all her memories gentle but firm. He had been the sort of person who gave spontaneous compliments, rested his hand on their heads, on their hands, as he passed—as though to remind them both that, no matter the business at hand, he was still present. Still thinking of them.

It was so difficult, sometimes—this late autumn day in a strange city, for example—to imagine the world without him in it. Somewhere. Without either of their parents in it. But she would not allow those thoughts to intrude on this morning. Not of her parents' end. Rather, Aventurine forced herself to consider the look of those hands, so smooth and soft, long-fingered, the hands of an academic.

The touch of those hands. She wished for a moment that she could hold his hand for safety, while she crossed the street.

A woman's voice, calling, made her look up swiftly. A mother, calling some sort of warning or instruction to a small boy who had strayed too far away on the sidewalk. In brisk Portuguese, of course, so Aventurine could only guess at the words.

They spoke Portuguese in Brazil.

Aventurine slowed. The brunch restaurant was close, and she could see that neither Paul nor Lance were outside—perhaps they'd gone in to find a table? She checked her watch. Still early.

Her parents had had smatterings of all sorts of languages, from their travels for Daniel Morrow's research. Her parents had been able, she remembered, to speak just well enough to travel in Brazil, where they had driven to their deaths off the Rodovia da Morte, the road of death. Where Shep Genthner had had to travel to make arrangements to bring their bodies home for burial.

Had Shep known any Portuguese? Of course, he could have hired a guide, or a translator—he had the wherewithal. He could have drawn on the resources of his multinational employer. Or he could have just presented himself to the proper authorities and said the magic words: *Daniel and Michele Morrow. Rodovia da Morte.*

Aventurine shivered. It had been twenty-odd years ago. Still, it had been difficult to wake up one morning and realize she was an orphan. She and Micheline were all that was left.

Now, Nicola.

Who had laid hands on Nicola's head, on her hands, when she was a child?

Aventurine wished she could speak to her father. She had so many questions.

She was nearly finished with her first coffee and the *pastel de nata* she had ordered when Paul and Lance appeared, looking a bit worse for wear. Outside the window overlooking the *praia*, the wind on the tide seemed to have died down, and the sun was working its way out from behind the clouds. It would be another fine day for heading over to the festival.

The waiter appeared, and Lance and Paul stumbled through their order: *salada frango* for both of them. Then Lance excused himself for a moment, with a quick look at Avi.

"Lance told me," Paul said without preamble. His eyes, she had noticed when he'd shifted his sunglasses to the top of his head, were hooded, with deep circles beneath them. He narrowed his eyes, even though the morning light, in the cafe, was muted. Slanted. "About Genevieve. Disappearing. Everything."

Aventurine made a face, and looked down at her hands, spread on the rough-hewn table before her. They did not, to the best of her knowledge, look like her father's hands from the dream. Not long-fingered enough. Not delicate enough. More square, more built for heavy lifting.

"So you know Genevieve was trying to get you two here," she said.

"And succeeded." Still squinting, Paul looked off toward the water. "And Mom, I guess. Where is she? I feel like a pawn. Like you said to Lance. Moved around in some weird game of chess. But I don't know why I should be, Avi. And I don't see the end game. And that book Genevieve let you find implies that she's moved Mom to Lisbon as well. Somewhere." He turned back to her. "Did you go to the address on the box? No, of course you did."

"And your mother wasn't there. They hadn't seen her, didn't recognize her picture, didn't have her name in the register."

Lance returned, and a moment later, the waiter appeared with a tray laden with their breakfast and coffee. Paul lifted his napkin and shook it out, then stared at it as though he'd never seen anything like it before in his life.

"*Obrigada,*" Avi murmured. The waiter smiled and disappeared.

She sipped at her second coffee, served in a cup as wide as a soup bowl. Too hot. She wished she'd thought to order another *pastel de nata.*

"The thing I can't get over," Aventurine said slowly, setting the coffee aside, "is that she disappeared. Genevieve. Just did a flit out the window into the rain. And *I watched the house.* For three days. I don't think she came back."

"Until the fourth day," Lance agreed, spearing up a bit of mango with his fork. He chewed thoughtfully, but Aventurine noticed he did not look up at her.

"So she knew you were watching for her," Paul added. With the frown lines between his eyes, he definitely looked like his father. "She was watching you, watching her."

"Too much of a coincidence otherwise," Avi said. "And we all know that Genevieve does not believe in coincidence." She sighed. "After all this time with her—especially after the Mary Wentworth episode in Lincoln—I don't believe in coincidence, either." She narrowed her eyes at Lance. *Cynical.*

"She got us here," Lance said. "How'd she get you here?"

Aventurine shook her head. "It was easy, for the master manipulator. Like you said, she left that book in her upstairs closet. Addressed to Micheline. To a hotel here, in Lisbon. And let me find it, looking for you two in her house."

Lance nodded. "Yes. She certainly knew that would get you to Lisbon." His slight smile at her was sympathetic, and again Aventurine was struck by how much he understood: not just Paul, but her as well. And, the cynical comment notwithstanding, how little he seemed to judge.

Avi made a wry face. "It worked. You're right, she knew it would. After she disappeared, and looked as though she wasn't coming back, I had no other lead than that address. No idea what to do. So of course I came here." She shook her head. "It rankles. That I was watching for her, and all the time, she was spying on me. And I didn't peg that at all."

"She's a professional, Avi," Paul reminded her.

"And she was out in the cold." Her voice was bitter. *What the hell are you doing, Genevieve?*

Lance wiped the last of his lettuce around the dressing on his plate and ate it. He set his fork aside and wiped his lips with his napkin. "So. The book in the closet. The address. Where was it again?"

Aventurine fumbled in her pocket for her phone and then pulled up the photos. Scrolling through them with her thumb, she found the one she had taken from the box.

Micheline Genthner
Rua Vasco Da Gama Nr 13
Lisbon, Portugal 2685-244.

She held the phone out. The other two leaned forward across the table.

"And you said you went," Paul said.

Lance lay a hand on his arm. "Of course she went," he said. "And found out—what?"

"It's a hotel. They hadn't heard of her. There was no record of a reservation in her name." Aventurine pressed her hands to eyes, reliving the disappointment. To have had her hopes raised—that she was so close to finding Micheline—and to have them dashed so abruptly again. "No Genthners of any kind."

"What then?"

Avi shrugged. "I gave them one of my cards and asked them to call me should Mick turn up. So far, nothing."

"Maybe—" Lance frowned, as though trying to form his thoughts into something coherent. "Maybe we should go back?"

"I don't know what the point is. I asked them to call. They haven't called." The helplessness washed over Aventurine. She pushed her hair from her forehead with both hands. Her headache was dull behind her eyes.

Paul pushed the remains of his salad in her direction. She looked down at it in distaste and slid it back. He offered it wordlessly to Lance, who speared a piece of mango.

"Let's go back," he said. "Maybe they got busy. Maybe Mom's there now."

Aventurine drained her second coffee and got stiffly to her feet. "All right." It was worth a chance. Anything at this point was worth a chance.

They paid up and headed for the train station.

"*Desculpe,* I'm sorry," the woman at the desk said, as they entered from the street, holding up her hands as though to ward them off. "Full. No rooms." She tucked a strand of reddish hair behind her ear and pushed her silver-framed glasses back along the bridge of her nose. She seemed genuinely sorry to have to turn them away, unlike the young woman from Avi's first visit.

"I was here before," Aventurine said, approaching. "Someone else was at the desk?"

"Ah. Christiana. *Sim.*"

"I was looking for my sister. Her name is Genthner. Micheline Genthner. She hadn't—arrived yet."

The woman frowned.

"She's my mother," Paul added, smiling in a way that made the woman blush. "She said to meet her here to go for a drink." He leaned forward, resting both arms against the desk. "She told me to have you call up to her room when we got here?"

Again, her hand went to her hair. The woman smiled, and she, too, leaned forward. The logical flaw in Paul's request was nearly visible as it passed her by.

"Genthner?" She tapped the keyboard to her right and leaned forward to peer at the screen. The frown returned. "No one by that name here."

Quickly, Aventurine searched in her bag to draw out the photo of her twin. She held it out over the desk. "Perhaps she's using her maiden name."

"*Com licença?* Maiden name?"

Paul indicated the photo, which the woman had yet to look at. "My mother. Have you seen her?"

Now the desk clerk finally looked at the photo. Then she looked up into Aventurine's face, puzzled.

"We're twins," Avi said. *"Gêmeas."*

The clerk nodded.

"Have you seen her yet?" Paul prodded, turning up the wattage of his smile. *Where had he learned to do that?*

The woman's face fell back into the frown, which might have been her normal expression. *"Sim.* But not Genthner." She glanced again at the computer screen. "Morrow. Aventurine Morrow." She looked even further confused.

Aventurine froze.

She and Micheline had traded places before. Slowly Avi commanded her lungs to breathe, her expression to remain neutral.

"Could you call her room and let her know we're here?" Paul asked.

But the desk clerk shook her head. *"Não. Desculpe.* She has gone out. Festival?" Her mobile face now became tragic, again, as though she were desperately sorry to have to deliver bad news. Especially to a handsome young man who was smiling at her as Paul was.

He threw up his hands and laughed. "Well, I guess we'll have to find her there." He winked. "Thank you. *Obrigado."*

They withdrew into Rua Vasco da Gama.

Five

"It's early. The big names won't be on yet." Paul looked at his watch, and somewhere a bell rang in a church tower. Another answered.

"Let's go to the Sé," Aventurine suggested, waving toward the top of the hill. "Kill some time."

"Sightseeing?" Paul scoffed. He'd left off his mad smile as soon as they'd hit the pavement, and quite frankly, it was a relief.

"I was talking to Genevieve about patience," Lance said slowly. He had taken out his phone, and now was looking up directions to the Cathedral. "Last night."

Aventurine's jaw dropped. "You talked—to Genevieve—last night."

"She told me we should do some touristy stuff," he continued, as though she hadn't spoken.

"What, to take our minds off Mom and Dad?" Paul demanded.

"On the contrary. We were talking about where I imagined your mother might go if she were trying to imagine where your father might go."

Paul grimaced. "Genevieve always thinks in the most convoluted ways."

"No. She sees big pictures. She sees the whole forest when we only see the trees in our flashlight beam."

Aventurine's headache was growing; either she needed another coffee, or she'd had far too much already. "You were talking to Genevieve last night," she repeated. She felt one step behind the game, whatever one it was they were playing now.

Lance shuffled his feet on the cobblestones. "I had to check. You had me worried with your talk of her disappearing."

"And she answered you." Of course, when Avi tried, the old woman had left her on read. She sighed. "It was ever so much easier when there were books to follow around. Now we're here, and there are no leads at all."

"So we might as well go to the Sé, then," Paul said. "*If* we imagine Mom imagining where Dad would go."

If *Shep were alive.* But Avi didn't add that.

Lance indicated the uphill route. "And we'll look harmless."

To Aventurine, the Sé appeared somewhat subdued after the soaring grandeur of Lincoln Cathedral, but she was grateful that it did not have the emotional reverberations for her. The three wandered along the nave, peering into the radiant chapels off the deambulatory. The inside was cold, the air a bit clammy, but Aventurine wondered whether that was simply her nerves. Footsteps echoed, though voices were hushed, sound both swallowed and amplified in the vast space.

What if they found what they wanted in here? she wondered, and bit her lip, jamming her cold fingers into her jacket pockets. What if they found Micheline? What if—and this was a further stretch, but at this point nearly anything seemed possible—what if they found Shep? Even Genevieve was willing to entertain the idea that Shep was still alive, in hiding somewhere for reasons known only to himself; and Genevieve was no slouch. *She knew things.* And she had had the copy of *Passion in Portugal* in her upstairs wardrobe. Damn it: the copy Avi had forgotten to get back from Brian; she'd have to try to remember later. Now Aventurine shook her head and hurried to catch up to Paul and Lance, walking close enough together to lean into one another, though they did not hold hands.

The cloisters were closed for archaeological excavation work. They ascended into the high choir and had a look along the nave to the chancel. She felt better about the view from here, her eyes slipping along the arches on either side and up into the dimness where they curved together to round the ceiling. At the same time, the view gave her shivers, as she couldn't help but think of Magnus Etheridge tumbling to his death from the gallery in Lincoln. *Stop,* she ordered herself. Next to her, Paul and Lance were gazing down into the nave, but they hadn't been in Lincoln Cathedral, and they didn't have this visceral reaction.

Aventurine took a deep breath and blinked to clear her mind's eye. Very few people wandered below them; apparently this wasn't a popular destination today for tourists. Still, Avi stared downward, looking in vain for the form of her twin; what would she do should she see Mick? Shout, but would the sound be lost in the echoes? And would that give Micheline warning, and—Avi glanced back over her shoulder and tried to remember how many stairs led back down to ground level—a chance to escape again?

Paul grimaced, shaking his head. "Nothing," he said. "She's not here. He's not here."

Lance put a hand on his shoulder.

Slowly they made their way out onto the balcony looking down over the Largo da Sé.

Avi imagined Dominic Burroughs's expression, if he were to see the three leaning against the stone rail for the view from just below the rosace. *Another high place.* If only he knew how poorly she handled heights—it was far less likely that she'd hurl someone to death from a high place, and more likely that she'd get dizzy and topple off herself. She clutched Lance's arm and concentrated on the number 28 trolley, lumbering up the hill toward them.

He let her lean into him and said nothing. She squeezed his arm again. Seriously: if he hadn't been so much younger than she, and gay, she would have gone for him herself, he was so kind. Even to the point of recognizing her queasiness.

Paul had moved further along the wall, finding a space to lean forward and look down into the Largo da Sé, which, even under this sullen sky, was bustling with foot and tuk-tuk traffic. Aventurine slid in beside him, letting go of Lance's arm to grasp the stone balustrade, and leaning carefully away from it at the same time. A quick glance to her right showed Paul rapt in the scenery. She wondered how, after the terrible night on the wall in York, when they had watched Neil's body tumble down into the darkness, he could bear to look. Far below them, the Tagus flowed away with the tide. The river, too, was teeming with boats large and small; she wondered, also, after his repeated declaration to Phil Newlan that he would never sail again, how Paul could bear to watch the progress of the craft on the water. On her other side, Lance seemed to be paying more attention to the pair of them than to the action below. He had been there, too, in York, but somehow—and this really puzzled her—Aventurine didn't have the same concerns about Lance's fears. Lance gave the impression of a person who had seen things and didn't shake easily. He shot her a quick reassuring smile, all teeth and dimples, and she wondered, not for the first time, about his history. She didn't think he would mind if she asked; rather, he'd probably tell her if he wasn't prepared to answer.

Slightly to the west of zenith, the sun broke through the clouds and cast a brilliant ray on the Plaça do Comercio down the hill from which they had come. Another trolley was climbing toward them. Avi felt uncomfortably warm in her jacket; what was unseasonably warm here in Lisbon? This was her first time as a visitor, after all, and Aventurine had no context. She supposed she could take out her phone and look it up, but she wanted, despite her shaky knees, to gaze out on Alfama spread below them, a colorful tapestry, even in its late autumn.

Still, she took out her phone and stepped back from them. "Let me get a picture."

Lance and Paul dutifully moved closer together, their hands touching, but just barely.

She centered them and pressed the button.

"Love is love," she said.

Lance laughed, and kissed Paul on the cheek. She snapped that picture quickly, too.

But when they huddled together to look at the photos, Aventurine noticed the glare from the sun, off to one side. Paul's face was partially in shadow.

"Switch places," she ordered. "I want a better one."

They shuffled around obediently, laughing. A family with three small children surged past on their way to the stairs, and Aventurine waited for them to get out of the frame before she looked up and called, "Smile!" Then she snapped another picture, and a second to be on the safe side.

"One of you two," Lance suggested.

They reorganized themselves, making the cell phone exchange so Lance could take the photo on her camera. Aventurine was pleased when, once they were side-by-side, Paul put a light arm around her shoulders.

"Say *pasteis de bacalhau!*" Lance said. Both Avi and Paul grinned, albeit a bit foolishly. "One more for luck," Lance commanded and turned the camera on its side.

Once more they gathered around the phone to look at the results. Paul and Lance together looked comfortable, as though they had momentarily forgotten why they were in Lisbon to begin with. Paul, now his entire face could be seen in the photo, looked flushed, perhaps as close to happy as Aventurine had seen him in ages. She thumbed over to the first of her and Paul, his arm around her shoulder, as it would have been naturally, before all their world went to hell. Maybe he was really coming around. Maybe he really was considering his behavior, his attitude, and how it affected the world around him? Genevieve had seemed to think it would happen, on the other side of his grief. She had had faith in him and had believed it more than likely.

She swiped to the last photo.

And there she was.

Peering out of the stone doorway to the stairs, as though she'd thought to slip out but found them taking photos. Her face was a round pale oval beneath the swing of shoulder length blonde hair.

"Is that your mother?" Lance gasped.

Paul met Aventurine's eyes. "No," he said. "Look again."

Aventurine took a deep breath. "It's Nicola."

Six

They dashed down the stairs as quickly as possible, what with the foot traffic moving both ways. Much complaint and cursing followed them down. At the bottom, there was no sign of her. They hurried along the nave, scanning the chapels as they went. She could be anywhere; she could have fled out into the street. She could have blended in among the tour groups, could have slipped behind a curtain in one of the chapels, headed back into the museum—anywhere at all.

Tourist thing.

Aventurine would have laughed at Genevieve's prescience, if she had the breath in her lungs. Finally the three burst out onto the landing at the top of the waterfall of steps to the Largo da Sé, glancing down the hill, to the left and right. The foot traffic was brisk now, pedestrians dodging the oncoming trolley and the tuk-tuks. There were any number of shaded doorways out of the wind, and a few cafés, that Nicola might have slipped into to keep watch on them.

"Damn it," Aventurine hissed through clenched teeth.

"What does she want?" Lance demanded.

"Why is she hiding from us?" Paul asked.

They stared at one another, unable to come up with an idea.

Aventurine's legs ached from the rush down from the balcony; she cursed herself for growing older. Neither Lance nor Paul seemed to show any after-effects; Nicola had probably handled the stairs just fine as well.

"There's only one thing for it," Avi said, sinking to a seat on the cathedral steps. She still had her phone in her hand. Quickly she clicked through to Nicola's contact and texted.

What do you want?

After a moment, a laugh emoji. Aventurine was struck by the contempt in the gesture.

I want Shep.

Aventurine nearly dropped her phone in shock. Instead she held it out in an unsteady hand. Lance took it from her grasp, and he and Paul leaned their heads together over it. Their expressions were nearly identical, eyes and mouths open in surprise and confusion.

"What does this mean?" Paul demanded, his voice so low it sounded painful.

"Text her back," Aventurine ordered roughly. She didn't think she'd be able, with her shaking fingers, to type anything coherent. "Tell her I want to see her. Tell her I want to talk to her."

Lance looked up, his dark eyes probing his face. "You told me you thought she could be dangerous."

Avi nodded. "I still think that. More so right now. But we have to find out what she's doing. What she knows. What she wants, Paul, with your father."

Nicola, too, obviously believed Shep to be alive. But why would that even be a matter of interest to her, beyond the newly discovered relationship to his wife?

Paul took a deep breath and nodded as well. He took the phone and swiftly tapped his thumbs across the screen. Then he licked his lips. "I told her this: 'I want to talk to you. Face to face.' How's that?"

"We'll see what her answer is, shall we?" Lance frowned with a sudden thought. "Screenshot that conversation, will you? And send it to me."

Aventurine opened her mouth, but Paul was already following directions. When Lance's phone buzzed with the message, he quickly began typing. At last he looked up again.

"What?" Paul asked.

"I've forwarded it to Genevieve."

"Genevieve?" Aventurine felt her eyes widen. The old woman got back to him. Again.

Lance's gaze was inscrutable. "My great-grandmother."

A laughing group of uniformed kids was streaming along the cobbles toward them.

"Here." Lance took her arm and pulled Avi out of the path; she found herself leaning against the railings of the front steps to an ornate doorway. Paul leaned in close; at the very least he acted as a sort of windbreak. "The next train along to Oeiras leaves on the hour. We'll need to hustle."

Aventurine nodded. They were taking her seriously. She had conveyed her urgency to them. "You've still got your wristbands on?"

Both held up their arms to show the orange strip held in place by the bead.

"A taxi might get us to the train more quickly," Paul suggested. He looked along the street, first uphill, then down. "I think that's one coming there." He threw out a hand to flag it down.

"Light's off," Lance objected. He jerked his head to the right. "We'll probably have better luck down at the next intersection."

"Wait. It's pulling over."

The cab was indeed pulling to the side of the street and slowing. As they watched, a blonde woman in a green jacket skated her way through the people on the pavement and leaned in toward the driver's window.

Paul gasped. "Mom—"

"No." Aventurine grabbed his arm before he could move from the shadow of the doorway. The woman ahead moved in the wrong way, and it jarred. "Not Mick."

"What—"

"Nicola."

Before she could say anything else, Paul jerked away and hurled himself along the pavement toward the woman and the taxi. She looked up as he approached and then yanked the door open to slide into the car. Even as Paul reached it, it squealed away from the curb. As it pulled away, Aventurine saw Nicola waving from the back seat. Her smile was triumphant.

"Shit," Paul hissed as he turned back to them.

"Shit," Lance agreed.

Aventurine blew out a long breath. "Let's get to the festival," she said.

Nothing else from Nicola.

They made their way down to Cais do Sodre and boarded the train. It was crowded, and they ended up standing at the end of the car, clinging to the poles. It was only about half an hour out to Oeiras; Avi checked her watch. They'd be plenty early for Mobius, who were on at six; she pulled her schedule, dog-eared now, from her bag, and ran her finger along the lineup. Paul leaned over her shoulder to look at the name of the evening venue and then called up the maps on his phone.

"Maybe ten minutes' walk," he murmured.

"Was that your stomach growling?" Lance laughed.

"Might be." Paul tapped the screen of his phone. "How long before your friends are on? Time enough to grab something to eat?"

"We're going there to look for your mother," Avi reminded him sternly. "And maybe stumble upon Nicola into the bargain."

"Or maybe not," Lance interjected. The train slowed and he put a hand on Paul's arm. "But we can find a place along the route to the venue, and sit by the window." He made a face. "We're flailing, after all. Anyplace we look is as good as any other place we look."

He wasn't wrong. Aventurine closed her eyes and tried to imagine her twin, tried to somehow connect with her. Mick could be anywhere.

And something in her said they had to find Mick before Nicola did, though why, she didn't know.

The desk clerk at the hotel had mentioned the festival. It was the only lead they had.

They left the train at Oreiros and headed in the direction Paul's phone suggested. There was still plenty of time before Mobius went on at the venue; Aventurine was bringing up the rear when the others stopped at a restaurant on the corner.

"Here," Paul tossed over his shoulder to her. "How's your Portuguese?"

"Minuscule." Aventurine fit herself in between them to look at the selections on the menu posted at the door. It was lunch time, and the sign on the door indicated that this particular restaurant did not close for the afternoon but served food straight through. That part was good, anyway. The menu had a fair mix of things she could decode, for the most part. She pointed out the *bife*, the *peixe*, the *frango*, the *sopa com pão e salada*. "Basically, everything you need for lunch."

"Fries?"

"*Batatas fritas*," she told them, pointing.

"This is our kind of place," Paul said. "I'm hungry."

"You're always hungry," Lance observed.

Inside was all blue and white checked tablecloths, and ladder-back chairs. They were shown to a table near the front windows and handed menus; the waiter asked for drink orders and then sailed away. All three fell to further examination of the menus; when the server returned to rattle off the specials, Aventurine estimated that she caught every third word. Lance eventually settled on something that roughly translated to beef and sweet potatoes; Paul chose octopus, and Aventurine opted for a salad of shrimp and greens.

"Octopus," Avi said to Paul once the waiter had retreated again, promising—she thought—to bring their drinks from the bar as soon as possible. Or frequently? "That's no burger and fries."

He gave her a look from under his drawn brows. "Genevieve would kill me if I ordered a burger and fries in a Portuguese seafood restaurant."

Lance snorted.

"What?"

Lance shook his head. "Genevieve. Killing people."

"Oh," Paul said. "Right." He cleared his throat and adopted a serious face. "Genevieve would be ever so disappointed in me, should I order a burger and fries in a Portuguese seafood restaurant."

"So much better," Lance laughed; the look he cast on Paul was unbearably sweet. "Much more concise."

The *caipirinhas* arrived, delightfully pale green and sporting lime slices.

"So what are we going to do about Nicola?" Aventurine asked. She leaned forward to look out on the street. The drink was sweet and spicy, and tangy with the lime. She had a feeling she should drink it slowly, and definitely only have one. "What are we going to do about Mick?"

"We're going to take a moment to consider," Lance said. "We're not going to rush into anything when we get to the festival site."

"You sound like *your great-grandmother*," Avi protested.

"It's the genetics." The corners of Lance's dark eyes crinkled. He too sipped his drink.

"What's to consider?" Paul asked. "We eat lunch, we keep an eye on the street, we keep an eye out, inside and outside the venue."

"But what if we're at the wrong venue?" Aventurine once again dug out the dog-eared schedule.

"No," Lance said, sipping his drink; he had abandoned the straw on the tablecloth. "We won't be wrong. Mobius is a constant. If Nicola wants you, or to be you, she'll go where they are—you've seen that already."

"But—Mick? Where would *she* go? And what if Nicola's following *her*?"

"I think," Lance said, frowning, "that Nicola might be playing a weird cat-and-mouse game with us. She wants to find what we want to find—"

"My sister—"

"My father—"

Lance shrugged. "Either? Both? We need to figure out why. We need to figure out what's in it for her. *We need to figure out how it's all related.*"

"I just don't understand what she would want with Dad."

Aventurine bit her lip. *Passion in Portugal.* When she looked up, Lance was watching her and tipped his head nearly imperceptibly.

"I mean, this is the second time she's insinuated herself into something to do with Dad. First the boatyard, and now here." Paul leaned back in his chair, his eyes scanning the street: neither Nicola nor Micheline seemed inclined to make an appearance. "It's like she knows he's not dead. But why would that be interesting to her? She doesn't know Dad. And we none of us knew anything about *her* until just recently." He frowned, as though chasing an idea. "She had to have been the one to leave the book in the filing cabinet at the boatyard. But the clue was 'Your Mother Should Know.' *Mother.*"

Again Lance turned to Paul, his brow, under his tumble of dark hair, furrowing. "Maybe we're coming at all of this from the wrong end. We're here, looking for Micheline and Nicola. Maybe we have to go back to the beginning and start with the reason your father chose to disappear. Begin at the beginning."

The food arrived, and they murmured appreciatively to the server, waiting until he had gone again to resume conversation.

Aventurine watched Paul closely. He took a bite of his octopus and chewed it carefully, once again appearing to consider the taste, the mode of cooking. When he offered some, Lance waved him off.

"Where cilantro is concerned, I'm team soap," he said, grimacing.

"Genetics, huh?" Avi gibed.

Lance rolled his eyes.

At last Paul took a sip of his *caipirinha*. "Back to Dad, though. I keep veering away from that—why he would disappear."

It was an admission, but today it lacked rancor. Avi found herself relieved, and she wondered how much Lance had had to do with this attitude adjustment. However much it was, Aventurine was grateful.

"It could have been an accident," she offered. "The foundering?"

But Paul shook his head. "Maybe. In the beginning. But the *Máquina* debris was found, and Dad wasn't. There were no reports of anyone matching Dad's description found anywhere. Which precludes his—I don't know—his having amnesia or something? It's not like there were any Gilligan's Islands out there for him to wash up on."

Aventurine took another drink, then pushed her glass aside. The *caipirinha* was as strong as she had imagined, and her head was already threatening. She needed to stay clear-headed for this conversation. And for the afternoon and evening in the venue.

"Someone could have found him and not reported it," she suggested. *Unless he went down with the wreck.* The filament of understanding between them, though, was so fine, and still so fraught, that she did not voice the thought. Or perhaps it was because she was beginning to be ambivalent herself?

Again the headshake. Lance, chin on hand, was apparently going to let Paul take the lead in this guesswork, probably the best course of action. "I don't see how. Any innocent bystander—anyone just sailing by—would probably know to be looking for him and would have reported it had they found him." He cleared his throat, obviously uncomfortable. "Which means that, if Dad is alive, he *meant* to disappear."

This time it was Aventurine's turn to shake her head. "But why would he do that? Why would he put you and your mother through that? The people he loves most in the world?"

Paul's expression grew bleak. "Does he, though?" His meaning was clear, and she had to agree with him. This was not a way to show love. It was cruel. One of the cruelest things she could think of to do to a loved one. "Does he?"

Aventurine took a deep breath.

"Yes, Paul, he does." She squared her shoulders. "I've known him nearly half my life. I did the most important thing I could do for him, and for your mother. I know how much the pair of you mean to him. If he's done this disappearing act willingly, there has got to be a damned good reason for it. A damned good reason."

Seven

Aventurine glanced at her watch. "We need to go."

They paid the bill and slipped out in the street, where the crowds seemed to be growing as the afternoon drew on into evening. The shadows were longer now, and the air had a bit of a chill to it. Avi had an anxious look around, but there was still no sign of either Mick or Nicola. As they moved along, she could feel her heart pounding. They were so close to Micheline, she knew it. For the first time she thought of Genevieve and was grateful instead of annoyed, that the old woman had left the package with the Lisbon address. Genevieve had been moving them all around like chess pieces—to get them all back to Micheline. Right?

"Wait," Lance hurried to put a restraining hand on her arm. "Hold on. We're clear how we're going to do this?" When Paul drew up, he placed his other hand on his arm.

"We need to go," Avi repeated. The afternoon acts would be done by the time they got to the venue; there would be a dinner break before the evening performances began. With no act on, it would be easier to move around, looking for Micheline, but by the same token, everyone else would be moving around as well, in search of their evening meal.

"Aventurine—"

Paul cut Lance off. "Mom doesn't want to be found." His throat worked. "She's doing something—looking for Dad, or clues about Dad, we don't really know—but she doesn't want us to know what she's up to. She's made it clear we're not welcome to come after her."

Lance nodded. "So we have to approach this carefully, Aventurine. If she's trying not to be found—"

"But why? Why doesn't she want our help?" The built-up frustration filled her words. They were right; she knew they were. If she had her way, she'd bulldoze everything in her path to get to her sister and then deal with what Mick wanted when she got there.

"It doesn't matter why she's avoiding us," Lance said reasonably. "It only matters that she is. We can't risk spooking her. We've got to come at this search carefully. Come at *her* carefully."

"I just feel like—we have to hurry."

Paul and Lance glanced at each other, but she turned away again, impatiently.

They split up once they reached the hall, where the doors were not yet open for the evening performances. Paul passed on down the street in one direction, Lance in another. Aventurine skirted the front and slipped down the alley toward the rear of the building. They had paired up their phones on the Find My app while in the restaurant, and all three had portable chargers and cords in their packs. For just in case. Just in case.

Only a few people were in the alley, eating offerings from food trucks; she had been right about the ebb and flow of the crowds in search of food and drink between sessions. The atmosphere was as much carnival as festival, and she was glad to escape the worst of it as she rounded the back and came upon some equipment vans, including the one she recognized as belonging to Mobius.

It would be a simple thing to recognize Micheline even from a distance: not just her appearance, but the way she moved. Aventurine knew in her bones the way her twin would walk down the cobbled pavements, the way her arms would swing, the way her head would turn. She checked her phone, tight in her right palm. Nothing from either Paul or Lance yet. Avi took a deep breath and pushed on, past the trucks; at the intersection she glanced first in one direction, then the other. Micheline was here somewhere, if what she had told the hotel receptionist was true. They would find her. Then they would execute the pincer movements they'd settled on, using their phones, circling, circling, keeping her all the time within their sights, until they all appeared at her sides. They would find her, and she would not be able to escape.

Then they could find out what Micheline was doing. And why.

It was all about Shep, of course. She had been lured to Lisbon in a search of information about her husband, and perhaps been sworn to secrecy. That was the only feasible reason for her behavior. For Mick had never given up hope that Shep was still alive, in the world, somewhere.

That made Micheline vulnerable. To whomever was doing the luring.

Evil. That was the word Dominic Burroughs had used. Aventurine, at this point, had to agree. Someone was using her sister to some dark end, and that someone was evil.

Perhaps that someone was Nicola.

The three had circled, met up, circled again. Nothing.

Now Aventurine flashed her wristband, hoping the volunteers at the back would not pay too much attention, and slipped into the artist's entrance. Wrong color, but they'd gotten so used to her—and Nicola's—back and forth at the venue that no one seemed to care. That and wearing stagehand black seemed to do the trick.

Are you coming? Linny had texted. **I need you.**

With Linny, that need could be for a deep heart-to-heart, or for help putting her hair up. Aventurine half-smiled to herself, thinking that, in spite of all the anxiety, it was good to be with Linny again. Good to be among friends. And Mobius being invited to play at the Festival do Fim da Estrada—that boded good things for them in the music world, she hoped. She could probably ask Ruth about it, but she would no doubt be rebuffed.

Mobius had this one other show early evening, she knew, and then they'd be heading back home out of this Portuguese sun and into the English winter. "Come with us," Linny had urged the other night on the beach. But it wasn't that easy. Not without Mick. And the clues to her possible whereabouts had so far turned up a whole lot of nothing.

So hard was she thinking about this that she ran into Gio's chest before she realized.

"Whoa, there," he said, his deep voice coming from somewhere above her ear.

She looked up at him, his handsome face, his silvering hair.

"Which one are you?" he asked.

She jerked away. "I ought to punch you."

I can tell you apart, Burroughs had said to her that afternoon in Sioned's library in Hay.

She pushed that thought away.

"Don't be an ass, George," she said bitterly.

He laughed and tipped her chin up with a finger. "Ah. Aventurine. I should have known."

Avi pushed his hand away. He was a charmer, would always be a charmer, but now she was resistant. It was as though she had been vaccinated.

"After all these years," she said, "you should have known. But maybe you weren't paying all that much attention."

She turned to walk away, towards the open door further along the corridor, where she could see Ruth conferring with Pete and Brian over a piece of paper. The playlist for the evening, probably. Much to her annoyance, Gio fell into step beside her, crowding the hallway.

"I didn't expect to see you here," he said. Genially, though she sensed the probing behind the statement.

"Nor I you."

He shrugged and smiled. "I'm a musician. I play festivals. I particularly enjoy warm ones when it gets cold at home." He laughed.

"I enjoy a warm welcome, too."

"Find Nicola. I'm sure she'll be willing to oblige." Aventurine quickened her pace, then spun back. "And don't you dare pull that line about the couch."

Gio held up a hand. "I wouldn't dream of it." He glanced around. "Nicola's here at the festival, too?"

Right.

"She didn't tell you?" Again she moved away. At the doorway at the end of the hall, Brian had spotted her. And Gio. His expression turned sour. "She was here. Probably still is. Pretending to be me, which is apparently her game these days." She jerked her chin. "Had Brian convinced, anyway."

She felt a tiny niggle of satisfaction when Gio's face darkened. But, ever the consummate glad-hander, he affixed the genial expression again.

"You always said you had to turn Brian down."

"Every woman has to turn Brian down. Except Nicola. Apparently she didn't get the memo. And Brian's pretty annoyed about it."

Even now Brian had turned his back on the pair of them, retreating further into the green room. Pete called something to him and received a dismissing wave over the shoulder.

Aventurine heard her name, and Linny appeared, fluttering her eyelashes at Gio. She kissed Avi's cheek, and blushed when Gio leaned down to kiss both of hers.

"Ah, the lovely Linny," he crooned.

She looked from Aventurine to Gio and back again; she had always been a good reader of a tense situation. She edged a fraction of an inch closer to Avi, and, though she never lost her smile, it lost some of its warmth.

"Mr. Constantine," she greeted him.

He raised his eyebrows at her formality.

"I was just trying to convince our Aventurine to work my stage crew this evening," he said.

Aventurine crossed her arms and stared at him challengingly.

"She can't," Linny said, linking arms with Avi. "She's working for us."

"A shame." Alan had appeared and lifted a hand in their direction. "If you ladies will excuse me," Gio said, and left them for Linny's brother.

"Walk with me out to the van," Linny ordered. "Tell me what's going on there. The sweetness and light factor seems to have dimmed."

"He slept with my sister."

Linny let out a screech, and quickened her steps, out through the door and into the darkening alley, past the volunteers. At the van, she leaned against the side panel and crossed her arms. "Your *sister?* Micheline?"

"Not that one."

"The new one?"

"See, she knew. Nicola knew that Gio and I had—a thing. So that's what she did about it."

Linny dug a key ring from the pocket of her dress and unlocked the van, where she drew out a bag and rooted around in it. She cast a quick glance over her shoulder to the stage entrance, her pale hair swinging about her shoulders. "You told me once, or twenty times, that it wasn't serious between you two. Just friends with benefits, as the kids say."

"Yeah, but this is my *sister,*" Aventurine protested. "The idea makes me queasy. There's a lot of baggage there that isn't love, for God's sake." She leaned back and looked up at the sliver of city sky, where no stars were visible. "And it's the intent. She keeps trying to slip into my shoes."

"That's more than shoes, Avi," Linny observed dryly.

"A bit. But she keeps trying to commandeer my life. And then I find out about it afterwards."

Linny turned slowly, frowning, a curling iron in one fist. "Oh. Like with Brian, too."

Aventurine grimaced. "Exactly like with Brian. Except that she didn't realize I had never succumbed to his charms."

"He'd thought you'd finally given in." Linny's expression, in the half-light from the van's overhead, was almost comical, a mixture of laughter, disgust, and pity. "Poor Brian. What a trick to play on him. He thought, after all these years, you'd finally given in—"

"And it was someone else entirely. Someone who was using him to get back at me."

"But why?" The question might have been directed at the curling iron; Linny gazed down on it in confusion and finally jammed it back into the bag. "Why would she want to get back at you?"

Aventurine threw up her hands. "I don't know. I haven't got a clue what goes on inside that woman's head. I mean, I have only known of her existence for a month."

"And in that time she's—" Linny shuddered. She turned now, slamming the van door shut, holding up a slim tube of lipstick, which did not look like a curling iron at all. "Ick. I don't even want to think about it, Aventurine."

"Me, neither."

"No wonder you don't want to talk to Gio."

"He keeps telling me he slept on the couch, when they were staying together in his aunt's cottage in Lincolnshire."

"And you don't believe him?"

"He's backtracking, Linny. And his story is not the same as hers."

"But—surely you don't believe *her*. I mean, what reason has she given you to believe her about anything?" Now Linny bent to the side mirror—she didn't have far to go—and began applying the lipstick, examining her mouth carefully in the dim light. The red—and it came as a shock—was nearly the same Taylor Swift color Genevieve had foisted on Avi when she was transformed into Mary Wentworth. It looked much better on Linny than on Avi, though.

"Not a single one."

"So?"

It was difficult to explain. "I think she'd say the thing that would hurt the most. That she *thinks* would hurt the most. But more than that—I think she'd *do* what would hurt the most."

Linny smacked her lips together and replaced the cap on the gold tube. Then she turned her frank eyes on Aventurine. "You really don't like her, do you?"

The question was hard to answer. "I want to," Aventurine said slowly. "I *wanted* to. But she makes it harder and harder. And—" she swallowed. "She wallows in it, Linny. She *enjoys* it."

After a moment, Linny nodded. "I get it." She smiled, that sweet smile that Aventurine had learned to count on over the years. The smile that spelled out loyalty. And love.

They linked arms again and turned back toward the stage entrance.

Eight

"Earn your keep," Ruth ordered as they reached the door. She tossed a ring of keys, similar to Linny's, in Aventurine's general direction. "Alan wants the rest of his cases." Her eyes shifted. "Linny, get in here."

Linny shrugged and pushed her way past Ruth into the venue. Aventurine picked up the keys from the ground and turned to find Lance and Paul.

"Earn your keep," she ordered.

She unlocked the back liftgate and looked immediately to the left: Alan always loaded first, early, and his cases were always to the left, no matter what vehicle they used. The bag with his auxiliary electronics was on top.

"We didn't see anyone," Lance said.

"I didn't, either." Aventurine sighed. "What if we're on the wrong track altogether? What if we're looking in all the wrong places?" She hefted the bag and passed it back to Lance.

"We've got no other leads. The hotel clerk said Mom had mentioned coming here." Paul was sounding defeated, the sound that always put Aventurine on alert. "She *had* to be coming to look for Dad. We *had* to come here."

Aventurine threw up her hands. "I just hate this feeling. What if we're all wrong? I can't get away from that."

"But you still think Dad's dead." A challenge.

"I didn't say that."

"But you thought it. You think Mom and I are on some wild goose chase." Paul's hands were on his hips, his feet wide apart. A fighter's stance. "Lance, let's get out of here."

Aventurine knew what this was: his frustration at their failure to find any trace of either of his parents, and he needed to channel that frustration—but why always at her expense? She glanced over at Lance, who returned her look with sympathy. *You're safe,* he'd told her. *He lashes out at you because you're safe, and you're here.* All right, but that didn't make it feel any better.

"You know what, Paul?" Aventurine said. She wiped her grimy hands down the legs of her jeans—how did this equipment make such a mess? "You need to grow up."

There. She'd said it.

Paul looked shocked and drew back. Lance pointedly turned away, still holding the equipment bag.

"I'm sorry, Lance, that you have to keep witnessing this," she said. She squinted in the dimness of the alleyway, the better to see her nephew's expression. "But you, Paul. Every time you get mad at me, every time you get upset about something I say, something I do—you run away."

"I don't."

"Even with Lance. You had an argument in Southampton with him, about me, in the summer, and you took the rental car and ran away. To York."

"But—"

Aventurine plowed right over his protest. "You had an argument with me about your father, so you took the train at Paddington to God knows where—somewhere *away* from me."

Again her nephew opened his mouth, but she held up a hand. "No. You need to listen to me. You are nearly twenty-four years old. You're not a kid anymore. You can't just get mad and storm off. Even Genevieve says this: there will come a time when you have to stand up and face what's coming. You can't just run away when things get uncomfortable."

Under the dome light from the van, she could see the color washing in and out of Paul's face. Aventurine turned back and pulled out a mandolin case. She thrust it into Lance's free hand and turned back for another. "Run these inside, Lance," she said. "Those people will love you forever."

Lance shrugged and headed toward the stage door.

"Why are you talking to me like this?" Paul demanded at last.

"No, darling," Avi said, and her voice softened slightly. "The real question is—why *haven't* I talked to you like this *before?*"

"But—"

"Paul. Your family is in trouble." She hefted a case in her left hand and decided she could handle another in her right. "Not just you. You're not the only one who's been hurt here. You're not the only one who's suffering, and you need to understand that and stop lashing out at the people who love you. You've spent far too long up your own ass, to put it mildly, and now it's time to look around and see what you can do to help everyone else. Your mother. Your father, should there be any help out there for him. And maybe me."

They stared at each other for a long moment. Aventurine vowed she would not be the one to break the gaze: she was in the right here, and it really was about time Paul grew up. Took some responsibility.

He said nothing.

She waited.

Finally, he reached into the rear of the van and pulled out the last two cases.

"Come on, then," Aventurine said.

She spent the show up back near the sound desk, Paul and Lance on the rail. Her eyes grew accustomed to the darkness quickly, and she scanned the crowds repeatedly, paying special attention to the edges, near the walls. She'd recognize her twin by movement, but she was less certain of Nicola.

At the break when Mobius abandoned the stage before the encore, she felt rather than saw Gio slip in behind her shoulder. Still she scanned the crowd between the desk and stage, refusing to turn.

When at last the lights went up, she made to push to the front to help with breakdown, but Gio put a hand on her arm.

"I've got to go back to work," she said.

"I just want a minute."

Aventurine crossed her arms and waited. Around them the tide of people moving toward the rail, the merch table, the exit, ebbed and flowed.

"Outside?"

She did not move. "Here's fine." Her voice was flat.

For a long time he did not meet her eyes.

"You hate me," he said at last. There was sadness there, but Aventurine could not help but feel that there was an element of falseness—as though he were expecting her to reassure him that she did not, indeed, hate him.

Aventurine looked at him in the full light of the auditorium. She felt her own sadness as a little knot sitting below her collarbone. The hit-and-miss nature of their former relationship, she knew, was over. His handsome profile, those soulful eyes which were, at the same time, self-knowing. She had grown used to him, and fond of him, realizing that he was all showmanship, even in his private life. Even in his relationship with her.

"I don't hate you," she said, and before he could relax, she added, "but I do think you're an ass. And a gullible one at that."

Gio looked taken aback.

"You know she played you, right? Nicola?" Aventurine shook her head. "And you fell for it, hook, line, and sinker."

When he opened his mouth to protest, she held up a hand.

"Don't, Gio," she said. "She told me you two were lovers. She thought that that would hurt me."

"And did it?"

The hopefulness behind the question made her laugh.

Slowly she dropped her arms to her sides, tipping her head to look at him. "I thought it did. But then I realized that it wasn't hurt at all I was feeling. It was anger."

"At me?"

"At you, for falling for Nicola's manipulation, so easily."

"Are you *really* saying I'm gullible?"

"Where Nicola is concerned? Yes."

They were a little island in the wash of people; no one came near. The conversation was not going the way Gio had envisioned, that seemed obvious. He glanced away, and Aventurine studied his profile. It was dear to her, she supposed, but not because she was in love with him. She wasn't. At this point, knowing how open he had been to Nicola's machinations, she wasn't even in lust with him any longer.

"And are you angry with her?"

"Oh, yes. Very much so." Aventurine's voice was forceful. "Because she knew about us, and she purposely tried to ruin it. Just like she did when she slept with Brian, only she was mistaken there." She sighed. "I guess she thought that it—what you and I had—meant more than it did."

There was a very long pause. Over in the corner, Ruth was busy packing up the merch.

"What did it mean, then, Aventurine?"

She ran a hand through her hair and looked up at the ornately painted ceiling above the rails holding the light bars. There were stylized constellations there, perhaps to mimic the overhead sky outside, but Avi didn't recognize any of them, and didn't know whether that was her own ignorance, or the painter's perspective. Because that was all what it was about, wasn't it? Perspective?

"It meant we were friends, Gio," she said at last.

He bowed his head.

"Are we still friends?"

She let out a tiny rueful laugh. "Oh, Gio." She leaned in to kiss his cheek, and then turned and walked away toward the stage, not looking back.

Nine

No beach party session afterwards: Ruth was hurrying her charges into the van, to pull an all-nighter on the road. The three waved them off.

"Absolutely nothing," Paul groaned, watching until the taillights disappeared. "No Mom. Nothing."

"I need a drink," Aventurine said.

When they headed back along the street, they found their dinner restaurant still open and ducked in for a second round of *caipirinhas*.

"I've got this one," Paul said, reaching into his pocket for his wallet. When he drew it out, a scrap of paper fluttered to the floor beneath his chair.

Lance scooped it up and slid it across the tablecloth. "Fell out of your pocket."

Garishly colored, the ochres and yellows found on Moorish buildings around the city; the edges were ragged, as though the fragment had been torn from something larger.

"This isn't mine," Paul protested.

"What was it doing in your pocket, then?"

Aventurine leaned closer. Across the scrap, in yellow letters that contrasted with the background, it read *Você já visitou Sintra?* She drew in a breath.

"What?" Paul demanded.

She pointed to the question. "Have you ever visited Sintra?"

Lance pushed his half-empty glass away.

Paul looked up from the paper, at each of them, and then at the torn bit again.

"No," Lance said, "but I guess we're going to now."

They argued. How had it got into his pocket? The venue had been crowded, but could someone have slipped the scrap in without being noticed, a reverse kind of pickpocketing?

"It's the manipulation again," Avi protested. "Someone wants us to go to Sintra. And I'm willing to bet that someone is Nicola. But I don't feel like being moved around like a pawn by someone who is no doubt laughing behind my back."

"But what if Mom's there?"

Aventurine shrugged. "What if she's not? We've only had a possible sighting, tentative though it may be, here, in Lisbon."

"At the guest house. And they directed us to the festival, where we didn't find her." Paul wiped his hands across his face. "We've got nothing to gain by staying here, nothing to lose by going there."

"Genevieve would probably tell you to sit tight."

"Genevieve's not here."

Aventurine took a deep breath. Something about this felt wrong. Well, something about everything for the past several months felt wrong. But she had to dig her heels in, somehow. Had to stop feeling like a marionette.

"What if—" Lance paused, chewed his bottom lip. "What if Paul and I go to see if we can find anything there, and you stay, to see if anything happens here?"

"I don't know if splitting up is the answer. I don't know if splitting up is safe." Aventurine had a flash of her plunge from East Pier, the water closing over her head. *Did she fall or was she pushed?* Well, they could probably figure out the answer to that question. She brushed her hair out of her eyes.

"And if I go," Paul said with a touch of bitterness, "Avi will only accuse me of running off again because I'm angry."

"Not if you keep in touch," she corrected him. "Not if you come back."

Lance nodded. He leaned in. "Listen, Paul. It's all right to be angry. And you have all the reason in the world to be angry. But it's not all right to run from it and expect it to be better. It won't be. Not until we find some answers."

"Maybe not then," Paul said, looking down into the depths of his glass. He used the straw to stir the ice around.

"Maybe not," Lance agreed. "But we can figure that out when we get there."

Slowly Paul lifted his head. His eyes, so like his father's, sought Avi's, and he nodded. Then he turned to kiss Lance.

"That's settled, then," Aventurine said, swallowing back the lump in her throat. "You two get the train to Sintra tomorrow, and I'll keep looking around here." *If there was anything to see.* "But be careful. Nicola can't be in two places at once, but it's almost certain she'll either follow you there, or try to get to me while I'm on my own."

"Will you be okay with that if she does?" Lance asked.

She met his gaze. "Oh, I'll have to be." Avi felt her jaw harden. "And I have a few things to say to her if she appears." She pushed away from the table. "And you, Lance: tell Genevieve what's happening. Tell her where you're going. Because you appear to be the only one she'll talk to."

Aventurine waved off Lance's offer to walk her back to her hotel.

"I'm not that drunk," she said. "I'm not drunk at all."

Paul shook his head.

"Let me know what you hear from your great-grandmother," she added to Lance. He nodded.

She felt like she had missed a siesta that afternoon, and was enervated because of it, as she headed away from the *praia*. She paused for a moment to listen to some faraway bells and then trudged on. She felt exhaustion deep in her bones. It was becoming more and more clear the longer she stayed in Lisbon exactly why everyone closed their blinds and took a nap in the afternoon. It was a relief to gain her room, though she let herself in cautiously with an eye for anything untoward. The bed was made, fresh towels set out at the end. Everything was neatened up, edges squared. It didn't look as though anyone other than housekeeping had been in. Still, she checked the bathroom, checked the closet, opened the drawers to see whether her clothes had been rifled. Satisfied, she turned the deadbolt lock, slid the desk chair under the knob. Only then did she strip off her jacket, kick off her red Converse, and lie down across the comforter.

It might have been that last *caipirinha,* but she dozed off almost immediately. Her dreams were random, musical, with repeated images of unidentified people walking away from her toward distant mountains where the sun was setting. When she awoke again, her watch was dead, but her phone told her it was 2:42. She'd left the overhead light on, and now she blinked against it, turning it off and switching on the desk lamp instead. Well before sunrise and any reasonable waking hour. A lifted curtain showed her a narrow street below, in shadow, with streetlights dropping small, disconnected beads of light onto the pavement.

Aventurine did a quick inventory: her neck cracked when she stretched, no doubt the result of sleeping the wrong way. Her eyes felt grainy when she rubbed at them with her fists. Thirsty—her mouth was dry, so she filled a glass of water at the sink in the bathroom. But she did not feel hungry: surprisingly, the shrimp salad from earlier had filled her up, and she felt no urge to eat yet. She carried the water glass back to the desk and got out her laptop. She opened it, stared at the blank screen for a matter of moments, and then began typing.

At one point, she thought she heard a brush of movement from the hallway, but nothing further. She held still, listening, but the sound was not repeated. Just the wind, or a late-returning guest, then. She returned her attention to the page.

Ten

Aventurine awoke with a start from a nebulous nightmare as the daylight crept into the room. She grabbed up her phone, yanking it off the charger. There was nothing else from any of them; why had she thought there might be?

She lay back, wondering what to do with her day—whether to stay locked in and safe, or to go out and make herself a target for her half-sister. To look for Micheline—but where? She debated returning to the Sé, having seen so little of it, and paid attention to so much less. Doing the *touristy thing.* But of course, that had not really been the impetus behind Genevieve's suggestion, had it? To enrich themselves, to explore the world? Aventurine's head was aching—probably the results of the *caipirinha,* she thought ruefully. No, the old spy had wanted them to visit the places Micheline might visit because *she* thought *Shep* might visit them. The bunch of them were all running around Lisbon after one another, without ever catching up. Circles.

Except for Nicola.

Either she was a very bad operative, or she had intended that they should spot her at the Sé. Aventurine went back and forth in her mind between either possibility. If Nicola had wanted them to see her, then why?

I want Shep.

Aventurine thumbed back to that text and stared at the three words.

Well, he obviously wasn't with them. Either dead or alive. *Schrödinger's Shep.* Aventurine grimaced. There was no way to know what Nicola meant. *Want,* as in *to find?* Or *want,* as in *hand him over?* Or *want* in the physical and emotional sense? Avi could feel herself cringe inwardly. She thought fleetingly of the book from Genevieve's closet—still with Mobius, damn it—then banished that thought. No, Genevieve, no. Not Shep and Nicola.

But the thought hovered.

Nicola had gone to the boatyard, had convinced Phil Newlan that she was Micheline. To leave a book... but what if there was another reason? What if she really *did* want to be Mick?

What if she already had been?

Aventurine sat up abruptly, looking about the hotel room desperately, as though to find the embodiment of the thought lurking in the shadows. The laptop on the desk was still open, though the screen had gone dark; she had flicked off the light before she'd fallen back into bed. She didn't want to follow her train of thought to its logical conclusion; she wanted it—*needed* it—to disappear. Instead she thought of Lance and Paul, the kiss they had shared in front of her, the way they had clasped hands as they walked down the street beside her. But those intertwined fingers morphed in her mind's eye into those of her sister and brother-in-law. No. Shep wouldn't have done that. Avi knew as a certainty that he wouldn't have, what with the depth of feeling the pair of them had shared. If Nicola wanted Shep in that way, it was wishful thinking on her part.

Avi thought again of Lance and Paul's hands, which became again, just their hands. They had looked good together last night, and again, she hoped that they could stay good together. It was Paul she worried about—though he had shown that he might just now be turning back into the person he had been before Shep's disappearance had rocked his world—because she already sensed the steel of Lance's loyalty, and she admired it more than she could put into words.

Then Aventurine realized that, as she had followed them around the corner at Rua dos Bacalhoeiros, the more she looked at their clasped hands, the more she missed Dominic Burroughs.

Aventurine pushed aside the curtains to look down the road toward the water, grey and restless under the early fitful sun. The room was warmer than she was used to, warmer than it would be at this time of year in her apartment on the Back Bay, warmer than it had been in England. She had slept fitfully, throwing the light blanket aside.

Now her dream flitted away in wisps, like clouds or phantoms, and the bits she remembered made her uneasy. The slight noise outside her door? A woman with her mouth open in a silent scream? The sound of the tide retreating? A metallic thunk, like that a car door made in closing? She closed her eyes and rested her hot forehead against the cold glass.

What was she even doing here, in Portugal? Not for the first time did she ask herself this, and this time as with all the others, she was unable to formulate a satisfactory answer. On a wild goose chase, no doubt. With her eyes closed, she could see again the box in the closet in Genevieve's townhouse, the box addressed to Micheline in Lisbon, in Genevieve's spiky hand, at a hotel in which *someone* had registered under Avi's name. The box containing the bodice ripper written by Nicola.

Micheline. *Missing.*

Genevieve. *Missing.* Or was she? Lance had seen her. Lance was now in touch with her.

Nicola. *Missing.* Or hiding. Taunting.

This in addition to Shep, missing, and Lance and Paul, this morning, off to Sintra, on perhaps another wild goose chase. They were flailing, and this alone made Aventurine anxious. Frightened? As though something was coming at them on the event horizon, something they were totally unprepared for and could not stop if they wanted to.

Again she circled inside her head. Lisbon was the only clue she had. And now she was here, what was she to do? She had checked the hotel, twice. She had checked the festival, twice. Where else to look? She couldn't imagine where to move next. But to wait? For what?

A thin ray of morning sun warmed her face and reddened her eyelids. Slowly she turned back to the dim room, letting the curtains fall. Again she thought of the sound she had dreamed, of someone or something outside her door. The desk chair was still wedged under the knob. She stared at it for a moment, then dislodged it and undid the bolts. The hallway was brightly lit, and empty; she blinked, looking to either end, before realizing there was a newspaper outside the door. Had she ordered a newspaper? Some of the other rooms had one as well; she must have, she supposed, though she didn't remember it—probably an accident, checking off the wrong box or something. She stooped to pick it up and found a key fob beneath it.

Again Aventurine looked up and down the hallway. There was no one in sight. Obviously the person who delivered the morning newspaper had dropped it and not realized. She picked it up and brought it back into the room with her. She'd bring it downstairs when she went out for breakfast, leave it at the reception desk. She dumped the newspaper on the desk, and after a moment slid the fob into the pocket of her jacket, so she wouldn't forget.

Aventurine started the coffee maker and then went into the bathroom to splash some water onto her face. She was still headachy—hungover, she thought again, from the *caipirinhas* of yesterday. Too much of a lightweight. She opened the curtains now, and the milky early morning light entered the room. A glance at her watch on the charger told her it was not yet seven. She wouldn't be sleeping again, she knew; perhaps a quick walk down to the beach was in order, before she washed and ate and tried to figure out what to do with this day. Again she peered down toward the beach, and a glint across the Avenida Marginal caught her eye. A car. Silver. She squinted. Perhaps someone else had had the same idea: an invigorating early morning walk on the beach. She hadn't noticed it at first, as there were cars up and down the road, parked in front of guest houses and hotels. But this car was the only one parked in the few spaces above the *praia*, and there was something about the careless way it straddled a couple of lines that made her look again. Perhaps the driver had been drunk in the night and had just left it there to wander down toward the water, in which case, she hoped he was dressed for a night on the beach. She wondered fleetingly whether he would come back for his car before someone called the police, or the parking authority, or whoever had jurisdiction over that sort of thing.

A key.

A car.

Coincidence, probably. Still, Avi pulled the fob out of her jacket pocket again, and, approaching the window, clicked one of the three buttons. Nothing. She was probably too far away, or the battery was too weak, or the key was to some other car entirely. Stupid idea. Still, she held the fob closer to the window and pushed the bottom button.

The taillights on the car flashed. She leaned even closer to the glass and pressed the bottom button a second time and thought she heard, faintly, the answering toot of the car horn.

Eleven

Aventurine threw on some clothes, dragging on her coat and gloves against the cold, and then after a thought, jamming her hair up under a hat. She rushed downstairs. In the early morning street, she turned and hurried toward Avenida Marginal, where the traffic was still quite thin. Her hands were stuffed in her pockets, her gloved right fist curled around the key fob. No one else walked the street, not even a dog walker, though behind her she could hear the sound of an engine—a panel truck, making a delivery. She crossed the avenue against the light, and purposely walked past the car, a Peugeot, to the wall, to look down at the waves caressing the shingle. She didn't turn until she heard the truck leave, then gave it a few more minutes before retracing her steps to the car.

It was empty. Avi leaned forward, hands still in pockets, careful not to touch it. There was no one inside; the interior was remarkably clean, not a gasoline receipt or other scrap on the seats or floor mats. No trace of a driver; it was as though the Peugeot had mysteriously made its own way to the beach-side lot in the night.

The wispy dream memory: the thunk of a car door closing?

Aventurine looked quickly up and down again; two cars passed, heading toward the city center, but no one else seemed to be stirring. The watch on the inside of her left wrist showed her that the time was just coming up on six thirty; the sun wouldn't rise fully for another half hour.

Her hand sought the key fob in her pocket again, and she clicked the button twice, rapidly, in succession. Thankful for her gloves, she felt along the ridge of the trunk until she hit the latch.

The smell hit her first: something dark and feral, both sickly sweet and sour at the same time. And metallic. The smell of blood, and a lot of it. She held her breath and pushed the trunk open further.

The body lay curled, knees to chest, the left hand with the all-too-familiar wide wedding band thrown out to the side. The eyes were open. A trickle of blood trailed from the side of the slightly open mouth. His expression, frozen, was one of surprise.

Shep.

Juegos del gato y el ratón

Twelve

Aventurine staggered back into her room, slamming the door behind her, just in time. In the small bath, she dropped to her knees before the toilet and vomited until she felt turned inside out. She didn't know how long she knelt there, shuddering, dizzy, and sick. At last she became aware of the stink, and the cold of the tiles beneath her knees, the cold of the toilet seat against her forehead. She slumped back against the wall, pulled the lever, closed the cover. Tried to breathe.

She wasn't prepared for the sobs. They came suddenly, and she pressed her hands to her mouth. She wasn't sure how thick the walls were, and she couldn't risk anyone else hearing her cry.

Shep.

There was absolutely no doubt now. No room for hope.

There was absolutely no doubt that Shep Genthner was dead.

The sun rose. The shadows shifted in her room, and the muted light crawled across the ceiling. Aventurine lay on her bed and watched, fearing to doze, knowing that each time she closed her eyes, Shep's surprised expression would rise before her. She could not risk the waking nightmare becoming the stuff of her dreams. She felt feverish and sweaty. Her stomach was empty, and she knew both that she had to eat something, and that if she did, she would only make herself sick again. She got up, shakily, hung the *não perturbe* sign on the outside knob, then locked herself in again.

Her hands were shaking. Aventurine re-started the coffee maker. She shifted the curtain away from the window and peered out again at the silver Peugeot: Shep's coffin. The thought of her discovery roiled her stomach. She drank the coffee black, though it scalded her tongue, and, finding that it stayed down, made another one and drank that, too. Her shaking didn't stop. It might have become worse.

She lay back down on the bed and wondered what to do.

Aventurine had no idea how much time had passed before she became aware of the first disturbance. She got up and pulled the curtain aside again. A police car had pulled into the space beside the Peugeot. A pair of uniformed officers climbed out and walked slowly around the car, looking at it from all angles. One kept leaning into the radio set on his shoulder, while the other wrote things in a small notebook. They both donned gloves and tried the doors: locked. Aventurine had had the presence of mind to click the fob before she threw it into the Tagus and fled.

She kept watching, unable to look away. After a while a tow truck appeared. The driver slipped a thin metal bar into the window, and in a moment, had the door unlocked. The two officers looked inside, and one hit the button to pop the trunk. That's when the proverbial shit hit the fan.

The two officers held the tow truck driver until reinforcements appeared: an unmarked car with a suited man and woman; a van from which poured a collection of people who donned sterile suits and booties. Photographers. A tent was set up around the car, as, by now, a number of curious people had appeared in the beach-side parking area, craning for a look at the action.

Aventurine couldn't bear to watch any more. She dropped the curtain and threw herself back down on the bed. She had witnessed this machine groan into life before, near the Old Bishop's Palace in Lincoln, the night Alyona Morozovna had been killed. Avi had been horrified then at the ruthless efficiency flying in the face of someone's tragedy, and that feeling had not changed. Now, if anything, it was worse, because she knew the victim. She knew the man whose body was stuffed in the trunk of the car. The man whose hands she had touched in life, whose cheek she had kissed. She had stood up for him—for them—at his and Mick's wedding. Shep. Her brother-in-law. Dead. She was horrified, and somehow in awe of the enormity of it.

Aventurine's thoughts skittered back to Alyona Morozovna and away again. That night Aventurine had first met Dominic Burroughs, who didn't trust her, and whom she would not think about.

Either you're always in the wrong place at the wrong time, or you're a killer.

Well, he'd already made up his mind about her. So she wouldn't think about him. She wouldn't.

Except that *he* would think about *her.* The discovery of Shep's body would be news, and it would reach him, and whatever suspicions Burroughs had would be confirmed. And because he was a policeman, he would probably convey what he knew—what he suspected—to the ever-widening network of investigators.

Because Shep had been murdered. There could be no doubt about it, as a man who had been missing, declared missing and presumed dead for more than a year, would not otherwise end up bloody and dead in the trunk of a car more than 3,000 miles from where he had disappeared.

She had to tell Micheline. She knew she couldn't do it over the phone. How did one call up one's twin sister, whose life had been overwhelmed by grief and uncertainty for such a long time, and baldly say *oh, by the way—I came across your husband's dead body today*? How cruel that would be. Of course, with the way things were going, it was unlikely that Micheline would answer the phone anyway. A text? Even more cruel. Mick had left her on read over the past couple of weeks.

And Paul. She caught her breath, pressed the balls of her hands into her eyes.

Paul, who had stormed off on her in London when she had suggested—when Nicola had suggested through her—that Shep might have died by suicide. Might have wrecked the *Máquina* intentionally. Paul, with whom she finally had words about his fleeing when things went bad. Now she was the bearer of the worst news: that his father was actually dead, but not from the wreck of the boat, and most certainly not by his own hand. How would Paul take this? How would he take it, coming from *her*? Again Avi drew in a long breath. Lance—maybe Lance could help? Paul was lucky to have Lance in his life, and as Genevieve had said—it seemed like ages ago now—the two of them were inextricably linked together by Neil's death and the aftermath.

No matter what she did, or did not do, it would be wrong. It would be an impossibility.

Aventurine struggled to her feet and peered out through the gap in the drawn curtains. More strobing lights: blue, red. Police tape. An ambulance. A handful of people, the numbers growing slowly, looking on in morbid curiosity. As she watched, more people gathered and were held back by the cordon, leaning into one another, gossiping. She felt a wash of hatred toward them, just looking down toward the *avenida*. Ghouls, all of them, gawking at the death of someone who had been so vital, so dear. Her sister's dearest love. Her nephew's—son's—father.

Oh, God. Shep.

The light was streaky, with only a couple of hours of daylight left before sunset. Emergency flashers strobed the *avenida*, and then the klieg lights were set up.

Aventurine groped for her phone, but the battery was dead. Hurriedly she plugged it in, fumbling with the cord. Why hadn't she plugged it in before? She turned back to the window looking over the street, where the blinding false noontime of the crime scene lights now blazed. People moved back and forth below her. At some point someone questioning people door-to-door would come to her room, to her door—or would all the guests be summoned to a common room downstairs to give statements?

Another run-in with the police. Aventurine felt the net tightening about her. She'd done nothing—*nothing*—and still she was caught up in this trap. Almost as though someone were setting her up. So far she had escaped, had remained free—but she felt it only a matter of time before she would be unable to work herself out of the situation.

Coincidence? Burroughs had asked that, of himself, of her. And had come to the conclusion that he could not believe her protestations of innocence. At this point he was hardly a stranger. How would someone who did not know her—those police officers out in the street, for example—take her involvement in these deaths?

The wave of terror made her rush again to the toilet—but there was nothing left to come up out of her empty stomach.

She had to talk to Micheline.

Micheline.

She had to call her sister. No. She had to see her sister. Face-to-face. She couldn't just break the news of Shep's death over a text, or by phone call. Avi coughed into the toilet bowl, clutched by the horror of it. Shep was dead. She knew it. Mick didn't. And the news would kill her twin. But it would be better for Micheline to learn it from her, wouldn't it? Rather than from some stranger? Rather than from the news?

She reached for the phone again.

Thirteen percent battery now. She hit Micheline's number on speed dial and held her breath.

The phone rang and rang and finally went to voicemail.

"Call me," she said helplessly. "*Call me.* Mick. It's an emergency." Then, after a moment of indecision, "It's about Shep."

She held the phone, still tethered to the charger, and waited. Outside there was the sound of yet another siren, and she winced.

Finally she texted the same message. Waited.

No response.

She tried Paul.

Nothing.

A little later she watched furtively as a handful of police officers fanned out along the street, talking to people, taking notes. They'd be coming to the buildings shortly, all the hotels and guest houses along this stretch, to ask if anyone had seen anything, heard anything. Aventurine chewed her lower lip, scanning the windows across the way, hoping against hope that no one had seen her in the early morning semi-darkness. That no one had seen her rush down to the beach and hurl the key fob into the incoming tide.

She had been early. She tried to remember. Earlier than the joggers. Earlier than the dog walkers. The street, and the avenue below, had been deserted, save for the occasional car. She had had her hat on against the morning cold. As long as no one had been watching the sunrise from their windows overlooking the street, she should be fine.

There was no more coffee. She made some tea.

A knock came on the door. Aventurine let the curtain fall, took a deep breath, and called out, "*Quem é, por favor?*"

A woman's voice "*Serviço de limpreza!*"

Aventurine unlocked the deadbolt but kept the door on the chain. In the corridor, a young woman in blue, holding folded towels over her arm. Avi took the door off the chain and held her hands out for the towels. Her words were painstaking. "*Eu estou bem hoje. Chá? Café?* More?" She looked down at the *não perturbe* tag on the door, which the chambermaid hadn't seen, or had ignored.

The young woman smiled. "*Mais?*" She held up a finger, and turned away toward her cart, then almost immediately returned with a handful of tea bags and coffee packets in her cupped palms. "*Leite? Açucar?*"

Aventurine forced a smile and took the offering. "*Obrigada, não.*"

The woman peered at her face, and her expression turned sympathetic. "*Sentir-se melhor! Tchau!*"

She turned away again, and Aventurine shut and locked the door behind her. She leaned against it, exhausted, having used up all her knowledge of Portuguese.

When Avi nudged the curtain aside again, she could see that the police were still moving about purposefully. It wouldn't be long before they were inside, asking their questions. She rinsed out the coffee maker and started more water. It would only be a matter of time.

The darkness fell, and Avi did not bother to turn on the bedside lamp. The brilliant lights from across the *avenida* still played across the ceiling, even though she had not opened the curtains. At a loss, she finally dialed Genevieve's number.

There was no answer.

She started to type in a text message, then deleted it. Tried again and deleted that, too. Finally, only two words. **Shep's dead**. She hit send before she could change her mind.

Thirteen

Aventurine turned on the television, looking for a channel carrying the news.

When she found one, the program was in the middle of a weather forecast, a perky young woman in a yellow cap-sleeved dress, waving a hand at the coastline. Bands indicating isobars undulated behind her. Avi understood very little of it. She picked up the remote control to surf some more when the weather announcer threw it over to a man and woman seated behind a desk, looking very grim. A banner scrolled at the bottom of the screen, too quickly for her to read more than perhaps every third word.

Sintra.

She sat upright, hitting the volume button as though raising the level of sound would raise her level of understanding. *Acidente.* That word was obvious. *Ferimento.* Injury, she thought. She dropped the remote and leaned forward. What kind of accident? Who was injured? The screen cut to some dim footage inside a well: *Poço Iniciático na Quinta da Regaleira.* It was slightly unsteady, and she could see the ornate carving on the pillars at the other side of the well, and the shadowy forms of people descending; she could hear echoing footsteps, drips, voices. Then suddenly, chaos. There was a jolt, and people were falling, knocking one another down like dominoes on the circular stairway, with screaming echoed and re-echoed in the cramped space. After a few terrifying moments, another cut to someone interviewing a rescue worker, who spoke far too quickly for Aventurine to translate. But the figures behind him, seated on the ground, being tended to by other paramedics—there was Lance, holding out a bandaged arm, blood on his face; behind him, Paul, with a protective arm around his shoulders.

She grabbed her phone again, dialing Paul. The call went straight to voicemail. "Are you all right?" she gasped out. "Is Lance all right? What happened? Call me. I need you to call me." Avi realized she sounded borderline hysterical. She hung up, dialed Lance's number, which, too, went through to voicemail. Frustrated, she left the same message.

On the television, there was theme music, and the news was over. Quickly, Aventurine snatched up the remote and flicked through channels, looking for more news. But it was the top of the hour, and she was unable to find any. She shut the TV off and opened her phone to the browser. Typing in *Poço Iniciático na Quinta da Regaleira*, she flipped through the results, but apparently this news was too fresh to have been put up on any news outlet's website yet.

Nothing to do but wait.

The knock on the door came shortly thereafter. Aventurine expected a uniformed police officer but instead was faced with the hotel manager. He wrung his hands apologetically.

"You will come downstairs?"

"What's happening?" *Give nothing away,* Genevieve had always said, though at the time, Avi had thought she was speaking of her time in occupied France. Now Aventurine knew that the old spy had been talking about every facet of life.

"Emergency. *Emergencia? Uma occurencia?*" He seemed particularly distressed. At the incident, or at the disruption at his hotel, it was impossible to tell. He pointed toward the stairs. *"A polícia está no saguão."*

"Police?"

But he was gone, heading to knock on the next door. Aventurine turned back to gather her bag and key, then headed downstairs. No help for it. She squared her shoulders, hoping her pale face and weepy eyes wouldn't give her away; but if the chambermaid thought she was sick, perhaps the police officer would, too.

There were already several people in the lobby; all available seating was taken. Aventurine found a spot to the side, leaning against the wall near a young couple, and a man who smelled like he'd just come from the gym. She surreptitiously held a hand before her nose. She saw that the young woman was doing the same.

After a few minutes' wait, the manager appeared once again, looking more flustered than before. He conferred with an officer, which the policeman frowned at, then folded his hands away into the pockets of his coat.

"*Ola, boa tarde,*" the officer called, and the noise level in the lobby dropped immediately.

"Good evening," a woman next to him said. A translator? Most of the people in the lobby of this little hotel seemed either Portuguese or English, with a few American outliers like herself—but what did Aventurine really know? She looked between the two. Maybe this woman was a guest with better Portuguese than most of the other English speakers.

The policeman barked out several rapid sentences, the woman beside him frowning slightly in concentration. When he paused, she said, "There's been an incident on the avenue, and someone has died."

Several people gasped. One older woman in a chair raised her hand. The policeman ignored her and continued. Then he nodded to the translator.

"The police would like to ask anyone who has any knowledge of a car parked in the area above the beach sometime last night to speak to them immediately. Anyone who saw anything out of the ordinary overnight and into this morning."

The woman in the chair still waved her hand in the air and now cleared her throat loudly.

The policeman spoke. Aventurine recognized the words *seu nome* and *passaporte,* but the rest flew by her too quickly. The meaning was obvious, however. The sweaty man next to her unzipped a pack and drew out a passport with a red cover.

The translator picked up. "If you would form a line and give your name, present your passport to the officer, and indicate at that time whether you might have seen anything, he would appreciate it."

The woman to the side hefted herself out of the chair and pushed forward. "Will this take long?" she demanded in English. "I have dinner reservations."

The policeman turned and stared at her blankly. If he didn't understand the words, he certainly understood the tone. The woman who had been translating smiled beatifically. "Why don't you just come up to the front of the line, ahead of everyone, so you can go to dinner and not be inconvenienced by this tragedy."

Aventurine wanted to kiss her.

Avi got into the line, trying to put a few people between her and the sweaty man; it fell to the young couple to fill the space between them, and she almost felt sorry for them. The line itself moved slowly but efficiently; ahead she could see the officer jotting down names, addresses, passport numbers from people who presented them. When she finally reached the head of the line, she held hers out, debating her expression. A little nervous? She was an American tourist in a strange country with limited language ability: how would a perfectly innocent person present herself?

"Você viu ou ouviu alguma coisa ontem à noite ou esta manhã?" the officer asked.

Apparently her expression of confusion was convincing. "He'd like to know whether you saw anything last night, or this morning," the translator said.

"No," Aventurine replied. "*Nada.* Nothing. I was sleeping."

They both nodded, and having copied her information into his notebook, the police officer handed her back her passport.

"If there are any more questions, the police will be in touch."

"Thank you." Aventurine nodded to the officer. *"Obrigada."*

"Obrigado," he said. And did not smile.

Aventurine headed for the stairs.

She didn't feel at all like Mary Wentworth. As she opened the fire door at the top of the stairs, she half-expected the police officer to shout her name, come thundering upstairs after her.

Aventurine wondered why she wasn't used to lying to the police yet.

Her phone was nearly fully charged. She ordered a pizza online, then went out to pick it up. Her legs were wobbly all the way to the next street and back.

The police tent and lights were still in place, guarded by a pair of officers. The flatbed tow truck was gone. So, too, it would appear, was the Peugeot. Aventurine let herself into the hotel, shuffling purse, pizza, and keys about.

Once inside her room, she threw the bolt, clicked the chain into place, and then, once her hands were empty, shoved the desk chair back under the knob. It might not keep a determined intruder out, but at least it would make a terrible crash, should anyone attempt entry.

She slumped onto the bed and drew out a slice of pizza. It tasted like the cardboard of the box in her mouth, but she forced herself to chew and swallow: the first food she had eaten all day. She clicked on the television and scanned the channels, looking for news from the beach, from Sintra. All she could find were police dramas and a football match. She left the sound down. The pizza was sitting in her stomach like a rock. She forced herself to take another bite. That didn't help. She set the slice back in the greasy box and closed it up. Maybe later. Maybe tomorrow. Maybe never. She closed her eyes and willed her phone to ring.

There had been no ring, no vibration from the phone for the entire time she'd been in the street. Still, she took it out now and checked, a compulsion, in case there was something she'd missed. Nothing. Of course. She stared at the icons, all cheerfully colored, all indicating she'd missed nothing except for her Duo Lingo lesson for the day.

Call me, Mick. Paul. Lance.

Nothing happened.

Resisting the urge to dial them—any of them—again, she moved to the window and lifted the edge of the curtain. The two officers both had their arms crossed over their chests; they both scanned the windows of the hotels and guesthouses along the street. She dropped the curtain quickly, not wanting to be seen. Then she chided herself. She probably wasn't the only person keeping an eye on them, up and down the street. But she certainly was the one with the guilty conscience.

No, not guilty, exactly. But the one with more knowledge of the goings-on than was healthy. The one with the most at stake here.

She bit her lip and dialed Genevieve. The call went straight to voicemail.

She refilled the kettle and put the water on for tea. More tea. Digging through the little basket on the tray, she found a couple of decaffeinated tea bags. It was probably too late: she was probably going to be staying up all night. She groaned and squeezed her head between her hands.

The phone buzzed, on the bed where she'd tossed it.

Avi crossed the room with a bound and grabbed it up. *Please be Mick. Please be Mick.*

It wasn't Micheline. It was Dominic Burroughs.

Burroughs, who had walked away from her on East Pier, it seemed a lifetime ago, because he couldn't trust her. The man who had just walked away.

Leaving her to be shoved into the water. Leaving her to be nearly drowned.

Where are you?

She pressed her lips together, furiously. Why does it matter? she texted back.

I need to see you.

For a long time all she could do was stare at the screen agog. The nerve. Seriously.

You walked off and left me, and I nearly got killed.

And now Aventurine almost threw the phone, in her frustration and fury. It didn't matter that he had had no idea that someone was there, waiting on a chance. Getting a chance. It didn't matter. What mattered was that suddenly she felt the water in her nose, in her mouth, filling her lungs, making her gag, making her cough. She could have died. She almost wished he stood there in front of her, so she could wring his neck.

All the more reason why I need to see you.

The kettle was boiling, and it shut off with a click. She dropped the phone and moved to pour herself a cup of decaffeinated tea. *Decaffeinated.* She could have spit.

The police were still out there; as she watched, one set off along the pavement, leaving a single officer outside the tent.

Aventurine had had enough of police. She'd had enough of Dominic Burroughs. This was just one more secret she'd have to keep from him. This was just one more unexplained propinquous death that he would, no doubt, lay at her feet.

"Damn you, Burroughs," she hissed.

The tea was too hot and burned her tongue. When she set the cup back down, the liquid sloshed all over the tray. Still cursing, she fetched a towel from the fresh supply housekeeping had brought and used it to sop up the mess. Only then did she retrieve the phone and respond, peevishly.

It'll be difficult, since I'm in Lisbon.

Take that, Dominic Burroughs.

Still no reply from Micheline, or the others.

Aventurine stripped off her clothes, and, turning off the light, slid between the sheets.

Fourteen

The morning dawned grey. Or at least, it was grey when, after a night of tossing and turning in a half-sleep, waiting for phone calls that never came, Aventurine opened her gritty eyes. Her first instinct was to check her phone for messages, but the battery, again, was dead. She put it back on the charger and resigned herself to wait until there was at least a smidgen of power.

Another day in Lisbon. Another day of Shep being dead.

Aventurine shut her eyes again in frustration and despair. She needed to check the news, to see what there was about the discovery of Shep's body. Had he been identified? Perhaps he had had some sort of identification in his pockets, in his wallet? She should have checked. She cursed herself for her stupidity. Then asked herself *why?* *Why* should she have checked? She had been in shock. She was still in shock. Her first instinct had been to protect herself; there was nothing, at that point, that she could have done for her dead brother-in-law.

And what about the incident in Sintra? What about Paul and Lance? Why hadn't they called? What had happened?

She groped for the remote and turned on the TV; it was early morning, there would be news broadcasts. Both of these things were big news. Should be. She frowned, wishing she could keep up with the newscasters, with normal conversational speed. Of course it would be easier to check the online news; she instinctively reached for the phone, but of course the battery was barely above one percent. She leaned back against the pillows and stared at the television.

Her head spun. She'd tuned into the news right at the sports segment; she'd have to wait for the program to come around again to the hard news. Shep, dead in the trunk of a car on the beach. Paul and Lance, caught up in some sort of accident at the Initiation Well. No way to contact Micheline. No way to contact Genevieve. She looked over at the table, at the kettle, and realized that if she drank any more of the abysmal tea or coffee, she'd make herself sick again. The pizza sat in its grease-stained box on the desk; she didn't even bother to look inside before jamming the whole thing into the trash.

Avi peered through the curtain. Nothing had changed across the avenue.

She turned back to the television when she heard the word *testemunha:* witness. The footage was a long-distance pan of the scene at the beach: the tent, the car on the flatbed. Someone in a uniform was speaking rapidly: witnesses to the crime? Witnesses should come forward? Then *identidade*. That one was easy enough to figure out, but what about the identity? Of the victim? Of the perpetrator? Aventurine wondered whether the police would be back to the hotel today, to question the guests. To question her. *Say nothing.* She heard Genevieve's voice repeating the words, a sort of mantra. *Say nothing.* Of course, that was easy to do when your Portuguese was so rudimentary. But the police could engage a real translator; then things would be exponentially more difficult.

She hardly had time to consider these questions when the announcer segued into the next story. She caught the words *Regaleira* and *Sintra* and moved closer to the screen. The reporter spoke too quickly, but she recognized the footage she'd seen before, and she concentrated on the background, where the paramedic was bandaging Lance's arm. Then it cut to what appeared to be an eyewitness interview: a woman with an incipient bruise on her cheek, waving an arm back toward an opening in the hillside, near a waterfall. She kept shaking her head as her words tumbled out. The camera pulled back to show a small child, jacket muddy and torn, clinging to the woman's leg. Then it was back to the newscasters at the broadcast desk.

The only thing for it was a newspaper. There was a newsstand around the corner at the other end of the street, and—she glanced down at the pizza box crushed into the trash can—she could probably find some *pasteis de nata* and a decent cup of coffee at the same time. Stiffly she dragged open the bureau drawer and rifled through it for some clean clothes.

Her portable charger, too, was drained, so she had to go out without the phone. Aventurine found herself hurrying, feeling lost and exposed. What if someone called? She quickened her steps, listening for the echoes of footsteps behind her, but there were none. She found the newsstand and bought a paper, and there was a pastry shop, it seemed, on every corner in Lisbon, so she soon had coffee and a bag full of *pasteis de nata* to bring back. When she turned onto her own street, she passed a uniformed police officer heading the other way—perhaps one who had stood watch all night, in which case, he must be exhausted. She nodded, trying not to look too shifty. She felt his gaze on her until she turned into the hotel.

Did it make more sense to play the gossip and ask the receptionist for news, or just sail on by? Which would seem more suspicious? She cast a glance at the young woman at the desk; Avi had seen her before and thought she might be a relative of the manager. Daughter, perhaps.

The girl beat her to the punch. "*Ola,* good morning," she said with a wide smile. She had gorgeous dark eyes and wore her hair, the blue-black of a crow's wing, pinned back.

"*Bom dia,*" Aventurine returned.

The girl's smile widened further.

Aventurine crossed the lobby to the desk and leaned in, lowering her voice. "Any news? About—" She tipped her head toward the street.

"*Não,*" the receptionist said, and shook her head. "*Uma tragedia.*"

"No one knows who he is?" Aventurine asked.

The girl shook her head, looking puzzled.

Aventurine searched her brain for the word. "*Identificacão?*"

"*Não.*"

Aventurine too shook her head and thanked the receptionist, then turned to the stairs.

Once in her room, she set the bag and the coffee on the table below the window. She clicked on the desk lamp, not yet up to opening the curtains. Still, wouldn't closed curtains be more suspicious to the policemen in the street, the ones scanning the windows or the hotels and guest houses? She paused. Were they still doing that? She hated this—all the second-guessing she had to do. If she did open the curtains, the officers would no doubt see a woman sitting at a table, drinking coffee and eating pastries over the morning newspaper. Harmless enough.

The phone buzzed. She dropped everything to pick up. Paul.

"Oh, my God, are you all right?" she gasped. "And Lance—how's Lance?"

"You've seen the news, then," Paul said.

"Yes. Last night and this morning. I tried calling—"

"I know. My phone died. And it was complicated, getting back here, and having Lance's wrist looked at at the hospital."

"Is he okay?"

"A sprain. We thought at first he might have broken it in the fall, but the x-rays were negative."

"The fall. What happened at the well? It was all over the news. I didn't understand much of what they said. What happened?"

A long indrawn breath. "Aventurine. Avi. Calm down. We're okay."

"And there was blood on his head—"

"Just a scrape. He's okay. Resting right now. We're both okay."

Aventurine sank into the desk chair. She took a deep breath. Another. "Tell me. Tell me everything. I won't interrupt."

"Hold on a minute." His voice grew muffled, as though he were holding the phone away from his mouth. Avi heard her name, and something that sounded like *I'll turn off the light*. Then he was back. "Whatever it was happened so quickly, Avi, that neither of us know exactly what happened. We'd gone to the Initiation Well and were just starting down when there was a shout, and people began to fall down the circular stairway, just like dominoes. The steps were wet—there were warning signs everywhere—but people just kept falling. Then everybody was screaming, and it was so echoey in there." Paul took a deep breath. "Lance grabbed me, tried to break my fall, and ended up taking my weight when he went down. We fell into some other people, and they pitched forward—it seemed to go on forever, Avi. In the dimness, it was downright terrifying."

"It looked it on the television," she said. "Maybe it was worse because I didn't understand what people were saying. But you're all right, and Lance is all right." She didn't know why she needed to keep being reassured.

"We're okay," Paul repeated. "There were some people who were hurt worse—some broken bones, I think a concussion. But we were lucky, Avi. We were all lucky."

She sensed the hesitation behind his words. "What is it?" she demanded.

"I don't—" he stopped and started again. "Avi, I can't get over the feeling—that it wasn't—an accident."

"What are you saying?"

"I don't know what I'm saying."

Her response was quick. "Listen. I need to see you. We need to talk."

"This is all I know—"

"No," Avi cut him off. "A lot has happened since yesterday morning when you left. Not just this—thing—in Sintra. Things here."

"Nicola?"

Worse. Far worse. But she couldn't say it over the phone. "How fast can you get over here?" She peered out the window into the street, just as another police car slid to a stop at the curb. "No. No—don't come here. I'll come to you."

"But Lance—"

"This involves him, too." She bit her lip. Lance's were the only calls Genevieve would take. "And I need his help."

She grabbed the bag of pastries and the unread newspaper on the way out, along with her charging cord—the phone wasn't even up to 50% yet, but she could charge it in their room. Their hotel was about a half mile away, and she put its address into her map application and stepped out, choosing a route that led away from the beach, and the police. No one stopped her; no one spoke to her. The sky overhead was grey and ominous, portending rain later, but for now, the air was just sticky and humid. Unless that was just her nerves playing tricks on her.

Paul was waiting at the door. He straightened when he saw her.

"I expected you to come the other way," he said, pointing in the direction of the avenue.

Awkwardly she threw her arms around him.

"I—couldn't," she said. She found she was shaking. How was she going to tell him? "The police—"

"Traffic accident or something?"

Aventurine extricated herself and looked up into his face. She saw so much of Shep in him this morning: the shape of his jaw, the worry lines beneath his eyes. It was hard to bear, and she stifled a sob. *Not now. Don't break down now.*

Paul stilled, his hands on her arms. "Avi, what is it?" He leaned closer. "It's okay. I told you Lance and I are okay. Tired, but lucky, I guess."

She swallowed. "Can we go to your room?"

He glanced over his shoulder, toward the windows on the upper floors. "Can we just go get a coffee or something? Lance is sleeping. I don't want to bother him."

Aventurine shook her head. "No. Paul, please. And I told you I need Lance's help as well." Her voice was shaking now, too. She felt the sweat break out on her forehead. "Please."

Shrugging, Paul turned to lead her inside. There was an elevator; they took it to the fourth floor. When he let them in with the keycard, the room was darkened. Lance stirred in the bed and sat up slowly, rubbing his eyes with his right fist, endearingly.

"Did you find breakfast?" he asked groggily. He turned on the bedside light and squinted, turning his head away.

"I found Avi," Paul said.

"I've got some pastries," Aventurine added, finding her voice still shaking.

"What's wrong, Aventurine?" Lance asked quickly.

Paul shook his head and, closing the door behind them, went to sit next to Lance on the bed. "I told her we're—mostly—all right."

Aventurine licked her lips and took a deep breath. She crossed to set the newspaper on the table before the window. "Paul. Lance. *This.*"

Something in her voice finally got through. The two came to her side slowly, as though swimming against some underwater current. The story was on this morning's front page. Avi steeled herself to look at the photograph, taken with what passed nowadays as a telephoto lens—probably just a really good cell phone camera. It revealed next to nothing she hadn't already looked at repeatedly the previous day, or seen on the newscasts: the trunk of the car, the milling policemen, the sullen water of the river beyond the beach—all telescoped into the appearance of being much closer.

Polícia Busca Informações Sobre Morte Suspeita.

Aventurine dragged out her phone again, and the charger fell to the floor at her feet. When she had looked up *busca*, she was able to figure out the rest. A suspicious death. The three of them scanned the article; Avi picked up some information and put a hold on the rest, but the name she wanted was not there. Nowhere did it say "Shepherdson Genthner." She went back again, translator in hand, and figured out the gist of it: nowhere did it say the police were withholding the name of the victim pending notification of family, either. So it was probably safe to say that they had no idea yet whose body they had on their hands.

Quickly she texted Micheline again. With Paul and Lance. URGENT.

"What—is this?" Paul asked hoarsely. "Why are you showing us this?"

Lance moved closer.

Aventurine held on to the table with both hands.

"It's your father," she whispered. "It's Shep."

Fifteen

Carefully she explained everything that had happened since sunrise the previous day.

"You didn't call me right away?" Paul said. He had sunk into the hard chair next to the table, and now sat, rocking gently, his hands clasped between his knees. His face was tracked with tears.

"I'm sorry," Aventurine said. "I—I was in shock, Paul. I hardly knew what I was doing." She wanted to take him in her arms but knew she couldn't. Lance had drawn up the second chair, and he sat stiffly in it, close, but not touching Paul. He would wait until invited. "I hardly know what I'm doing now."

"It's understandable," Lance said.

"It was Dad. You're certain it was Dad."

Aventurine nodded. "I'm sure." She didn't want to—couldn't—bring herself to speak the details: the surprised expression on the face she knew so well, that ring on his wedding finger, the match to Micheline's own.

"And you didn't call the police."

Avi shrugged helplessly. "There was no help for him. There was nothing I could do. And we couldn't be involved, not any of us."

"The authorities are going to get to us eventually," Lance said. *When he's identified*—but he didn't speak those words. "It's only a matter of time. Because you all are his family."

"You were trying to save your hide," Paul said. He wiped angrily at his face.

"And yours," Avi reminded him.

The look Paul shot her was agonized.

"We're all in this together," Lance said.

"Except Mom," Paul said. His tone was tinged in horror now.

"Except your mother," Aventurine agreed. "I've called and texted and she won't answer me. I can't—" another sob—"bear the thought of her finding out from the newspaper, or the television."

She leaned forward and pressed the balls of her hands to her eyes. Why didn't Mick call back? What if the emergency Aventurine was trying to reach her about had to do with Paul? What if the emergency had to do with Aventurine herself? Didn't it matter?

Avi, too, was crying now, hot tears that coursed down her cheeks. She wiped at her face with her hands. Hadn't she just said, a while ago, that Paul had to let his mother do what she needed to do? Hadn't Avi pointed out that while Paul was important in Mick's life, Shep was even more so? Shep was more important to Micheline than anything in the world. And Micheline was convinced that she was working toward finding out where her husband was. But didn't the word *urgent* mean anything?

Maybe Aventurine simply wasn't being clear enough. Maybe Micheline thought Avi was playing tricks in an attempt to have Mick call her—though, why would she think that? That was cruel; that sort of thing was simply not done. Aventurine picked up the phone again.

News about Shep.

Maybe that would do it. Aventurine didn't want to have to break the news over the phone: they had to arrange to meet.

Call me.

Meeting Lance's dark gaze, she texted the same message to Genevieve, not knowing what to do if she was left on read again.

Her phone rang almost immediately.

Genevieve drew in a long breath. Aventurine could imagine the old woman, seated in that wing-backed chair, stroking that evil cat, her eyes turned inward as she thought. "Tell me all of this again," she said over the speaker when Avi had finished. "Start at the beginning. Don't leave anything out."

So Aventurine did, glancing between Lance and Paul for support, starting with her arrival in Lisbon and finding no Micheline at the address she'd copied from the box. The other two chipped in as the story progressed, through each encounter with Nicola, at the Sé, at the festival.

"Then the key fob," Genevieve prodded.

"It was under the newspaper outside my door. I thought whoever had delivered the paper had dropped it there. I meant to bring it down to the desk."

"But you tried it through the window."

"And it worked."

"Did you order a morning newspaper?"

"No, I didn't."

"So in all likelihood, whoever left the key fob took someone else's paper to cover it up. Did you hear anyone in the night?"

Aventurine covered her face with her hands for a moment, trying to remember. "I don't know. I think I heard something, but it was mixed in with bad dreams."

There was a pause, then a meow and a thump from the end of the line. "So what we've got, Aventurine, is someone parking that car down by the beach, then bringing the key fob to you."

"Yes." The idea was sickening.

"Someone who wanted you to find Shep."

Paul stood abruptly and turned to look out the window. It was Lance's turn to look agonized.

"Yes." Avi's voice was failing.

"Someone who was hoping to implicate you."

It seemed obvious when Genevieve spoke the words. Someone had done this intentionally. *There were no coincidences.*

"Nicola?" she asked hoarsely.

"We don't know," the old woman said. "The reasoning behind her actions is cloudy, but it doesn't seem out of the realm of possibility."

"The text. After the Sé? She said she wanted Shep."

A small noise, like a wounded animal, from Paul.

"Yes. So the question becomes: did she find him, or did someone else find him first?"

It was like a kick in the gut, hearing her put it so succinctly. This time, when Paul made a noise, Lance was at his side immediately, pulling him into a one-armed embrace, where Paul seemed to collapse, with great gulping sobs.

There was a long pause. On speaker, Genevieve had to have heard. The silence from the other end stretched.

"I'm sorry, Paul," the old woman said at last, sounding truly contrite. "I forget that not everyone has my training and experience."

The words were a surprise to Aventurine. She had never heard Genevieve apologize for anything—wasn't sure that was even possible. But then again, this was, figuratively, a new dawn. Nothing was out of the ordinary.

Genevieve cleared her throat. "Back to the car, Aventurine. Walk me through that."

So Aventurine did: the pre-sunrise cold and anxiety, the car straddling the spaces across the avenue. How she had thought originally of the driver down on the beach, maybe walking a dog, maybe jogging. The wondering whether the car and the fob were related. The fateful click of the button. Closer examination, opening the trunk to find Shep. The smell of the blood, mingled with a cloying sweetness she couldn't quite identify and really didn't want to. And then returning to the room to wait for the knock that would indicate police questioning. How she'd have to lie.

"You didn't meet anyone."

"No one. I'm just hoping no other early risers were looking out their windows."

"Yes. It would complicate things if someone saw you at the car. If someone saw you exit or enter the front door of your hotel. But you had your hood up?"

"Hat on. It was cold."

There was a familiar tapping sound, fingernails against something hard: Genevieve thinking. Aventurine realized that it was a tell. Nervous habit? Genevieve didn't do nervous. "That's good. One of the first things anyone mentions about someone's appearance is the hair. If they didn't see it, that's all the better for you." Another pause. "And the key fob?"

"I threw it in the water."

Over the line, the old spy's sigh was audible. "It's better than having it on you, I suppose. That would be really hard to explain."

Aventurine didn't appreciate the wry humor. She crossed to the window, where she looked out blindly, one hand on Paul's back. The *praia* here was impossible to see, and it was just as well. She thought of the flatbed truck backing up to the crime scene tent. They'd have to do a vehicle autopsy. Along with the autopsy on Shep's body.

"They'll be searching the beach, no doubt," Genevieve continued. "The police. They might find the fob, and they might not. Tides and all. Did you wipe it before you threw it?"

"I—don't remember." Aventurine pressed her eyes closed and tried to envision her movements, step by step. Going down to the shingle, trying not to look as though there was any urgency to her movements. In case someone—anyone—was watching. Going down the beach and coming back up to the avenue by a different way. "Wait," she said. The cold air on her cheeks, any exposed skin. "I was wearing gloves. I was wearing gloves, Genevieve."

"The entire time? No prints on the car, then?"

"No. I don't think so. I didn't take them off."

"You've learned something from me, then." There was a hint of satisfaction in the old woman's voice.

Taking a deep breath, Paul extricated himself from Lance and Avi, and, going into the bathroom, shut the door behind him. They heard the water start running in the sink.

"But Genevieve," Aventurine protested now, lowering her voice. "I don't understand. It was Shep. It was *Shep*."

"I believe you."

"But how could he be here? How could he be here *now*?"

"That's what we're going to have to find out."

"How can we do that?"

"I don't know yet. He was certainly traveling under the radar, as it were." Genevieve clicked her tongue. "I'm disappointed. I thought my contacts might have picked up on something in the past year and however long. But they didn't." A system failure, obviously unexpected and unappreciated. Heads would roll.

"Or they weren't telling you."

The old woman made a scoffing noise. "They don't have to tell me," she pointed out. "There are ways."

"If you're a professional."

"If you're a professional. Still, I can't believe I've been putting out these—feelers—and got nothing."

Again, Aventurine had the sense of a spider, in the center of her web, waiting for a vibration, a movement, along one of the many strands she had cast out. This time, apparently, nothing had been caught in the fine filaments. The web had failed Genevieve. Perhaps, though, she had simply missed something. She was, as she kept telling Aventurine, an old woman. Perhaps she simply wasn't as sharp as she used to be. But entertaining that thought made Avi uncomfortable, and she dismissed it quickly.

"What do we do now?" she asked. "Paul's taking it very hard. And how do we tell Micheline?" Avi knew this would kill her sister.

"That's delicate."

Down on the avenue, a police car passed, lights flashing. Aventurine shuddered. Were they headed toward the crime scene tent? Were they asking questions at the hotel? She leaned her forehead against the window. It could be a traffic stop. Just a traffic stop.

"It will destroy her."

"Or not." There was a slight pause. "Aventurine, both Micheline and Paul have been balanced on the knife edge of possibility for ages now. That didn't destroy them as it would have done weaker people. Now there is definitive knowledge. Shep Genthner is dead. They don't have to wake up to hope every morning, only to have it dashed at night."

There was the sound of a flush from the bathroom.

"So, they wake up every morning hopeless, now?" Avi's tone was bitter. Lance slipped in beside her and put his good arm around her waist.

"For a while. And then they push on."

"What if they can't?"

"Oh, Aventurine. I'm disappointed in you. Surely you know that your twin sister is stronger than that. And surely you know that Paul is as well—and even if he weren't, Micheline has it in her to be strong for both of them." Genevieve sighed. "And then of course there's you, who has the strength of ten lions, as they used to say in the Resistance. Now: I will call you back—"

"Will you?" Aventurine's tone was disbelieving.

"—after I've checked on a few things here. Stay out of trouble."

Just like that, the phone went dead.

Aventurine found herself staring at it.

"Come and sit down," Lance urged.

She looked up at him. "We—didn't talk about your accident."

He held the chair for her, and she sank into it. More sounds of the faucet from the bathroom. Now Lance looked down at the bandage on his left arm. "We didn't need to," he said slowly. "She—already knew."

Of course she did.

"You talked to her last night."

"This morning, before you got here."

The bathroom door opened, and Paul emerged, looking pale and gaunt and sick. His eyes were red and swollen. He seemed to have aged enormously. He held up a shaking hand to forestall either of them coming to his side, speaking any words of comfort or sympathy.

"No," he said. "We don't have any time. We have to do something."

"Like what?" Lance asked gently.

Paul drew himself up. "We need to go back to Avi's room. I need to see—the place."

Sixteen

They argued almost all the way back to Aventurine's hotel.

When they reached the far end of the road, by mutual agreement, Avi turned left down the road, while the other two kept on.

"Don't be seen," she hissed angrily. "And like Genevieve said, *stay out of trouble.*"

Wordlessly, Paul pulled the baseball cap further down over his hair. Lance pulled up the hood of his sweatshirt.

She entered the hotel to find the door to the small dining room to the left closed. The black-haired receptionist looked less than confident today, and her eyes kept drifting to that door. Avi nodded in greeting and turned up the stairs.

Her room had been serviced, and she was grateful for the removal of the pizza box with the trash. It didn't smell quite so stale, anyway. She had had the foresight to bring back the pastry bag, too, and she pulled one out now, cold and a bit squashed, but her stomach was growling. She saw with relief that the coffee supply had been replenished. The curtains had been drawn open.

She flung off her coat and edged closer to the window, wondering whether to close the curtains again. What would look more normal? Probably open, she decided, since it was the middle of the day. There were the flimsy privacy curtains, of course, so she most likely wouldn't be seen by anyone watching the street. And even if she was? There were still small knots of people wandering past the end of the street, gawkers, looking at the police tent. She would just be another ghoul.

The phone buzzed.

"Are you alone now?" Genevieve asked abruptly.

"What the hell?" Aventurine couldn't see any figures who resembled Lance and Paul, the baseball cap and the hood. Good. They were staying out of sight. "Yes. I am. For the time being."

"Our young men are—where?"

"On their way to my hotel. What have you found out?"

"Nothing yet. I just wanted to check in with you personally."

Aventurine snorted. "Yeah? Now? That's nice. You've hidden from me, spied on me, scared the hell out of me. You led me to believe, weeks ago, that you knew where Micheline was."

"Take a deep breath, Aventurine," Genevieve advised. "You're getting worked up." She paused for a moment. "Lance and Paul— you're getting along all right now?"

"Don't change the subject on me."

"It's all the same subject. You found them. You're talking. Working together." They were questions, disguised as statements, and despite her mild tone, Genevieve seemed to care about the answers. Unless that was Avi's imagination.

"We're talking."

"Good. Three brains are better than one." Another pause, with a rush of background noise, as though the old woman was standing in a wind tunnel. "Now you three can find Micheline, and the four of you can bend your attention to Shep's story."

Story. "You know Mick wasn't registered at the address you left for me to find in your closet."

"That was the address I had at the time. She might have thought someone was on her trail and opted for another hiding place. Or another alias."

"Like mine."

"Unless that was Nicola Hallsey."

"Mick might have just up and gone. To go haring after the next clue. Whatever that might be. Another book, maybe?"

"Aventurine, who left the books?"

"I think you did. And I think you're playing me."

Genevieve laughed shortly. "I'm only responsible for the one in the closet. I know nothing about the placement of the others, though I have my suspicions."

"I don't believe you."

Again with the tutting. "Your belief or disbelief makes no difference to the facts of the matter. You should know that by now." She sighed along the line. "You believed that Shep died in an Atlantic crossing. I thought that might not be true. As did Micheline and Paul. And now we've found that that scenario was absolutely incorrect, and that somehow, the foundering was staged."

Aventurine again peered out the window. A dog walker, with four energetic charges, passed below; a golden retriever inspected each doorstep for a moment before being urged forward. Avi leaned her head back and stared up into the unrelieved slate of the sky. No, there was a sliver of bright blue to the south that seemed a lie. Everything seemed a lie.

"He's been alive all this time. Until recently," she said bitterly.

"Why was it so hard to accept that possibility? Your sister did not accept that Shep was dead; your nephew"—that delicate pause—"did not accept it. The only thing anyone knew for certain was that the *Máquina* foundered. There was absolutely no proof that Shepherdson Genthner was on it when it did."

"Then where did he go? How did he do it?" Avi demanded. "Why did he do this to Mick?"

"The *why* is what we have to determine now. Once Micheline has learned about the death of her husband."

The silence stretched out between them. The dog walker was returning, finding the police presence apparently too exciting for his charges. Avi fancied the retriever cast the hotel entrance a longing look. Probably he just wanted to mark the door.

"But why Lisbon?" Aventurine asked at last, subdued. "Why here?"

There was a series of metallic clanks before Genevieve answered; Avi couldn't identify them.

"Because of Nicola Hallsey," Genevieve replied at last. "The book she published a couple of years ago."

"The one set in Lisbon."

"The one set in Lisbon. Micheline asked about it. I found her the copy. I read it first."

"And?"

"The main female character has a clandestine affair with a married man. A married sailor. Who is in Lisbon on business."

Aventurine felt her knees buckle. She sat quickly. "I need to read this book. I—lost my copy."

"Check with Bertrand Bookstore. Or, if you have to, overnight it from Amazon."

Aventurine cursed herself for letting Brian take off with Genevieve's copy. She looked around the room as though it might somehow reappear. The pain in Avi's gut was growing. "This is going to kill Mick," she said, echoing her words of earlier. "All of it."

"It's not. We need to find her, though, Aventurine. She needs you. She needs Paul."

Next to her ear, the phone buzzed with an incoming text. Paul and Lance were, as planned, nearly to the rear fire door of the hotel. "They're almost here," she said.

"There's one more thing I want you to think about very carefully before I ring off, something that bears mentioning again," Genevieve said. "That's that someone parked that car at the end of *your* street. Near *your* hotel. Left the fob outside *your* door."

"I was supposed to find Shep," Aventurine agreed. She gulped for air. "I know. We'd discussed that."

"And I don't for a moment believe it was just to make you feel better, give you that new-agey *closure*."

Avi shivered. As always, Genevieve was able to give voice to her own fears. "I know."

"It's someone who wants you implicated. *You.* Someone who knows where you are and wants to direct attention to you."

"I know."

"You think very carefully about who that might be; I think we might already know. We've discussed before that whoever was raising your sister's hopes about her husband was being *cruel.*"

Aventurine did not mention that she had herself directed that adjective at the old woman.

"I would posit that whoever left Shep dead on your doorstep is not just cruel, but vindictive. You figure out who is that angry with you." Genevieve's voice hardened. "And you watch your back."

Aventurine had no time to reply before the call ended. She stuffed the phone in her pocket, grabbed the room key, and headed downstairs to admit Lance and Paul.

When they were safely in her room, she locked the door and turned to Paul.

"Call your mother," she ordered. "Say whatever you have to say to get her here."

Seventeen

It was dark when they went out to find dinner. No police detectives had called to ask Aventurine to come downstairs to make a statement. The news was still vague: the name of the victim had not yet been released. With no addendum *pending notification of next of kin.* So the authorities had not yet identified Shep. Still, the three let themselves out through the fire door into the alley all the same.

Micheline had not answered Paul's call. Nor had she returned it.

"Come back to the room," Avi invited wearily. "We can wait there."

But the two had decided to return to their own hotel, to get some sleep, if it was possible. Paul still looked like hell, and there were pain lines under Lance's eyes.

"Keep your phone charged and your ringer on," she said. "And call me at any whisper."

But the night passed with no whisper. Aventurine dozed, and woke, and checked her phone, then did it again. The broken sleep, she decided, was worse than no sleep at all. When dawn broke, she dressed and headed back out through the fire door.

She made it to the beach using a roundabout route, not looking back over her shoulder at the police tent now some half a mile away. She followed the walking path toward the west until she reached the steps leading down to the sand. The wind had died back, but the air was still a bit sharp, with the tide coming in, a steady susurration. Aventurine thought of the other times she'd been on the beach, with Lance and Paul and the members of Mobius, and the time before that, a couple of weeks ago, in Whitby. The time she'd met Ernest Swales, and the time he'd rescued her by pulling her from the water below East Pier. She shivered. Had she drowned, there would have been no question about her possibly being involved in her brother-in-law's death. That thought, however, was not comforting.

Perhaps Aventurine should have gone to the police then. But would they have believed her? *Did she fall or was she pushed?* That would have focused their attention even more closely on her, something she needed to avoid at all costs.

She shoved her hands into her pockets and trudged on.

Only a couple of other figures were in sight, a person who had taken a seat on the sand, further down the beach to her left, and a pair of women walking a terrier. Aventurine slowed her pace so she would not have to speak to them, would not have to nod. Once they had gone, she turned away to her right and, head bowed, made her way slowly to a large stone protruding from the beach itself. She settled onto it—it was dry but would probably be underwater later— and turned her attention to the waves, trying to calm her anxiety. Just beyond the spot where the waves broke over themselves, four gulls bobbed lazily on the water.

Micheline had not called her. Had not called Lance and Paul, either, for they would have let her know.

Aventurine dropped her head into her hands. It was all too much. All she had ever wanted to do was to research, and to write books. She had not wanted to get involved in any of this, had never in her wildest imaginings pictured anything like this. She wanted to curse the moment she had received the first email from Genevieve, asking her to call and discuss the possibility of doing a book on the old spy's adventures, but she really couldn't bring herself to do that. Genevieve had somehow come to mean far too much in her existence since the summer, and Avi wasn't even sure how that had happened. The woman was infuriating, but even her maddening nature had enriched Aventurine's life in a very short time, made it seem somehow less flat. Just this morning had come the notice that the first article had been contracted; but now, would there ever be another one?

Her old computer, stolen from the hotel room in Whitby, had drafts, but at least this time everything had been backed up to the cloud. Should she ever be able to write again. Which was questionable; the stuff from the other night had seemed stilted at the reading.

She looked back up the beach in the direction of the police tent. *Oh, Shep.* This writer's agony was just diversion. Shep was dead. The Peugeot was gone away on the flatbed, and even the police presence had thinned out. Had Shep's body been removed first, to be taken to the morgue, or had he gone with the car to the police auto forensics facility? She had no idea how any of that worked and was not sure she wanted to know.

Instead, she thought of Shep as she had known him, from the time she and Micheline were in college. From the first time she had met him, when Mick had brought him to dinner. She thought of their wedding, at which she had been the maid of honor. She thought of the day they had come to her, to ask her to carry their child, the day she had agreed to give birth to the son who was never to be hers. How alive Shep had been. How humorous, how loving to her sister, how kind to her, how good a father he had been to Paul. How helpful when Mick's and her parents had died in the car accident in South America.

How he loved to sail. How excited he had been to solo, finally, the Atlantic.

And then he had disappeared.

Now he had reappeared.

He was dead. She knew it, and now Paul did, too. But Micheline did not. And until her sister contacted them, there was no way to break the news to her. She would go on living in that limbo of not knowing.

Aventurine pressed her hands into her eyes, trying, again, to hold the sobs in. She couldn't be breaking down like this. She couldn't be crying on the beach, where anyone could wander by and see her. Not far from where a murder victim had been discovered and then rediscovered in the past days. She fumbled in her pocket for a tissue to blow her nose, and found only her cell phone, her not-ringing cell phone.

"Hello, Aventurine."

She looked up sharply and found herself staring at a neatly pressed handkerchief.

Burroughs sat next to her, heavily, using both hands for balance as he settled on the far end of the stone. She stared dumbly at the handkerchief in her hand for a long moment, before flicking it open to wipe her eyes and blow her nose. Only then did she cast a sideways glance at him, sitting so carefully apart. His face looked pale, his features harder than she remembered; there was more grey in his hair. She might not have seen him for years, rather than for weeks.

"What are you doing here?" she asked at last, refolding the handkerchief.

Gulls wheeled overhead. A pair landed a safe distance away on the sand, eyeing them warily.

He didn't answer for a long time, the space filled by the hush of the waves. He had his hands, with those long, elegant fingers, clasped on his knees. He stared out at the early morning river shipping traffic.

When she had last seen him, it had been night, and cold, and he had been walking away, leaving her on the deserted East Pier. Because he knew she had not told him everything, because he knew he could not trust her. For a moment, that still stung. For more than a moment.

"I'm on leave." There was something odd in his tone, something angry, and bewildered.

"Leave?"

"Indefinite leave." His lips pressed together tightly.

Aventurine stared at his hard profile. Something of his mood rubbed off on her. She felt uneasy.

"Why? What's happened?" Her voice was shaking, and she quickly put a hand to her mouth, as though to steady herself. *Indefinite leave.* She found she was shocked by the words: to her, he was defined by his profession, and without it, what was he? Her eyes locked on his face; she wondered if he held that same definition of himself in his own mind. That would account for his bewilderment. If he wasn't a police detective, who was he, actually?

Avi caught her breath. *If she wasn't a writer, who was she, actually?* Damn it.

Something *big* had obviously happened over the past couple of weeks, after he had left her in Whitby. And now, here he was. Again. Following her.

"But why *here?*" she asked, her voice low.

"In Lisbon? It's beautiful. It's warmer than home."

"You're dodging."

He sighed and wiped his hand across his pale face. "Why do you say that?"

"Because the world is large. Because there are many warm places to visit. And of all the gin joints in all the world, you walked into mine."

"Coincidence."

"No. I don't think it is." *There are no coincidences.*

Aventurine knew she was pushing, and at some point, she would reach a boundary—and possibly overstep it. She could feel his resistance just as she could feel the breeze, rising again from the rising tide. But, irrationally, she needed to *know.* After all this time of being cut off from people who were important to her, Burroughs's reappearance might be a lifeline.

Now he threw up his hands. "What do you want me to say, Aventurine?"

There it was, the boundary. She froze.

The silence stretched.

Finally, she held out the refolded handkerchief. "You don't want this back. I'll get you another one."

His laugh was a bark. "Don't even worry about that."

"Tomorrow," she insisted. "Tell me where you're staying."

For the first time, he turned his blue gaze to her face.

Why had she ever thought that gaze icy?

"This afternoon," he said. "I'll be here. On the beach."

"No." Slowly she got to her feet. "Right now."

He looked up slowly.

"I think," she said, before she lost her nerve, "that you had better come back to the hotel."

For the longest of moments, he only looked up at her, his expression inscrutable, and she began to feel somewhat of a fool. As though she'd read everything between them, since the first moment, all wrong.

Then his face closed down, as though a shutter had fallen. He held out a hand.

Eighteen

In the room, she locked the door behind them, then crossed to pull the curtain. She set her bag and the key on the dresser, then slipped out of her jacket. When she turned back, Burroughs was watching her. He had not moved since entering.

"Well?" she said.

He looked down, held out his hands for a moment, then dropped them to his sides.

Letting out an impatient sigh, she came to him, cupped his rough jaw in her hands, and pressed her mouth to his.

He seemed possessed by an incredible stillness.

"Do I have to do it all?" she murmured against his lips. When he said nothing, she slid her hands down and pushed his coat from his shoulders to let it fall to the floor. Then she began on his buttons. "Inspector Morse says the sexiest word in the English language is *unbuttoning,*" she said, undoing one, then sliding her hands down to undo another.

Burroughs gasped, and she paused.

"Do you not want this?" she asked.

"I do want this," he said. Now he met her kiss, open-mouthed, and she shuddered as he pulled her shirt from her waistband to run his hands up the bare skin of her back.

The room grew lighter, and then darker, as they explored each other hungrily. Afterwards they dozed, and, exhausted, Aventurine forgot everything: Shep, her sister, her nephew, Genevieve. She awoke before Burroughs, and fought back the tang of bittersweetness, that this might be the only time this would happen between them. She found herself tracing his profile with a light touch, trying to commit him to memory: his long straight nose, his thick brows, the strong line of his jaw, the shape of his mouth. She buried her face in his shoulder, trying to store up the scent of him.

Burroughs stirred restlessly, and she slowed her caresses. He turned over onto his left side. She shaped herself to him.

Beneath her hands, she felt a raised, rough line, just below his shoulder blade. She stopped, slid her fingertips over it again.

"What is it?" Burroughs asked groggily.

"What is *this?*" she countered. She sat up, flicked on the bedside light, and turned back to examine his skin more closely.

A scar, a couple of inches long, almost two fingers wide. New. Barely healed. The stitch marks stood out.

Aventurine touched it more gingerly, telling herself she had never seen his naked back before, telling herself she had no idea that he had a scar.

Barely healed.

When she ran a finger along it, this time he pulled away.

It was much redder than the surrounding skin of his back and felt warmer. It was raised as well. Most certainly a new scar. Only a couple of weeks old…

"*What is this?*" she demanded again.

Burroughs made a move to climb from the bed, but she grabbed his elbow to stop him.

"Don't you dare," she hissed. "Don't you dare shut me out here."

After a moment, he lowered himself again to the pillow, on his back, the scar safely hidden from her sharpened gaze. Avi propped herself up on an elbow and looked down into his face. His pale face, his hardened profile.

"Tell me what happened."

He closed his eyes. Waited, as though she might forget if he waited long enough. Then: "I was stabbed."

She sat up quickly. "How? When? What happened?"

Burroughs took a deep breath. "It doesn't matter."

"It *doesn't matter?*" Aventurine's voice climbed the register. "Someone stabbed you and it *doesn't matter?*"

"I recovered. I'm all right."

Aventurine fell back on the pillows. "You're on leave. Indefinite leave." *Of course.*

"Yes."

"And we just had mad passionate sex."

"I told you. I recovered."

Aventurine couldn't help herself. The laughter that erupted was borderline hysterical. Just as quickly, it subsided, and she found herself crying.

"It's not a joke. Damn it all to hell, Burroughs, it's not a joke."

Swiftly he caught her chin and turned her face to kiss her, hard. "Call me Dominic."

Again she pressed her face into his shoulder, feeling his skin dampen with her tears. "Dominic." She hiccuped. "It's not a joke. Someone tried to kill you."

"It comes with the job."

She would not be brushed off. "Who did this? Did they catch him?" She caught her breath. "It had to have happened really soon after I last saw you."

He nodded. "Very soon after."

Again, there was something in his tone which gave her pause. Aventurine saw again, in her mind's eye, his retreating back as he left her on East Pier in the windy night. Saw him grow smaller and smaller until he reached the top of the incline and turned onto Henrietta Street and was lost from her sight. So intent had she been upon his figure that she never noticed her own attacker, coming up from behind.

"What is it?" he asked, his voice low.

"Right after you left me on East Pier," she said slowly, "someone pushed me off into the water."

Burroughs stilled again. "How far out in the water?"

"The tide was over my head. I might have made it out anyway, but an old man was down on the beach and dragged me out of the water."

"You might have drowned."

"And been washed out to sea, and no one would have been the wiser."

He rolled over to face her, and she put a hand against his chest, working her fingers into his hair.

"I was stabbed in Whitby that night," he said. "On the way to the car park. After I left you."

"You could have been killed."

"*You* could have been killed."

Seriously. How could she have ever thought his eyes were icy? They were as warm and comforting now as a summer sky.

"We could have both been killed in the car in Wales," she reminded him.

Instead, his police driving training had earned them a place in a hedgerow instead of on the grill of a delivery van.

"We've got to find out for sure what's behind this," she said, her voice still low. "Before the next time. When we might not be that lucky." It mattered to her, his remaining safe, more than she would have thought.

"If that's the case," Burroughs said, "then I have to be able to trust you."

Aventurine tensed. "This again? Can you believe me when I say that I did not kill these people? That I neither attempted to kill you nor myself? That I have no idea what's behind all this? That I'm as confused as you are?"

His gaze traveled over her face, as though searching for answers. For reassurance. Though she had given him all she was capable of.

Finally, he nodded. Slightly. "I'm going to have to, Aventurine, aren't I?"

She blew out a bitter, disappointed breath. "Thanks for that, anyway."

He groaned. "Oh, Avi."

Then she was in his arms again, and he was kissing her mouth, her collarbones, her breasts. She pulled him to her, her palm flat against the rough scar on his back.

Nineteen

While Burroughs was in the shower, she checked her phone. Nothing.

She stared at it. Would she have broken from him in the middle of a round of mad passionate sex had anyone called? She knew she would have.

Once she had taken her turn and returned to the room, toweling her hair, she found Burroughs seated at the desk, looking at the newspaper she had left there yesterday.

"My Portuguese is not good," he said. He had buttoned his shirt—she felt a vague disappointment at that—but he was still barefoot. He leaned over and pulled the curtain aside, looked down toward the beach and the police presence, then turned back to her. He cocked his head. "You'd better tell me about this."

Aventurine swallowed. She sank down on the rumpled bed and crumpled the towel in her hands between her knees.

"The police—found a body," she said. She licked her lips. "Day before yesterday."

"A body."

Aventurine waited. *Another one?* But he didn't say it.

"The authorities haven't identified the victim yet."

The air between them vibrated with the tension. Avi dropped her eyes but then lifted them again.

"You're still here. So close."

"My first instinct was to leave. But that would call attention to myself." She hardened her jaw. "And—I haven't found Micheline yet." Her voice cracked; she couldn't help it.

Another long pause.

"I have to trust you," Burroughs said at last.

Aventurine said nothing.

He stood, tucked his shirt in, and then crossed to take a seat next to her on the bed, pushing aside a stray pillow.

"You'd better tell me."

"Shep," Burroughs said in disbelief when she had finished. "Here. After all this time."

Aventurine held her hands out helplessly.

She expected him to berate her. *Why hadn't she contacted the police? When they found out, it would only mean more trouble, that she had done nothing.* She put her head in her hands, her elbows on her knees.

"It had to have been a shock," he said instead. She felt his arm around her shoulders, felt him pulling her into his chest.

"It was horrible," she whispered. "I've known him more than half my life. He's my twin sister's husband. *And I already thought he was dead.*"

"And now he is."

"And now he is. And I still can't find my sister to tell her." In her resurging frustration and fear about her twin, Avi pushed him away abruptly. "And you're a policeman. I know what you're thinking. That I came across a crime and didn't report it. That I hindered an investigation." She sucked in a long breath and glared at him. "So go turn me in. Or better yet—" she stuck out her hands, fisted, the insides of her wrists up—"just cuff me now and get it over with."

"You're still in shock, aren't you?"

She pounded at his chest. "Stop patronizing me!"

Too late, she registered his wince. Aventurine pulled her fists in and crossed her arms at her chest.

"Stop patronizing me," she repeated.

He sat wordlessly, watching her out of those maddening blue eyes. Finally, a corner of his mouth lifted. "Aventurine, of all the things I have done and would like to do to you, patronizing you is not among them. And there's only one reason I'd handcuff you, but I'm sure we're not to that stage in our relationship yet."

She saw the glint in his eye. Maybe it was the near hysteria that launched her into the fit of laughing. He put his arms around her again, and this time she did not resist.

"I *am* a policeman, Aventurine," he said, speaking softly into her ear. "But I'm a policeman on indefinite leave, and way outside my own jurisdiction. Whatever you say to me in this room stays in this room."

She drew a breath, tried to gather herself. "Genevieve says—"

"Genevieve? That would be Lance's great-grandmother?"

"Yes. *That* Genevieve. She says that the person who—did this—to Shep is trying to implicate me."

Burroughs nodded against her hair. "I think that's a pretty fair surmise." He pressed his lips to the side of her head. "Who has it out for you, Aventurine?"

There was only one answer she knew. "Nicola."

"Your sister."

"*Half*-sister."

"But—what's her connection to Shep Genthner?"

Aventurine wondered whether she should tell him about the book. Or wait until she had found another copy, to show him? Suddenly the words *long game* appeared in her mind, much as if on a billboard. She closed her eyes, thinking again of the book in Brian's hands, his skimming through the text, his eyes widening.

"We've got to go to a bookstore," she blurted.

For a moment Burroughs looked taken aback, but he did not object. "In this, as in all else," he said, pulling on his socks—they were, once again, mismatched, one black, one blue—"I will have to trust you."

She pulled on her own shoes, her own jacket. When she reached for her phone to slide it into her pocket, it buzzed, startling her. She dropped it on the floor. Burroughs retrieved it and handed it to her, without dropping his eyes to the screen.

It was Paul.

Have you heard from Mom? Nothing here.

"It's my nephew," she said.

"Is he okay?"

Quickly she typed. Nothing. Then she looked up at Burroughs. "He's just learned his father's been murdered, and his mother is still missing." She grimaced, but it was painful. "He's as all right as someone in that position could be." A thought, and she quickly typed it: try Genevieve again. Then, "Let's go."

Aventurine thought about including their destination in the text exchange but decided against it: she didn't want to get into any convoluted explanation about her companion, nor did she want to lie.

They headed away from the beach, but Aventurine kept looking over her shoulder on the way to the station near the *Fundaçao*. Beside her, Burroughs stared straight ahead. She didn't feel safe until they'd boarded the inbound train to Cais do Sodro. They found a car with only a few other travelers, most of whom were intent on their phones, or books. Nearly everyone had earphones on.

"He had to have been into something bad," Burroughs murmured, leaning towards her from the seat to her right. "Whether he knew it originally or just stumbled into it."

Aventurine felt a wash of defensiveness, but that subsided quickly. "Tell me why you think so."

"Because he was in hiding for more than a year. Because everyone thought he was dead—including his family—and he made no move to disabuse anyone." Burroughs kept his voice low, but there was no one near them in the carriage. "Either that's because he was afraid for his life—and we know now, apparently with good cause—or he was afraid to endanger anyone else."

"Mick. Paul." Avi felt a stir of pity which she couldn't quite define: Shep in danger, Shep protecting those he loved best.

"Yes. But we don't know that. For all we know, he was aware of what he was getting into, and found himself in too deep. He could have been playing a dangerous game."

"But that doesn't fit in with the Shep I've known for half my life," Avi protested.

He touched her hand and didn't argue.

Aventurine leaned her head against the window. The train slid into the station at Santo Amaro, and almost immediately slid out again.

"Did he fake his death?" she asked aloud as the buildings eased by. She didn't expect an answer; how on earth would Burroughs know?

"I don't know," he said. "It would be complicated. I don't know how he could have done it on his own."

Someone would have had to have picked him up after he'd scuttled the *Máquina*. Someone who knew he was going to do it. Aventurine shied away from that idea. No. It was more likely that someone had taken him, then had scuttled the boat. Wasn't it?

But the intervening time: either he had been held against his will, or he was in hiding, unable or unwilling to contact his family.

Abruptly, she pulled out her phone.

"What is it?" Burroughs asked.

"I need to show you something."

Before she could second guess herself, Aventurine opened the letter on her phone and enlarged it as much as possible. Of course, she knew the contents now by heart, having read it nearly every day since Micheline had struck out on her own; but to make Dominic Burroughs understand, she had to let him read it. Still, the decision was a painful one, and she made it with some misgivings. She had betrayed Micheline's trust by taking the picture of the letter in the first place; and had betrayed it again by reading it. But Shep's death had changed everything.

She looked again at the familiar spiky handwriting, so sharp it might have been incised.

> *My darling Micheline,*
>
> *If you are reading this, then the worst has happened. The Máquina has foundered—perhaps the wreckage has been discovered. I've tried to protect both of you from the worst of it all.*
>
> *Whatever you hear, do not believe it all. Do not ever blame yourself for any of this. Know that my need to sail the Atlantic was never a choice, but a compulsion. Beyond that, know that I love you—and Paul—without measure. I truly believe that you and I will be together again someday.*
>
> *Holding on to you. Can you feel it?*
>
> > *All my love,*
> > *Shep*

Aventurine took a deep breath and held out the phone. Burroughs met her eyes, and she felt, somehow, that he read all her misgivings in her expression. But: they were trying, weren't they? Trying to build some sort of trust. He squeezed her hand gently before taking the cell phone from her fingers.

Avi watched him read the words, then frown, reading them again. Three fine lines appeared between his brows—she resisted the urge to smooth them with her fingers—and his lips thinned.

"You found this in the lockbox in Southampton. The one you told me about."

"At the shipyard, yes. Shep left the two letters, one to Mick, and one to Paul. You've seen the one to Paul."

"He keeps it with him?"

"Yes." She licked her lips. Was this next station Paco de Arcos, or Caxias? She'd lost track. The signage overhead wasn't working, and she hadn't been paying attention to the recorded announcements. "I don't have a picture of that one. He never lets it out of his sight." She cast Burroughs a sideways glance. "You've read it, though. It says pretty much the same thing, but in far less detail. No matter what he hears, remember that his father loves him."

Burroughs nodded, still frowning.

They left the train at Cais do Sodre, the end of the line, and exited the station to cross the Avenida 24 de Julho and head up the Rua do Alecrim. It wasn't long before the street began to climb, up into Chiado. When they finally reached the square, her legs were aching with effort, but she led Burroughs to the right, towards Rua Garrett. Shortly the bookstore loomed on their right. *The oldest bookstore in the world.* She pushed her way through the front door; Burroughs followed.

The shop was crowded. Aventurine locked away the location in her mind: someday, when she wasn't on a mission, she would come back. But for now, she scanned the first room, then passed through to the second. She was vaguely aware of Burroughs slipping through the groups of patrons in her wake, but she kept searching until she found a room with books in English.

She passed along the shelves, touching the spines of the books: hardcovers, paperbacks. Among the nonfiction titles, she found three of hers; she noted only that they were shelved spine out, rather than facing, before passing on to the fiction.

"For a minute there, I thought we were looking for your books," Burroughs said.

Aventurine didn't answer. She was looking for the *H*s. Only two of Nicola's books were there, and she allowed herself a minuscule preen before pulling the one she wanted from the shelf. She ran her eyes over the R-rated cover—neither of the characters on the dust jacket looked familiar, and she was grateful—before handing the book to Burroughs.

"Not my style," he said.

"Look at it, damn you."

His eyes roved over the cover, over the author's name, over the title.

Passion in Portugal.

Aventurine had never noticed before, the monument behind the two sex-starved figures: the *Padrão dos Descobrimentos.* The Monument to the Discoveries.

Burroughs whistled.

"This is the book Genevieve had in her closet."

"Lance's great-grandmother Genevieve."

Aventurine threw him a look.

She'd have to buy this book to replace the missing copy; Genevieve had said to read it. Nonsensically, she was annoyed at this; ten percent of the cover price would go to Nicola, and the purchase would up her sales numbers. She kicked herself for the fleeting thought. Petty, when there were so many other problems to face and to solve. She shook her head.

And caught sight of something, through the vacancy where the book had been. Something wedged behind it, and the second one.

"Hold on," she said.

Aventurine tried working her fingers into the space, but it wasn't wide enough. She pulled the second of Nicola's books out and handed it to Burroughs.

"We have to buy this one, too?"

Avi didn't answer. She slipped her hand into the crevice. Whatever was behind there was bound in paper and felt like another book. A smaller one. She quickly pulled out several other books until the gap was wide enough for her entire hand. She worked her fingers around it and pulled it out.

Book-shaped, book-sized. Wrapped in brown paper, neatly, though the cellophane tape holding it together seemed a bit yellowed. Hurriedly, she put the other books back onto the shelf.

"Let's pay for this—" she indicated the book in Burroughs's hand—"and get the hell out of here."

Twenty

Still nothing from Lance, Paul, or Genevieve. Burroughs rode the train back to Oeiras with Aventurine but planned to stay on until the next stop. His face was pale.

"Tomorrow," he said, and leaned in to kiss her. "Call me."

"That's what they all say," she shot back.

When she returned to the hotel room with the books in her bag, she flicked on the light to find Micheline seated on the chair by the desk, her hands between her knees.

Aventurine dropped her purse and heard coins rolling away under the bed.

"They thought I was you downstairs," Mick said dully. "I told them I'd lost the key. They'll be putting the replacement on your bill."

Avi took a few steps forward but then stumbled to a standstill. She desperately wanted to throw her arms around her sister, but Micheline seemed remote. Her face and hands were gaunt. She had lost so much weight. Her eyes were sunken, their expression shadowed.

"It—doesn't matter." Avi's words tumbled out. "I can't believe you're here."

Hurriedly, she pulled the other chair across the room and set it before her sister. She sank into it, only a few inches between them.

"You've come back," Aventurine said. So many questions, but she knew she couldn't ask. She had to let Micheline give her the answers in her own time, in her own way. The one thing she had to be certain of was that she didn't chase off her twin again. It was like dealing with a wild animal, one that could flee at any sudden movement.

"Genevieve told me to."

"You've seen her?"

"She sent a message." Michelin pressed her eyes closed. Her voice was low. *"Don't call. Just go.* She gave me this address."

"Did she tell you why?"

"She said—" Michelin licked her lips, which looked dry and cracked. "She said that you had something to tell me. Something urgent."

Aventurine now closed her eyes tightly. Her lids glowed red in the overhead light. The red of blood, the blood in the trunk of the car.

She felt the convulsive grip on her arm.

"It has something—to do with Shep, doesn't it?" Micheline's voice quavered. "You've found out something, haven't you?"

Helplessly, Aventurine nodded. She couldn't open her eyes. She couldn't look into her twin sister's face, meet her twin sister's gaze. She couldn't bear it.

"You have to tell me," Mick pushed. "Genevieve wouldn't say anything, only that I had to come to you."

Again, Aventurine cursed.

"Tell me," Micheline said urgently. The grip on Avi's arm grew tighter. *"Look at me and tell me."*

Aventurine took a deep breath. They had been together when the phone call from the Curicibo *Polícia* had come through, the one with the news of the accident and their parents' deaths. She had not had to break the news then. Neither had she had to break the news of the *Máquina* being lost in the Atlantic. She really didn't know how to say the words now. *Damn Genevieve.*

"He's dead," she whispered. "I've seen him."

Micheline closed her eyes again, but the tears squeezed out anyway, following the wrinkles carved into her skin. New wrinkles.

"Where?" she asked, her voice barely audible. "When?"

Quickly, so as not to lose courage, Aventurine told her sister about the key fob, the car, the trunk, the body.

While she expected the grief from Micheline, Aventurine was unprepared for the form it took. Mick seemed to grow smaller before her eyes, quieter, as all the anger and all the steel which had kept her going for the past year or more left her. Only the tears, still making their way down her face and into the collar of her coat, remained steady. Increased, even. Micheline did not sob; she did not shake. She simply collapsed in upon herself.

Aventurine found herself measuring the distance between them: the barest of inches which separated their knees where they sat facing one another; but the great gap which had widened between them over the past weeks. She wanted to bridge that gap—her arms shook with that want—but would she even be welcome? Avi remembered the times Micheline had snarled *you don't know* and now knew that her sister was right. Aventurine didn't know, and there was no way she ever would, except through Micheline's words, Micheline's expressions. *You don't know.* In a guilty sort of way, Aventurine realized that she was grateful for that ignorance.

"You saw him." Micheline said at last. Her voice broke.

"I did."

"And it was absolutely him."

Aventurine nodded. "Without a doubt. Even had I not recognized him, I would have known that ring anywhere."

Micheline grasped her left ring finger and its identical ring convulsively with her right hand. "He was still wearing it."

"He was."

It was clear that his wearing his wedding ring, after all this time, was important. Something for Micheline to hold onto. Something of their partnership.

"But—you left him there. You *left* him."

"I had to Micheline. I had no choice."

There was a spark of something in her flat green eyes. "You—"

"Micheline," Avi interrupted forcefully, leaning forward, but not—quite—touching. "Micheline. *Paul.*"

The realization dawned across her sister's ravaged face. Paul. There was always Paul to think about. There would always be Paul to think about.

"I knew an abandoned car at the beach lot would spark an investigation. So I left it. I let someone else *discover* it." Aventurine wiped a hand across her forehead. "Mick, there was nothing else I could do for him."

After a long moment, Micheline nodded. Then she lowered her head, gazing down at her hands, spread palms-up on her knees. The wedding ring shone dully in the light.

"This is what Genevieve told me to come to you for." The words were so thin, so quiet, that it was difficult to hear them. "She knew."

"She knew." Aventurine nodded. "From me."

"You told her first."

"Mick." This time Aventurine placed a hand on her sister's knee. "Micheline. *I didn't know where you were.* You never answered my calls or texts."

"You could have said it in a message."

Aventurine sucked in a horrified breath. "Oh, my God, Mick. *Message you?* To tell you that I just found your husband, and that he was *dead?*"

It was too harsh. Micheline covered her face with both hands. The movement seemed to cause her pain. Or the words. The one word. *Dead.*

"Aventurine," she whispered.

Aventurine bowed her head. "I'm sorry. I'm sorry, Mick." She took a deep breath. "I had to tell someone. It was hard enough to break the news to Paul." She shuddered. "I had to figure out what to do. And as you so often have told me, Genevieve *knows things.*"

After a moment, Mick nodded again.

"She knew where you went, didn't she?"

The box in the upstairs closet. Addressed.

"Not at first," Micheline admitted. "But then after I got here, she messaged me the one word. *Lisbon.* I should have known I couldn't hide from her. I should have known she would pull her strings and find me."

Again, the image of the old spy, a spider in the center of her web back in York, tugging at the strands.

Except she wasn't in York anymore.

Or maybe she was?

"She told me—without telling me—that you were here," Aventurine said. She shifted on her chair, moved a tiny bit closer to her sister. It was like attempting to get a wild animal to trust you—one careful, very slow move at a time. She'd already made one mistake. "I went to her, looking for Paul and Lance, and she told me to search the house for them. I found a box, addressed to you on the Rua Vasco da Gama, with one of Nicola's books in it."

There was a sudden cold stillness.

"What book was it?"

Why did that matter? Had Mick received a copy, read it?

"It was called *Passage to Portugal.*" Aventurine stood quickly to go through her bag and withdrew the new copy. This time, when she resumed her seat, she sat with her knees touching Micheline's. Her sister did not draw away. "It's one of her bodice-rippers." A stupid thing to say—as far as Avi knew, Nicola published no other genre. She looked down at the front cover: the shirtless man, the woman leaning back against his muscled chest in an attitude of utter abandon. In the background, the Monument of the Discoveries.

"So, she told you."

Even had she not read the blurb online, the anguish in Micheline's voice was enough to tell her of one of the plot lines.

"No." Aventurine was surprised at the anger in her own voice. "When I came back downstairs, after finding the box and the book, she was gone. Right out the French windows into the storm.

I haven't seen her since."

"But you've talked to her."

"Not until yesterday. I messaged her, just like I messaged you, but she didn't answer me, either. I didn't even know what happened to her until Lance told me he'd been to York to see her, after she'd disappeared. And then I thought—maybe—since she and Lance—" Aventurine shook her head. Genevieve and Lance—*what?* "He got to her. And she got to us."

"And then she got to me."

"Yes. And I was waiting for the next contact—from her, from you—which is why I'm so surprised—so shocked—to find you here." Avi dropped the book to grasp both of Micheline's bony hands in hers. "But I'm grateful to that old bitch. Oh, God, I'm so grateful. Micheline, I've missed you so much."

Her twin nodded.

"I wanted to help you. I needed to help you."

Micheline looked away. "The books—"

"I know about them. I don't know who sent them, but I found yours, and then there were ones left with my name in them, and ones for Paul and Lance—"

"The last one I got—there was a message for me—"

"I know about all the underlining."

"No, there was an actual message. I was to go, if I wanted to find Shep, and I was to tell no one. No one. Not even you, Aventurine." Now Micheline broke down into wild sobs, leaning over their clutching hands. "And so I went, and I searched, and each new clue sent me further, until I wound up here. And look what it got me."

She threw herself into Aventurine's arms, shaking and crying. Aventurine pressed her twin sister to her heart, caressing her hair, kissing her head. Helpless.

Because to someone, it had all been a game. *Look what it got me.* Led around blindly, to Llanthony, to Southampton, and then to Lisbon, where, finally, Shep actually *was* found. Dead. In the trunk of a car.

And not found by Micheline. By Aventurine.

Wheels within wheels, Genevieve would point out.

Aventurine rocked her sister, made soothing noises.

Things they knew. Things they didn't know. And things, it would appear, that they'd never find out.

"Don't tell Paul yet," Mick pleaded as they sat in the dark, leaning against the headboard. Aventurine had coaxed Micheline into the bed, where she had wrapped her in all the available blankets, even pulling an extra one from the shelf inside the closet. She had also gotten her sister some Panadol and a glass of water, and now Mick huddled, the glass in both hands, looking as though she'd never be warm again. Never be happy again.

"Mick, he needs to know you're here. He needs to know you're safe."

Aventurine sensed rather than saw the movement as Micheline scrubbed her hands across her face.

"No, Avi, not yet. Let me have a bit to feel this before I have to feel it for Paul."

"He's alone."

"He's not alone. He's got that boy Lance."

Aventurine sighed, feeling the wrongness of her sister's request even as she understood the feeling behind it. "Okay. Until tomorrow morning. If you don't contact him, I will." Then a thought struck her. "You know I told you that Paul and Lance got messages. In books? I did, too."

Mick didn't answer.

"We tried to figure them out, what they were telling us, but then— we had the argument—"

"Argument?"

"About Shep. Dying by—"

"Suicide. I remember." Micheline gulped. "Well, we know that didn't happen, don't we?"

"No." And then to lock himself in the trunk of an abandoned car on the beach on the Tagus? "No," Aventurine repeated. "But—" and the memory of that afternoon in Paddington began to coalesce. "It was Nicola who suggested that to me."

"Nicola."

"Yes." Aventurine hitched herself up further against the headboard. "It was so strange. I hadn't seen her since—we three were together last, in Lincoln—and yet I kept hearing about her, from Lance, from a lady at a cafe. And when she finally sent me a command to meet her for lunch, she dropped her bombshells. That suggestion, and also telling me that she'd read her mother's hidden diaries, and that Daniel Morrow was in fact her father."

Slowly, Micheline turned her head, her face still a death mask in the strange lighting. "So, she is truly our sister."

"Yes. And she wanted me to believe that Shep died by suicide."

"Before he was even—" Micheline could not seem to bring herself to speak the word: *dead.*

"Yes. Before then."

There was a long silence. Aventurine let it go on, let her sister process all the new information. So much. Whatever Micheline needed to hear, she would tell her.

"You and Paul had an argument," Mick said after a moment.

"Yes. Paul has had—a difficult time—" the words still tasted odd— "with me. We fought; he left again."

"But you found them again. You know where they are."

"I do. They were here, in Lisbon. I found them at the music festival."

"The music festival?"

"I know. I turned, and—there they were. After they'd been gone for a quite a while. It was almost as though—we were sent there to run into each other."

Their eyes met in the dimness.

Micheline set the water tumbler aside and then reached for the bedside lamp. She flicked it on, and the shadows pulled away slightly.

"Did Genevieve send them?"

Aventurine threw up her hands.

"I think she did. I wouldn't put it past her. After she disappeared on me that afternoon—when I found her copy of that book—" Her own was lying on the floor now, by the chair beneath the window—"I discovered she was still close by, and after I left for Lisbon, she came out of hiding and called Lance to her in York. To do—something."

"Something?"

"Lance was pretty cagey about it. He said she needed his help, and he went up to her for a few days."

"But—you trust Lance?"

Any number of emotions ebbed behind the question. Fear. Hope. Confusion.

"Implicitly," Avi said simply. She smiled gently at the thought of his dark eyes in his dark face, his kindness to her, his simple profession of love for Paul. "And I think we have to: he holds all of our futures in his hands."

Micheline slumped back.

"Damn Neil," she said.

Aventurine couldn't agree more. *Damn Shep,* she added to herself, wondering what he had gotten himself into. Not for the first time. What had gotten him killed.

Twenty-one

In the morning, Aventurine woke early to go out for coffee and pastries and the newspaper. Her Portuguese was meager and more Brazilian than that of Portugal—but she was getting better at decoding more than street signs and menus. Making change in Euros wasn't that difficult, either—but the shop took cards, and all she needed to do in the end was smile, tap, and say *obrigada*.

Micheline was stirring when Aventurine let herself back into the room; she could hear the shower running. Shrugging off her coat, she set the breakfast out on the low table beside the window. Quickly she texted Paul—come over ASAP; Micheline had not wanted to see him last night, but Avi couldn't, in good conscience, let him wait any longer. Then she settled into the desk chair to skim the front page. All world and national news, politics and things which might have interested her at some other time. She flipped the pages, running her eyes over the newsprint, unfamiliar as it was to do so; she got most of her news these days from online sources. Apparently, neither the murder of Shep nor the accident at Sintra warranted front page mention any longer. Aventurine was irritated by that. On the fourth page of the paper, she found what she wanted, however: *Polícia Ainda Busca a Identidade da Vítima.* Topping the headline of the story was a small picture of the car at the end of the road. Grainy, again as though it had been taken with a telephoto lens on a cell phone.

Aventurine was stumbling through the text when Micheline entered from the bath, a towel wrapped around her. Avi was again shocked by her gauntness, as evidenced by her prominent collarbones, but she said nothing.

"What have you got?" Mick's voice was taut as her glance took in the newspaper.

"Get dressed first," Aventurine ordered. One never knew how Lance and Paul would interpret *ASAP.*

Hurriedly, Mick gathered some clothes and disappeared again into the bath. She emerged in a matter of moments and came to Avi's side.

"How good is your Portuguese?" Aventurine pushed her coffee cup aside and smoothed the newspaper flat.

"Not good," Mick admitted cautiously.

"You'd better sit down for this." Avi pushed the second cup of coffee toward her sister.

But Micheline had caught sight of the photograph of the Peugeot, the trunk gaping like a toothless maw. A uniformed policeman stood nearby, hands on hips, as though the crime had not already happened, as though he was waiting for the show to begin. Mick groped blindly for the second chair and lowered herself into it.

"It's about Shep, isn't it?" Her voice was barely above a whisper, her eyes locked on the photograph.

"Yes. Do you want the gist of it?" Aventurine felt as though she were probing a raw wound.

Soundlessly, Micheline nodded.

"Police still looking for information about the identity of the deceased," she translated roughly, stumbling over some of the words, guessing on others. *"The body was discovered by officers investigating a complaint of an abandoned car."*

Painstakingly, Aventurine worked through to the end of the story, including the contact information of the officer in charge of the investigation.

"I've got to go to them," Micheline said when Avi was done. "I've got to go claim him. Shep."

"Yes, but how are we going to play this?"

Micheline met her eyes.

"Your husband, reported missing and presumed dead over a year ago, turns up in Lisbon at the same time you do."

"But Aventurine—"

Avi reached out and grabbed her sister's wrist. "I know you would never have harmed him. I know how much you adored him. But Micheline—the police here in Lisbon know nothing of this." She took a deep breath. "You've heard it as well as I have. That the vast majority of the time, when investigating a suspicious death, the police look first to the immediate family. Husband. Or in your case, wife."

Micheline's pale face whitened further.

"I didn't—"

"I *know*. But they don't."

When Aventurine's phone buzzed on the desk, so intently were they staring at one another that both jumped in their chairs.

Genevieve.

Call me, Aventurine texted back. **Now.**

The phone buzzed again.

We're at the back door. Come let us in.

"I'll do it," Micheline said.

The misgivings rose. "No," Aventurine said. "I can't have you running off. That's your son down there at the back door." She stood up. "Stay here. Stay right here."

Paul hurled himself at his mother. She was dwarfed in his embrace. Their mumblings were incoherent, but the grief was enormous: Aventurine felt as though it were expanding, pushing her and Lance to the walls. When she caught his eye, she knew he was feeling the same thing. She half-thought she should leave the room, and leave the two to their tearful reunion; but instead she looked out the window into the street.

Not much had changed.

And then the phone rang.

Aventurine had nearly forgotten that she had ordered Genevieve to do anything—call, not call, come, go. But this time—everything was different. Still, it had taken the old woman ten minutes. She put the phone on speaker.

"I need to talk to you," Genevieve said. "I've sent Micheline to you—"

"I'm here," Mick said quickly, without releasing Paul. "I know."

There was a delicate pause. Then, "I'm sorry." Genevieve's voice sounded subdued. Aventurine tried to imagine the spy, sitting in her darkened front room, but could not. Was she even there? Lance had said he'd left her there, but that meant nothing. She could be there, she could be here, she could be anywhere. Aventurine could imagine no context. It made her uncomfortable.

A deep breath from the other end of the line. "I'm sorry it had to end like this, Micheline."

"Yes."

"But now," Aventurine interjected, "we need to know what to do. We need to figure out a plan."

"Yes." Genevieve's momentary lapse behind her, she was all business again. "The Portuguese authorities are involved. The criminal investigative police."

"They're reported in this morning's newspaper as needing help identifying *the victim.*"

"I need to go to them," Micheline said again. "I need to tell them it's Shep. It's my husband. I need to claim him, and I need to bring him home."

Immediately, there was uproar.

When it began to subside, they could hear the familiar clicking of the tongue. "Not a good idea, Micheline."

The statement was bald, and Mick reared away from the phone on the table between them, staring at it, horrified. "I *have* to."

"Mom, no," Paul said.

"I told her," Aventurine broke in, "that as she is the spouse, doing this will definitely put her in the frame, as far as the police are concerned."

"It will indeed do that," Genevieve agreed. "And no doubt the police won't release Shep to you anyway, until they've completed the—examination."

"I can handle that." Micheline scrubbed at her face with her sleeve. "But you have to understand—both of you have to understand—that this is my husband. This is the person I love most in the world. I can't just ignore him in death."

"We're not asking you to ignore him—"

"Actually," Genevieve said, her voice cutting across the chatter, "that's precisely what I'm doing. Micheline, you need to leave Lisbon as soon—and as unobtrusively—as possible. You need to go back home to Connecticut and stay there. Shep's identity will be discovered through dental records, and then you will be contacted as next of kin. If they find out you've been in Lisbon all along, they will arrest you. They will hold you in a Portuguese jail."

"I'll get a lawyer."

"Mom, no," Paul repeated, his voice agonized.

But they were getting nowhere with Micheline, who could allow only one course of action, one line to follow. Aventurine could see it in her sister's demeanor, the moment she had begun to dig her heels in.

"Micheline—" Genevieve began again.

Aventurine cut her off with a single word. "Paul," she said, warningly.

He looked up, but then so did Lance and Micheline. Aventurine licked her lips, waiting for the realization to sink in, watching Micheline's expression closely. To have come this far, to have risked so much to protect him after Neil's death—and to throw it away? She waited.

There was only silence from Genevieve's end of the line.

"Shep is dead, Micheline," Aventurine said slowly, each word distinct and hard. "But Paul is alive."

"Paul." Mick turned agonized eyes on her son. "You would want me to do this, wouldn't you? This last thing I could do for your father."

Lance slipped between them. "Don't do this, Micheline," he said. "Don't make him make the choice between you and his father. Between *him* and his father."

"If you go down there, that brings Paul all the closer to the police," Aventurine reminded her. "You've been telling me since summer that I might have to sacrifice myself—my safety, my happiness, my needs—for Paul. Okay, but you can't tell me I have to do that when you're going to go ahead and put him in further danger by doing something so totally unnecessary."

"I won't say anything about him."

"Micheline. He's here. Right here beside you, in Lisbon. He and Lance both. If you become a suspect in Shep's death, they will as well. Me, too. Is that what you want?" Aventurine felt her voice rise in frustration.

"You're the one who was always bringing that policeman to our door, Aventurine," Micheline shot back in fury. "Don't you dare talk to me about endangering my son."

Aventurine closed her eyes. If only Micheline knew what she had done. But Avi knew her twin well enough to read the message in her words. *My son.* Hers. Micheline's.

"Stop it."

Genevieve had not raised her voice, but her words were forceful all the same. Aventurine felt the old wave of chastisement and fell back, but Micheline still looked rebellious.

"This is not the time for squabbling," the old woman continued. "This is a particularly delicate situation. My advice is for *all* of you to leave Lisbon. Go separate ways. Wait for the authorities to contact you, and then provide a positive ID. Because the authorities *will* be contacting you, once they've lined up dental records and fingerprints—Shep was a banker, so he was bonded, correct? His fingerprints are on file somewhere."

"I can't," Micheline said. Sadly. "I can't leave him."

"You have to," Genevieve insisted. She was not used to having her orders questioned, or outright disobeyed, and it was obvious from her tone. "Micheline. We are trying to keep you safe. We are trying to keep *all* of you safe."

His fingerprints are on file somewhere. TSA, Aventurine thought suddenly, and gasped. With all the traveling he had done, Shep surely had Global Entry, or at the very least, TSA precheck. And Micheline, too.

Aventurine, too.

That meant that their passports would be more easily traced, their travels noted in a state department computer database somewhere. They could stay, or they could go. But the authorities would be able to see, easily, that they had all been in Lisbon at the time of Shep's death. All of them.

"Shit," she hissed.

"What is it, Aventurine?" Genevieve demanded sharply. "Is someone there?"

"No. No, it's our passports. They'll know we were here."

"Precisely. That's why it's imperative to get you all out of Portugal—preferably away from Europe as a whole—before Shep is identified. It will be easier for you all to get lawyers, and more difficult for the Portuguese authorities to extradite you, should they decide that that's what they want to do."

Aventurine stared at her twin sister, who was in turn staring at the phone.

"I have to do this," Micheline repeated.

Genevieve let out a long sigh. "Then God help you, child, because no one else, sure as hell, will be able to."

Twenty-two

There had been no stopping her.

After the door had closed behind her, the remaining three stared helplessly at one another. Not knowing what else to do, Aventurine had at last speed-dialed Genevieve again. This time the old woman had answered.

"Should I go try to bail her out?"

"No," Genevieve said sternly. "Wait."

But the order went against every feeling, in every nerve, in Aventurine's body. She knew, intellectually, that the old spy was right, that it was in her best interest to stay as far away from Micheline and her dealings with the police as possible. Still, she wasn't dealing with any of this on an intellectual level. Pain was not intellectual.

"You don't know whether she's been arrested. Don't muddy the water before it's necessary."

"But how will I know?" The frustration was making it hard for Aventurine to breathe. She had been frightened for her sister when she had no idea where Mick was or what she was doing; but that was nothing to knowing that she was even now walking straight into the jaws of the monster. "She can't call me without giving me away. She can't call Paul."

"She can call me," Genevieve said quietly. "And I hope to God she knows that."

"But what can you do? You're so far away."

A mirthless laugh. "Perhaps."

Which begged the question: where the hell was the old woman anyway?

"We need to wait until we know what's going on," Genevieve repeated. "I wish I had been able to convince your sister not to do this, but she is as stubborn as you are, and I daresay, as loyal as you are."

"Is that a compliment?"

"Only sometimes."

It was almost a return to the familiar wry humor Aventurine had learned to expect. Almost. She felt a pang and wished to go back to that time. Was it only a few months ago? Back to the time before her trust in the old woman had been eroded. Before Aventurine had stood in the doorway of the darkened front room, watching Genevieve watch the rain outdoors. Before Genevieve had walked out into that rain without notice and disappeared.

"I miss you," she blurted.

"Don't." Genevieve's reaction was short and hard. A slap. "We don't have time for that sort of sentimentality. We've got much more pressing matters at hand. Saving your sister from herself, for example."

"Why? Why did she even come here?" Aventurine wrenched her attention back to Micheline's predicament. Self-made predicament. The thought nagged: the book still lay on the floor, and Avi bent to pick it up. She set it on the desk; almost immediately Lance retrieved it.

"You've got the book."

"I've got a copy."

"So you know it was obviously planned," Genevieve said darkly. "Someone—and I'm sure you have your guesses who now—lured her there. Someone was setting her up to take the fall for Shep's death. Or you. It seems the cat didn't care which mouse it caught."

There was a quick hiss of breath from Paul. When Avi turned, he was examining his hands, his head down.

"And she's taken the bait," Genevieve continued.

"Someone who knew she would react like this."

"So it would seem." The old woman coughed gently. "But I meant what I said earlier: the fact that the body was planted so near you—"

Another intake of breath from Paul. Lance moved to sit next to him.

"—that means that particular someone was gunning for *you*, too. You just didn't fall into the trap. That time."

"But you were the one who wanted me in Lisbon. You were the one who wanted me to find the book in your house."

"I wanted you there for your sister."

"You didn't know Shep would wind up killed?"

The old spy took a deep breath, which seemed to echo in the room with them. "A lapse on my part. An unforgivable lapse. I didn't see things playing out quite this way."

"None of us did." Aventurine sank down on the bed on Paul's other side.

Aventurine made coffee, which none of them drank.

Lance still held the book in his hands, and now he opened it to examine the inside flap. After a moment, he looked up again, to meet Avi's eyes.

"This," he said.

Aventurine lifted her hands and dropped them again. She nodded.

Paul took the book. Avi and Lance waited; it seemed to her that they both were holding their breaths. "One of her romances," Paul said. "Nicola's. But why would it make Mom come here to Lisbon?" Without waiting for an answer, he too opened the cover and read the inside flap.

Avi met Lance's eyes and looked away again.

"No," Paul said at last. "*An American businessman might hold all her secrets.' Her* secrets. The character's. It's fiction."

"But there are enough bombs in there to make your mother come investigate," Aventurine said helplessly.

"It's fiction. Dad loved my mom."

Aventurine nodded. "I know."

"It's just Nicola playing mind games," Lance suggested, an attempt at reassurance. "She seems to enjoy those."

She's playing a long game. But Aventurine did not speak the words aloud. The time between writing and publishing was a long time. Sometimes a couple of years.

Shep had been missing for a long time.

Paul stood abruptly. "I need something to eat."

Aventurine stood as well. "Let's go find a café or something."

But her nephew shook his head. "I'll go find something. Sandwiches, maybe. You stay here. Wait for whatever Genevieve says we're waiting for." His tone was bitter, helpless.

Avi stumbled back.

"Okay," she said slowly. She bit her lip. Lance's glance was sympathetic; he read her fear.

Paul blinked quickly and tossed the book aside. He leaned down and kissed her cheek. "I'll come back this time, Avi," he said. "I'll come back."

She stood in the center of the room, watching them gather their things and go.

Twenty-three

The knock on the door surprised her.

When she peered out through the peephole, she saw Burroughs, hands in the pockets of his coat, studying the ceiling. She unlocked the bolt and the chain and opened the door. He swept inside and kissed her.

"Not now," she said, pushing him away, frowning. "Too much is happening, and Paul and Lance will be back any minute."

"Damn it." He kissed her again, quickly. "Do you want me to leave?"

That he would ask that. She smiled, the first genuine smile she remembered wearing for a long time. "No. Stay. I need to tell you some things." She met his eyes. "Can I tell you some things?"

Burroughs stripped his coat off and flung it over the back of the desk chair. "Yes. You can tell me some things."

So Aventurine did, filling him in on Micheline's reappearance, Micheline's going to identify Shep's body. Genevieve's instructing them to wait.

Burroughs waited until she was finished and made a sympathetic face. "That's not sitting well, is it? Waiting?"

She shook her head.

He indicated the book on the bed. "Doing some light reading while you wait?"

Again she shook her head. "Don't joke about it. She—Nicola—is being intentionally cruel in that book. And Genevieve thinks it was meant to get Mick here and implicate her in Shep's death."

"Murder," he corrected. "I think that's more of a stretch than, say, attempting to implicate you by leaving you the key to a car which was left nearly on your doorstep. In which a murdered man was left."

"Yeah, well, there's that." Aventurine indicated the kettle. "You want some of this God-awful coffee?"

"No." Burroughs took up the book, and like the others before him, opened it to look at the flap, even though he had already done that at Livraria Bertrand. "So you've read this."

"Most of it. Last night, while Mick was sleeping." She looked away. "It's a cruel book."

"And the other one?"

Aventurine started.

"You haven't looked at the other book? The one you found behind the rest of Nicola's books, and smuggled out of the store?" He tipped his head. "Theft, you know."

"You saw me."

"I did. Perhaps you didn't notice me standing between you and the security camera."

Aventurine stared at him. He smiled.

"I didn't read it," she said at last. "I forgot it, in the midst of getting my sister back."

"Well, I'd suggest you get it and read it now, because obviously, it was something that struck you." He grasped his chin with his finger and thumb, an exaggerated gesture. "Something that made you take it."

Aventurine threw open the wardrobe, where her coat hung on the inside hook. She flipped it around, stuck her hand into the inside pocket, and withdrew the book.

At least, she had suspected it was a book, and when she turned it over and peeled away the brown paper in which it was wrapped, she found that she had been correct. She set the paper aside and turned the book over in her hands. Hardbound, worn at the corners, no dust jacket. Not a new book, by any means. Not anything which had slid behind Nicola's bodice-rippers accidentally. When she opened it gingerly, she found her brother-in-law's strong spiking handwriting.

La Máquina de los Vientos, she read. *S. Genthner.* And the date, a couple of years previous.

The logbook. From Shep's boat.

Which made no sense at all, for it should have been at the bottom of the sea, with the rest of the debris. Or, as paper, dissolved in the salt water of the ocean.

Aventurine glanced over her shoulder. Burroughs was watching her expectantly.

"Well?"

She sank onto the bed next to him, holding open the cover.

Burroughs whistled.

Slowly Avi turned the page.

September 9th

Arrangements made to overwinter in Hambleside. Sailing Saturday, Carl Brewster, Edward Rafferty crewing.

The fall before the fatal sail, when Shep was bringing the *Máquina* to the boatyard.

"Who are these people?" Burroughs had brought a notebook—that same notebook—from his pocket and now began to scratch away in it. "Do you know them?"

"I met Carl Brewster once, at a Christmas party at Mick and Shep's. He's dead now." When Burroughs raised an eyebrow, she shook her head. "Massive heart attack on a golf course in Miami that winter." She reached for her phone and googled his name and obituary. There were several results, and she clicked through the first entry: she had remembered correctly. "There. He died the December after this sail. He's not a part of the story of the foundering of the *Máquina.*"

"And this other person?" Burroughs touched a finger to the name. "Ed Rafferty?"

Aventurine closed her eyes. Big, with a booming laugh, and a tendency to be too handsy. Beyond that, she thought she remembered something else unsavory about him. Quickly, she searched his name on her phone. There were multiple entries, most from major news sources, naming him as a defendant in an insider trading trial. Hurriedly, she scanned the dates. No, he would have been in court in the days leading up to Shep's final sail. He had had nothing to do with this, either. She handed the phone off to Burroughs, who thumbed through the article.

It's come to this, she thought, a vaguely hysterical thought. Aventurine feared that she'd never go back to the person she was before, the one who took everything at face value. Shep's friends: people she had met, people who were sailing partners of her brother-in-law, but whom now she looked on with suspicion. Could this person have been involved in Shep's disappearance? Could *this* one?

And now, she noted, her own language had solidified.

He had not been lost at sea when the boat went down. He had simply—disappeared. To turn up dead three thousand miles away, over a year later. And here she was, seated on a bed in Portugal with Dominic Burroughs, holding a logbook that should not exist.

Aventurine took a deep breath and turned the page to continue reading.

Her head was spinning. She needed to text Micheline. She couldn't text Micheline.

Instead Aventurine texted Genevieve. Then sent an identical message to Paul and Lance.

We have the Máquina's logbook.

Too late, she realized she'd used the plural pronoun.

Midway through, Aventurine realized that the narrative—and the dates—didn't quite fit together.

"Wait," she ordered, as Burroughs reached to turn the page. She read the page she was on again, then flipped backward.

*Barometric reading
low on potable water.*

Aventurine looked again. Then she saw the finely cut edge between the two pages. Someone had sliced out the intervening page. "Look." She put her finger on the edge, easily visible now that she knew it was there.

Who had done this? It could have been Shep. It could have been the person who had placed the book behind the others in Livraria Bertrand. *Nicola's books.* It had obviously been a book drop of some kind, and more than that, Nicola had to have been involved: did she leave the logbook, or did someone leave it for her? Had Shep left it? *Or had she taken it from him?*

"Are there others cut out?"

Quickly, Aventurine flipped through the remainder of the pages, carefully running a finger in the interstices. Four were missing; each had been carefully cut from the book. Just as quickly, she turned back to the page she had left off on and skimmed through Shep's distinctive handwriting. All of it was straightforward—almost— mileage, weather, wind speed and direction, supplies, information from Hambleside, repairs. Aventurine had had some experience with logbooks, from back in the time she was working on the Alaskan fisheries manuscript. Nothing in Shep's logbook appeared out of place—except for the break that had caught her eye. So, what had been on the missing pages, that it seemed so important to *someone* to remove them?

The knock on the door startled her. Without thinking, she stumbled across the room and peered through the peephole. Then she opened the door to Paul and Lance.

Paul looked from her face to the book in her hands. "That's Dad's writing," he said. Despite being warned that she had the logbook, he sounded shocked.

Wordlessly, she held it out to him and then closed and relocked the door.

Paul stopped so quickly that Lance had to steady himself. "What are you doing here?" he demanded of Burroughs.

"Trying to help," Burroughs said.

"Read through the book," Avi urged.

With another wary glance at Burroughs, Paul took the seat at the desk. Lance leaned over his shoulder to read the pages. Aventurine clenched her fingers nervously as he opened the cover, read the name of the boat, the year, all written in his father's spiky handwriting. Paul's throat worked as he quickly read the next page and the next. The realization of what he was looking at was not long in coming. He lifted his eyes to her.

"Where did you get this?" he whispered.

Aventurine waved a hand in the general direction of Chiado. "I found it in a bookstore," she said.

The confusion was plain. "I don't understand. How can that be? This is the logbook from the *Máquina.* It went down with the boat."

"Apparently, it didn't. It was hidden on a shelf in the shop, behind Nicola's books. Like a message drop or something. I found it purely by accident."

"I don't understand," Paul repeated.

"And it was perfect timing," Avi said, the realization surprising her. "If I'd been in Livraria Bertrand earlier or later, it probably wouldn't have been there. I wouldn't have found it."

"We think," Burroughs said, "that it was either meant for Nicola to find, or that Nicola left it there for someone else to find."

Paul's jaw hardened.

"No, Paul," Aventurine broke in before he could object once again to Burroughs's presence. "He is trying to help."

"Someone else to find?" Lance echoed, breaking in. "You?"

"I don't know how she—if it was Nicola—would have known I would go to the bookstore. Unless she was trailing me again, but then, how would she get inside the shop before us? No. I don't think that's the answer. But I don't know what the answer is."

Paul turned his attention to the logbook again, his face hard, his jaw still working. While they waited, Lance hit the switch on the kettle, and once it had boiled, he poured a cup of tea and set it next to Paul's arm.

"Drink this," he said. "You look as though you've seen a ghost." He leaned down and kissed Paul's head in a gesture that made Avi's heart ache.

Finally, Paul looked up again. "I just can't figure out how this can be."

"Short answer? It can't be." Avi sank back down next to Burroughs. Their thighs were touching. He did not move away. "Long answer? That's what we've been trying to figure out. It has to have been a drop, but how?"

"You're thinking too much like a spy," Paul objected. Lance said nothing.

"I've been hanging around with a spy," Avi countered. "And I've taken lessons."

"I think it's about time," Burroughs said slowly, "that we face the reality that Nicola Hallsey is not on your side, whatever your side is."

"I've pretty much decided that she has to be behind most of the books we found all over the UK. Who knows? She might be behind *all* of them."

"Except for the one in Genevieve's closet," Lance reminded her.

"But that just takes us back to *why*." Lance took the teacup from Paul, took a sip, and handed it back. He grimaced. "*Why* Nicola would be jerking us all around like this. Making Micheline, and you, and us, high-tail it all over the place, when, if she just wants to tell us something, she could—I don't know—text you, Aventurine?"

"She wants something she thinks we have," Paul suggested slowly. He stood and peered out the window. The daylight was angling toward evening. "She wants information she thinks we might have."

"But what? Those letters your father left in the boatyard?"

"It obviously has something to do with Dad." Paul sat again, but his foot was jiggling, a habit from childhood. "Something he might have given us, or sent us, or left with us?" His face twisted. "He wrote to me that I shouldn't believe everything I hear."

"He wrote that to your mother, too," Avi reminded him. *And much more.*

"I thought he meant about—you, Avi. About you being—my mother."

"I'm not your mother," Aventurine whispered. She felt Burroughs stiffen beside her, but he did not move away. "I only gave birth to you. That's all. Micheline is your mother. I did that for *her.*"

But Paul continued on, almost as though she had not spoken. "But maybe that's not what he thought I'd be hearing. Because he—or someone—had worked very hard to fake his death." Paul ignored their expressions. "Which indicates that he was involved in something dangerous. His—*murder*—proves that."

Lance gripped his arm. Aventurine froze.

"Tell me I'm wrong," he challenged.

But Aventurine could not think of anything to say.

Twenty-four

When Paul had finished reading the logbook, he set it aside on the table and dropped his gaze to his hands. He still did not touch the tea.

Aventurine reached for the book. Beside her, Burroughs was busily scratching away in his notebook, a deep frown between his eyes. She felt the warmth of his thigh through her jeans, and it was somehow comforting as she opened the worn pages again. Ed Rafferty. Carl Brewster. Aside from them and the owner of the Hambleside yard, there were no other names outside of family written in Shep's spiky handwriting. No other leads. But where were the missing pages?

She checked her phone for a reply from Genevieve. There was none yet.

"Text Genevieve," she ordered.

"And tell her what?" Paul asked, his voice low. Almost despairing. Almost the voice he'd used in the summer.

"I don't know. Whatever you think she can help with."

Aventurine felt Burroughs's quick glance but returned her attention to the logbook. Nothing. No hint. Perhaps someone had cut the pages out and thrown them away, and perhaps she was imagining an intent where none needed to be. Shep had spilled coffee on the pages or something. But wouldn't he just have let them dry out, then?

There were several empty pages near the end of the book. Surely if he had used a page for something else, he would have sliced it out of the back? Absently she counted them. Twenty-four blank sheets. She looked at the last marked page, dated the day of last radio contact from the *Máquina*. Avi read the entry again. Blue skies, fair winds, good distance. And a single word, lacking all context.

Ironic.

"What is it?" Lance asked.

Aventurine touched the single word with an unsteady finger. "Ironic? What was ironic?"

The other three gathered around her.

"I saw that," Paul said slowly. "I just thought Dad might have been interrupted in the middle of a thought and had to go tend to something."

Burroughs shook his head. He pointed to the period after the word. "No. Punctuation. *That was* the thought."

"But that would indicate that he meant what preceded the word was ironic," Aventurine protested. "The weather? It seems ideal for sailing."

Paul pressed his lips together.

"Unless…" Lance crossed to sink into the desk chair, leaning forward, his chin in his hands and his brow furrowed. "Unless he means that it's ironic that the boat would founder in ideal sailing weather. As in, it shouldn't. *But he knew it was going to.*"

"What are you saying?" Paul demanded.

Lance looked up, still frowning. "I'm not sure what I'm saying." He rubbed his eyes with the balls of his hands, looking, for a moment, exhausted. But the expression was fleeting. "We know now that he escaped the wreck. But did he know there was going to be a wreck? And did he know he was going to escape?"

Aventurine sat back and bit her lip. "Planning. That would mean all this was planned."

"It would have to have been," Burroughs agreed. "There's no other way."

"If all of this is true," Lance said quietly, "he had to have an accomplice."

When Paul looked up, his gaze was burning. "Which means that there's someone out there who knows what happened."

They sat silently for a few minutes. Stunned.

Aventurine absently ran her fingertips along the cover of the book, feeling its worn edges. Perfect weather for sailing, and the boat went down. Shep did not go down with it. *He knew.* He had to know. Burroughs was right.

"Paul," she said suddenly. "Paul, no lifeboat was ever found."

He stared at her for a moment, his lips pressed together, high color in his cheeks. After a moment, he nodded.

Then her fingernail caught on the bottom edge of the binding.

Slowly she opened the back cover of the logbook and held it close, the better to examine the endpaper.

"What is it?" Lance asked.

"I'm not sure—" Avi prodded the glued-down paper with a nail. It seemed unevenly attached. She looked more closely. There was something awkward about the way it lay against the inside of the cover.

"A knife," she demanded hurriedly, holding out a hand and snapping her fingers. "Nail scissors. Quick. Something small and sharp."

There was nothing. They all looked around the hotel room helplessly.

"Oh, for God's sake," Avi said. She unclasped an earring and held it awkwardly open. The French wire was just long enough to poke between the endpaper and the cover. It slid sideways surprisingly easily. Then she dropped it to the carpet and worked her nail, then her finger, into the enlarging gap. After a tense moment, she lifted the endpaper more fully away and slid out the sheets that had been hidden inside.

Four pages. Cut to fit flat under the endpaper.

Her hands were shaking. Aventurine realized she was holding her breath—the others probably were, too.

Avi hitched over and spread the sheets out on the coverlet between her and Burroughs. Paul and Lance moved closer, Paul dropping to his knees beside the bed. Shep's handwriting, all sharp and spiky and impatient, a perfect match for the rest of the pages in the logbook. She flicked to the first cut in the book, and found which page fit there, after *Barometric reading* and *low on potable water.* Then she took a deep breath and began to read.

> *It started as a fragmented dream. I know now that I was drunk, or drugged, but then I only knew that Micheline was with me—even though I'd left her back at home—and that her kiss was sweet and hungry, and I wanted her more than I'd ever wanted her. Her skin. The way she arched her back and cried out my name.*

"Oh, Jesus," Aventurine whispered. She moved to put a hand over the page, but Paul stopped her. His face was pale, save for those two high spots of color.

"I have to know," he ground out.

> *And then I awoke, groggy and headachy, and rolled over to find her staring at me with those green eyes, a triumphant smile on her lips.*
>
> *"Good morning, Shep," she said.*
>
> *And it wasn't my wife. Dear God, it wasn't Micheline at all.*

Aventurine felt absolutely nauseated.

It was Nicola. It had been Nicola all along.

They had discussed, not entirely seriously, that Nicola had been trying to be Aventurine, and then had been trying to be Micheline.

She had succeeded. In the most sickening way. Either by getting Shep drunk, or by slipping a roofie into his drink. Aventurine flipped back to the first of the four pages to look at the date. A while before Shep's disappearance. Nicola had contrived to have sex with her half-sister's husband. Nicola had tricked Shep into bed.

Aventurine couldn't bring herself to pick up the second page, so sick was she from the knowledge of what she'd read on the first: the page Paul was reading now.

After all this, too: Shep had been unfaithful to Micheline. Mick hadn't believed the implications of *Passion in Portugal;* but this sure knowledge would absolutely shatter her. Shep had to have known that.

But he hadn't meant to, the tiny voice protested in the back of Aventurine's mind. Shep had thought he was making love to his wife. Avi had a flash of King Arthur, bedding his half-sister Morgan le Fey, a witch who had cast a glamor on herself to convince him she was his wife. Except with Nicola, it didn't need to be a glamor: she was identical in appearance to the woman she was impersonating. It hadn't been difficult to trick Shep. Nicola had simply appeared to him when he was under the influence of *something,* and the deed was done.

A couple of years ago.

Wheels within wheels.

Slowly, it dawned on her that what she had thought was the timeline—beginning with negotiations to write Genevieve's story leading to everything else—wasn't the timeline at all. Avi had pictured herself as the impetus, that she had been the cause and all else had been the effect. Now she put her head in her hands and squeezed. *Someone is playing a long game,* Genevieve had warned her. And now it was becoming plain that Aventurine herself had only been drawn into that game in the late innings.

This would still shatter Micheline. Not to mention what it was doing to Paul now.

Aventurine picked up the second sheet.

Twenty-five

I can see no way out. I can't hold her off forever.

Now the embezzlement. She'll ruin me personally and professionally. She'll take everything I've ever wanted, all the things I've earned over the years. How has she done this? How have I fallen into this trap? I always prided myself on being shrewd, a good judge of character, a person who avoided not only impropriety, but even the appearance of impropriety.

Embezzlement? There had been no hint of that, either before Shep's disappearance, or after, amidst all the investigation, and Aventurine would have heard about it had there been. She was an investigative reporter, for God's sake—or had been, before she had turned her hand to writing her books. She had come *this* close to earning national honors for her work on a journalistic corruption investigation. Until Neil—but she would not think of Neil.

At least, not with Burroughs sitting beside her.

Hold on a minute. Aventurine flipped back through the pages of the logbook, looking for that entry about Shep bringing the *Máquina* to Hambleside. His sailing buddies for that trip. Ed Rafferty. Yes, the insider trading fiasco. Ed had worked at the same investment bank as Shep and had been his friend for ages.

She grabbed her phone, saw the battery was in the red zone, and plugged it into the charger before remembering that she couldn't text Mick. So she turned to Paul. "Listen, what do you remember about your Dad's friend Ed Rafferty?"

"The one in jail?" Paul looked up, frowning. "He sailed with Dad a lot. Then he got into trouble after Dad retired, and I think that hurt Dad a lot. Insider trading? Something Dad disapproved of—he kept his reputation spotless. Dad had to back off that friendship." He shrugged. "Why are you asking?"

She handed him the page, then opened up her browser and began to search again for articles on Ed Rafferty.

I can't give her the information she wants, because I just don't have it. I've tried not to think of Daniel for twenty-two years.

It's the only secret I've ever kept from Micheline.

Until now. I'm going to have to tell her. God, what have I done?

But it was for her protection. And Aventurine's, and then Paul's. And I'd do anything—anything—to protect them.

If she tells Micheline, I don't know if she'll ever forgive me. I don't know how I will ever forgive myself.

Daniel?

Daniel Morrow had been dead for more than twenty years.

Of course Shep had not thought much about him. A dead man.

And what did Shep have to protect them from? Why was her own name included on this list?

Burroughs had been reading the pages she'd laid on the bed, upside down. Now, he glanced up at her, frowning. *Daniel?* he mouthed. She couldn't answer right away, because every word she had read from the hidden pages was a blow. Every sharply incised line that Shep had written, every page he'd tucked away against some eventuality which still remained unfathomable.

It's the only secret I've ever kept from Micheline.

Until now.

It sounded very much like blackmail. As though Nicola, having seduced Shep, was threatening to tell Micheline.

Until now.

But what was the first secret? How did Daniel Morrow's death enter into it?

"Here. Genevieve." Lance held up his phone, the screen of which had lit up with the text.

You've got three brains. Do some research.

"You didn't tell her I'm here?" Burroughs asked.

"Don't kid yourself," Lance replied. "She'd show up here and kill me."

Too late, he seemed to realize what he'd said.

The phone in his hand buzzed again.

I'm working some lines on this end.

Then: Stay together.

Twenty-six

So much.

"Write down everything you remember," Aventurine had instructed, handing them paper and pens from her bag.

"About what?" Paul had looked up, wariness in his expression.

"I don't know. Since Shep's disappearance. Anything. Then we can pool our info, and maybe some of it will jog other memories."

"I can't—" Burroughs had protested.

Aventurine had shaken her head. "Do what you can." She had glared at him. "Remember. You're on leave. Someone tried to kill you. Start there."

By the time she'd run out of steam, and her hand had cramped up, Aventurine had pages and pages. The room was in semi-darkness. She checked the time: her phone was fully charged now. It seemed like hours.

No further word from Genevieve. Nothing at all from Micheline. Avi bit her lip against the anxiety.

She re-read through her notes. Edward Rafferty was currently in a federal prison, serving an eight-year sentence for financial crimes. It was rumored that he might have had his sentence reduced, had he chosen to cooperate with prosecutors, and name co-conspirators; he had refused to name any names, however, insisting on his own innocence. This despite the trail of evidence presented at trial that led to contacts within the Russian mafia.

Russians.

Aventurine read through these pages yet again. She wished she had access to a printer, so she could lay out the news stories in front of her, but for now, this was the best she could do. She held out the notebook wordlessly, and Burroughs took it, frowning. His notes, in that familiar scratching, lay on the coverlet between them. Paul, still looking wary, gathered the pages to read.

Avi circled her neck and could hear all the clicks and ticks. It was always the Russians, wasn't it? Alyona Morozovna Davies, the dead woman who had been found in the Old Bishop's Palace grounds, Sioned Davies's sister-in-law. And there had been another Russian national, found dead, that she'd come across in her research. Aventurine flipped through the multiple tabs she had open on her phone browser and glanced over them all quickly. The second woman had been found dead in a theater. Avi looked again.

In York.

York.

She scrolled up to the dateline of the article and worked backward.

The night Genevieve had disappeared.

Twenty-seven

A quick tapping at the door.

Micheline burst in and closed the door quickly behind her. She looked pale and disheveled, her eyes wild.

Aventurine threw herself at her sister and gathered her into a crushing embrace. "Oh, God, am I happy to see you."

"I'm just here for a moment," Mick said. "My lawyer is waiting at the back entrance. He came through and let me in."

"Lawyer?" Paul pushed forward.

With a cry, Micheline detached herself from Aventurine's arms to embrace Paul. For a moment, all that came from her was incoherent, but at last she pulled far enough away to run a hand over his hair, his cheek, as though touching him for the very first time.

"Oh, Paul," she said. "Oh, Paul."

He nodded, without speaking.

"I'm sorry about everything. About Dad. I'm sorry about running off like that. I was—"

Paul lifted a hand. "I know, Mom. You don't have to explain anything to me."

Micheline still cupped Paul's whisker-shadowed chin in her hand. "I know you were frightened by my going to the police. But—" and now she buried her face in Paul's shoulder for a moment, before looking up again. "But I had to go to your father.

I hope you can understand that. I *had* to go to him."

"Don't," Paul said gently. "I mean it. You don't have to explain yourself to me, Mom." In that moment, Aventurine saw the steel of his father in him, and she began to see the other side of his darkness as a possibility. She hoped. She *hoped.*

Lance now approached, holding out a cup of—was that chocolate?— in his good hand. Where had he learned that? "Come have a seat," he said quietly, indicating the one comfortable chair in the room. "Tell us about this lawyer."

Now Micheline noticed Burroughs, who had risen to his feet at her entrance. "You," she mouthed. For a moment, she looked torn, casting a glance at the door, but her exhaustion was still plain, and she sank into the chair, accepting the mug with a hesitant smile for Lance. "Thank you. I can't—can't stay too long. The lawyer doesn't advise it." She glanced around and then took a sip from the cup. "He was against my coming back here to begin with."

"Why? Where'd you find him?" Aventurine asked suspiciously.

Another sip. "*He* found *me.*" Mick dug with one hand into her purse and pulled out a business card. Aventurine took it.

Abilio Pereira. Some abbreviations indicating degree. An address and a phone number.

"Ambulance chaser?" Aventurine asked, still skeptical.

"Turn it over," Micheline directed.

Aventurine did. Burroughs leaned over her shoulder.

Mary Wentworth.

"We're all Mary Wentworth," she murmured.

Paul took the card, and he and Lance examined the back.

"So much for Genevieve not being able to do anything for you."

"What's your status?" Burroughs asked. It was the first time he spoke.

"I've not been arrested," Micheline said. "The police were very polite. I had an interpreter. I—" Her voice shook, but she swallowed and carried on—"I made a statement in the presence of my lawyer.

But I'm fairly certain that they didn't believe anything that I said."

"Are they keeping an eye on you?" Paul took a seat on the end of the bed. Lance hovered close by, his good hand holding the arm in the sling.

"Doutor Pereira says yes."

A long pause. And then, "Dad?" Paul asked, the word strangling in his throat.

Micheline gripped the mug in both hands and looked deep into her son's eyes. "Yes. It was Dad." Her own voice was raw, but her eyes were dry, as though there were no more tears to be shed. She glanced over at Aventurine. "It was Shep." *Just like you said it would be.* But in front of Paul, Lance, and Burroughs, she did not say the words. What people knew, what they did not know—it was all so complicated. The less they knew, the less they would have to lie. In case—*something*—happened. Mick took a ragged breath. "The investigation is ongoing, and they will let me know when they can release—him. To me. For burial."

Aventurine might have said *I told you so*. But why bother? Knowing she had been right about what would happen with the police did not make the horror of Micheline's situation any less.

But the police response sounded familiar. She glanced at Burroughs. Like Avi's first meeting with him, back in Lincoln. *Keep yourself available.* The suggestion that was not a suggestion, carrying just enough threat to make it frightening.

Micheline had drunk up all the chocolate, and now she smiled gratefully at Lance as he relieved her of the cup. When he smiled back, it was a light turned on in the gloom. Mick patted his arm.

"Did they take your passport?" Burroughs asked.

For a moment, no one understood what he was asking.

"You're a policeman," Micheline breathed at last. Warily.

"I'm on indefinite leave," he replied. Aventurine was suddenly very aware of his closeness.

Micheline stared for a moment longer and then opened her purse to pull out her passport.

"Go home," Burroughs said. His jaw was taut.

"Home?"

"Harder to extradite."

"*Extradite?*" The gasp was Paul's. "That's what Genevieve—"

Burroughs did not reply but instead kept his eyes steadily on Micheline's.

"I don't—have any home now," she protested weakly. It was, to Aventurine, a terrible admission: that the home Mick had shared for more than twenty years with Shep was no longer the place to be, if there was no chance of her husband being there. A home that she'd held onto, these past couple of years, for his return. A return that was now an impossibility.

Lance turned his dark gaze on her. "Go to Genevieve. She'll know what to do. And you'll be away."

"Your great-grandmother," Burroughs murmured.

Lance cast him a look.

After a moment, Micheline nodded. She got to her feet slowly. "I've got to go," she said. "I'll try to figure out a way to get word to you tomorrow. Or you me. Somebody message Genevieve." She brushed her hair back from her forehead and squared her shoulders. "And if anyone hears *anything* from Mary Wentworth, I need to know."

Aventurine hugged her twin again, loath to let her go out into the hostile world. "I don't even know where you're going, whether you'll find Genevieve," she said into Micheline's hair. "How am I supposed to find you, now that I've finally got you back?"

"Keep your phone charged." A flash of knowing humor crossed Mick's face and then was gone again. She touched Avi's cheek. "Don't follow me now. Don't do anything to put yourself in the line of fire, as it were." She cast a hurried glance around at the four of them, lingering longest on Burroughs. "Any of you." She sighed one last time. "I know I've put you all in danger by going to Shep. But I hope you can understand. You have to understand. I had to go to him. There was no other way."

Paul pulled out a handkerchief and blew his nose. Then he nodded, his eyes suspiciously bright. "I understand, Mom," he said. He hugged her as Aventurine released her and kissed the side of her head. "I love you. I understand."

After a strangely shy moment, Mick and Lance embraced, and then she was gone.

The room seemed strangely empty without Micheline in it. Paul went out for food and came back with a couple of pizzas.

"Now what?" he asked, as he dealt plates like cards.

"Now we get out of here," Burroughs said.

Aventurine blinked. It made perfect sense. They'd found Mick, and they'd found Shep. There was nothing left for them in Lisbon. She found that she hated the place, beautiful though it was. She never wanted to visit the city again.

"Where do we go?" Paul said. He helped himself to a slice from one of the boxes. "I'm with Mom. I don't think I ever want to go back to the house again."

Lance put his good hand on Paul's arm. "Come back to the UK with me."

Aventurine's heart contracted.

For her part, she just shrugged. Her laptop, purchased after her other one had disappeared in Whitby, sat on the desk accusingly. She could, she supposed, go back to her plan of writing about the badass bitches of Britain; she'd just have to hold off on writing about Genevieve for a while. "I could go home," she said. She thought of her apartment, the books, the messy desk with its piles upon piles of papers. "I don't know what's left for me here. I don't know what I'm supposed to be doing now. I just don't know."

Beside her she felt Burroughs stiffen. She did not look at him. When her heart contracted this time, it was for an entirely different reason.

"But—" Aventurine broke off, trying to formulate the thought, unsuccessfully. "Nicola—"

Paul's hands fisted. "I'd like to kill her."

Aventurine caught her breath. He'd killed before. Hurriedly, she attempted to erase all expression from her face, before Burroughs noticed.

Burroughs's brows lifted as he gazed on Paul's white face. "All the more reason to get you the hell out of here."

Lance nodded, his hand on Paul's arm. Again. Still.

Aventurine took a breath, to try again. "I feel—like there's something unfinished there."

Now Burroughs turned that blue gaze on her. "You need—you *all* need—to let the police take care of Nicola. You don't need to get yourselves into any more trouble." He pressed his lips together for a moment. "Besides. If she wants you, she'll figure out how to follow you."

Lance's phone buzzed with an incoming text.

He glanced down, and then back up again. *Genevieve,* he mouthed.

Aventurine's buzzed. Then almost immediately, Paul's.

One by one they held the screens up so the others could see.

UK. But not together.

They stared at one another.

"I feel left out," Burroughs said after a moment.

Part III:

Breakwater

Twenty-eight

The wind was blowing off the sea. Aventurine jammed her hair up under a knitted cap and set off along the terrace toward the Whalebone Arch. The streetlights had come on already, and the tide murmured on the beach below. She thought she had seen Micheline walking in this direction from the hotel room when she'd first checked in, though it would be far too much to expect that she would still be down here. But receiving no immediate reply to her text—I'm here; where are you?—she couldn't help herself. She had to head out to look. Her heels clicked on the pavement.

At the top of the steps leading down to the Khyber Pass, Aventurine paused and looked across the river at St. Mary's and the silhouette of the Abbey. A gust of cold wind burned her cheeks. The lights were winking on in the Old Town, and she wondered where Mick was. Over there? Or here, on West Cliff, where Avi had—as a creature of habit—checked into the same hotel as last time? Their last determination, to regroup over a couple of days in Whitby, traveling by different means on different timetables, had been an attempt to throw Nicola off the track; Whitby had been Avi's suggestion, but she couldn't say why—just that the idea nagged at her. Only Burroughs, however, had looked at her strangely when she'd made it.

"Scene of the crime?" he'd asked.

"More like lightning never striking twice in the same place."

Now, aside from the wind and waves, and the occasional cry of a gull, Whitby seemed deserted. Lonely. The Goths had been and gone for their weekend, and now it was a summer destination buttoned up for the winter; it was late afternoon, drawing into evening. Aventurine pulled her coat closer around her throat, and, grasping the rail, headed down the steps. There were no other footsteps, but she stopped halfway down, only partly out of caution, and stilled her breathing to listen. She was alone on the steps.

She turned left to follow the sharp curve of the Khyber Pass and then took the next set of steps down past the coffee shop, closed up tight against the evening wind. From the bandstand, she could look across to East Cliff, but the angle meant the Abbey now was obscured by the square tower of the church. Squinting, she could make out some gravestones in the churchyard, and perhaps even a couple of benches. If Dracula were busily sucking the lifeblood from nubile young women up there, she might just be able to see the movement, but—and she cursed Bram Stoker once again for his exaggeration—probably not the vampire's bloody mouth. She looked down to the narrow passage between the ends of the East and West Piers, but no ghost ship was making its way along the river; no boats passed at all, until, with a rumble of engine, a shape she could dimly make out as the lifeboat, made perhaps its final pass of the evening, its running lights tiny stars against the roiling black of the tidal river. *Diamonds on the water,* she thought. But there was no music in the air, despite the Oysterband song. Only a sudden cry of a nightbird she didn't recognize.

Aventurine shoved her gloved hands into her coat pockets and moved down Pier Road toward the swing bridge. The wind tunneled here, between the arcades, and the fish and scampi shops, all dark and closed. She kept her head down against the grit in the air. She wondered now about that copy of *Dracula*. Genevieve had denied all knowledge of it; and how could she have got it to London, and into the Victoria and Albert, without following her? Which meant that someone had, and now the most likely suspect was Nicola. But why would Nicola have wanted her in Whitby?

To toss her into the North Sea.

But why do that, when, in Paddington, Nicola would only have to lure her to Little Venice, for example, and drown her there? So many available bodies of water—so much sea—between London and Whitby. Hell, so much water in Lisbon.

The drowning made sense, in a convoluted sort of way: after all, up until the last few days, they'd all believed Shep had drowned. All but Nicola, who, it would seem, knew exactly where Shep was and what he might have been doing.

But why would Nicola try to kill her, *and then* try to pin Shep's murder on her, by dumping him in a car to which she'd left Aventurine the key? Unless one hadn't worked, and so she'd tried the other? Just trying to figure this all out was making Avi's head hurt. She blinked and angled to her left just past the fortune teller's tiny shop. To her right, the Dracula Experience, closed, but with the black and red paint shimmering under the streetlights, reared up as though mocking her.

It all circled around to the puzzle of the books. She squeezed her eyes shut for a moment against the pounding of her thoughts. Or perhaps her head hurt because of the changing weather: to the east, above the Old Town, the sky was darker with clouds which, even as she looked, swallowed the last of the stars. She should have checked the weather before she headed out, but now, out here, the signal was weak on her phone. Stupid. Genevieve would have checked the weather. No self-respecting operative would leave something so mundane as weather to chance; Genevieve certainly hadn't the night they'd returned the Swynford Jewel in Lincoln. Probably, Nicola wouldn't have, either.

The ice cream kiosk was buttoned up tightly as well. It would be, in the nearly-winter, she reminded herself, as a gust of wind made her narrow her eyes. Even if some people came to see the sights, when it was *you know, not summer,* this wind along the water would probably discourage the delectation of a frozen treat. Aventurine wondered why they didn't do hot drinks, and then she wondered whether any custom would support that. And then she wondered why she cared. She didn't need any more coffee today, not if she expected to fall asleep. Even now, she held her gloved hand out to see whether she had the jitters.

When she reached the swing bridge, she looked back over her shoulder, warily, but the street was still deserted, save for a man in a puffer jacket walking a terrier, but he turned up the bank toward the cooking shop. There was a little bit of life in the pub on the far side, but she turned away and moved down the cobbled street until she reached the market. Aventurine settled on the top stone step, in the shadow of one of the columns.

What was she doing out here anyway, instead of being tucked into her warm bed?

She had come out because she had thought she'd seen Mick. Who had to be here in Whitby by now, hadn't she? Lance and Paul, she thought, were behind her in both time and distance, detouring, on the way, to Brighton.

Hiccupping, she pulled out her phone again and, taking off one glove, brought it to life with her index finger. Then she texted Dominic Burroughs.

I wish you were here. Then: hurry.

The shadows shifted, and there was a slight scrape and shuffle behind her and to her right. Aventurine stiffened, stilled her breathing, and tried to make herself small.

"Just me," a voice said, and Ernest Swales lowered himself gingerly to the step beside her and then set his cane aside.

Aventurine felt some of the tension slide away, but then it ebbed back. Who was this man, anyway? But then she reasoned that, with his limp and his cane, should he pose a threat, she could merely knock him down and run.

Unless he had a gun. *Or a knife.*

No, he had been with her when Burroughs had been stabbed, up at the top of the 199 steps; he couldn't be responsible for that. He was just an old guy, who kept showing up where she was in Whitby.

"Of all the gin joints in all the world," she murmured. Across the way, a light on the corner of a building flickered and went out.

"Okay, Rick," he shot back.

A couple passed unsteadily down the cobblestone square toward Sandgate.

"You keep turning up," she said, after they had disappeared.

Swales shook his head, and for a moment his eyepatch shimmered blackly in the odd light. "No, *you* keep turning up. *I* live here."

"Touché." She shifted. The stone was getting cold. "But—you always walk the streets at night."

"I can't sleep." He held his injured hand in his good one. "You walk the streets at night, too."

"I can't sleep."

Swales's chuckle was not amused. "Well, we've got that much in common."

"I keep looking over my shoulder, like some sort of paranoic," Aventurine said. "I would have thought this place to be a quiet town. A relatively safe town."

"It is, for the most part," he said. "Unless you bring your own danger with you."

Aventurine turned sharply. "What do you mean by that?"

Swales shrugged. "Just that I've lived here for years, and no one's ever tried to throw me off a pier."

Again, she relaxed. A little bit. "Or stab you?"

"Or stab me. Someone tried to stab you?"

"No. My friend. Up there—" she jerked her head—"by the church."

Now Swales nodded. "Yes, I heard about that, I guess. Later. After you'd gone."

Probably, he'd heard about the attack on Burroughs before she had; she'd only seen the aftermath—the livid scar in the skin below his shoulder blade. Had that knife gone into his back in a slightly different place, he would have been killed. Probably discovered the next morning among the gravestones. Aventurine shuddered. She could have lost Burroughs before she had really found him. She could have lost him for good. It didn't bear thinking about.

"How many years have you lived here?" she asked. Something niggled at the back of her thoughts, something she knew she knew, but couldn't quite remember.

Again the shrug. He was looking up now, where the sky was still cloudy, though those clouds were moving away quickly. They might get away without being rained on after all. "Almost twenty years. I moved around a bit before that."

"You don't sound English," she said. "Oh, there's a layer of that in your voice, and there's something that hints of Portuguese, but—" and she slewed a glance at him again—"you're American, aren't you?"

"You're good at voices," he said slowly. "I haven't been American in years. Left there after—a heartbreak—and never went back." He made a deprecating sound. "Melodramatic, and probably foolish."

Somewhere a church bell tolled the hour. Swales lifted his head to listen, and again she saw the dim light on his eyepatch. A sad smile twisted his lips. He picked up his cane and held it out. "Give me a hand up here, will you? I always forget how hard it is to get up once I sit down."

Aventurine stood and gave him her arm, bracing herself against the pillar. She waited until he'd got the cane underneath himself for balance before stepping aside.

"And besides," he said, looking away, "she probably wouldn't have liked life with the wreck I am now anyway."

"Give me your phone number," she said impulsively. "I don't know how long I'm in town, but maybe I could buy you a coffee. I'm still grateful for your saving my life at the pier."

He turned back and looked at her steadily with his one eye, then nodded. "Give me your phone. It's easier for me to put it in than to tell you."

Aventurine held his cane. He leaned against the pillar while he tapped in the numbers with his good hand. Then they traded back.

"You're okay to get back to your hotel?" he asked.

Aventurine nodded.

For a moment, Swales looked as though he wanted to say something else, but then he too simply nodded and turned away. She watched his slumped shoulders as he turned up toward Church Street.

Back at Khyber Pass, she gave one last glance toward East Cliff before heading up the stone steps. The clouds were gone. Some stars had come out. St. Mary's hulked across the river, among its stones.

That's when she remembered the old fisherman from the first pages of *Dracula*, the one she'd rediscovered on the bus to York. The old man who had been called Swales.

Twenty-nine

In the safety of her room, Aventurine once again faced the door, uncertainly.

Then she pushed the dresser in front of it.

There was no way to tell whether Nicola had followed her, or Micheline, or Lance and Paul—or none of them—from Lisbon. Perhaps her goal had been Shep all along, and with his death, she would leave the rest of them alone? But somehow Aventurine thought there was something more behind Nicola's behavior, something that was still, for her, left undone. What could it be, though? *What could it be?* Avi leaned against the dresser, her arms momentarily aching. Taking chances with Nicola, at this point, would be simply not done. She wondered what Genevieve would have to say about her choice of hotel.

Don't be a creature of habit.

Or maybe *she won't expect you to return to the same place.*

Well, in either case, if Nicola wanted to come for Aventurine, she'd have to shove her way through the furniture first.

But what then? Aventurine looked around. If Nicola had a gun or a knife, there wasn't much here for self-defense. Pillows. Her backpack and bag. None of that would really work.

With a sigh, she filled the electric kettle and flicked it on, then unwrapped a tea bag. She wished she'd bought some beer while she was out. Or some single malt.

What room?

The pinging of the text woke her from a doze. Groggily she checked the name, double-checked the name, and typed in the number.

The next she knew came a light tap at the door. Aventurine snapped on the bedside light.

"Hold on," she called, and pushed the dresser aside, with a horrible scraping noise, just enough to get to the door. She hoped she wasn't waking up her neighbors in the rooms on either side. She glanced at the watch on her wrist: dead.

When she finally got the door open, Burroughs slipped inside, then cupped her chin in his hand and kissed her. His eyes fell on the dresser.

"And this is what?" he asked.

Aventurine shrugged. "Extra security. You should know. You never know who's going to try to kill you in this village."

Burroughs closed the door, checked the lock, the chain, and the deadbolt, then turned back to her, peeling off his coat. The shoulders were damp. The rain had come.

"Put the dresser back, will you?" she directed.

The corner of his mouth curved upwards, but he shoved the piece back up against the door. "You know this is against all fire safety codes, don't you?"

Aventurine slipped into his arms, and it was, she thought, like coming home. "Then we'll just go up in flames, is all."

"All right, then." He tumbled her backwards into the rumpled sheets.

She dreamt again of the accident on the Rodovia da Morte. In the dream, she stood on the road, staring at the skid marks, the tracks through the dirt on the shoulder, the broken rail. She heard the sound of screams from far away—the bottom of the steep incline, perhaps— heard her father shouting her mother's name, his voice high and anguished. When she turned, she saw the second set of marks in the road, and as she stared at them, she heard the sound of an engine, and headlights strafed the air. It was instinct that made her dive from view, instinct that made her cower, peering into the road as a car stopped, and two figures climbed out. Then, somewhere below, there was an explosion, a flash of light. The two people returned to their idling car and drove away.

"What is it?"

The dark around her was elastic and suffocating.

Burroughs was shaking her gently. "Come back, Aventurine," she heard him calling, and slowly she fought her way into consciousness.

Whitby. She was in Whitby, in North Yorkshire, on the North Sea. South America was an ocean away. There was no accident. There was no fire. She felt herself shaking, partly in grief, partly in relief, and then she began to sob. Burroughs pulled her against his chest and let her, his murmurings soothing and incoherent, his hand stroking her back.

"It wasn't an accident," she hiccupped at last.

Much as she had done for her sister a couple of days ago, Burroughs wrapped her in the coverlet and set her to lean against the headboard while he fixed her a hot drink. He said nothing while she told him of Daniel and Michelle Morrow, and the car crash which had taken their lives.

"You both were in college," he said as he cupped her hands around the mug of tea, once her story had stumbled to an end. "You and your sister."

"Seniors." Aventurine said, feeling safe, and somehow ashamed of her breakdown. She wasn't supposed to do those things. She glanced at Burroughs's carved profile over the rim of the mug. She wasn't supposed to do those things in front of a policeman.

In front of her lover.

"And your sister was engaged to Shep Genthner at the time."

If there was a line to his questioning, Aventurine didn't know what it was. She nodded. The tea was still too hot to drink, but the heat of the mug felt comforting in her hands. "He was working in finance, for a company that had offices in Brazil. He volunteered to go down to take care of things for us—to bring our parents home. He knew people, you see? And we knew no one, we knew nothing."

"He arranged with the authorities to have your parents returned to the States."

"Yes. Like I said, he knew people who could help him get through all the red tape. He was able to help us navigate all those—difficulties." Even now, Aventurine could envision herself at that point, wandering through her days as though shrouded in cotton wool. She had been totally numbed. As had Micheline. Their family had been four, and then they were only two. Orphans. Avi remembered the feeling of being untethered; their parents had always meant stability, and now that was simply—gone.

Burroughs climbed into the bed to lean against the headboard next to her. She was very aware of the warmth of his thigh pressing against hers, even through the coverlet, and again, she felt safe—but a very different kind of safety than that she had felt with her parents still alive, somewhere in the world, all those years ago.

"They—their bodies—had been badly burned in the explosion when the car went off the road." There was an uncomfortable catch in her throat, even after all these years, and Aventurine swallowed it back. "We had their remains cremated before burial."

There was a long pregnant silence.

"What?" Aventurine demanded after taking a sip of the too-hot tea.

Burroughs was frowning, lines creasing his forehead.

"You dreamed that the accident—wasn't an accident," he said slowly, looking off into the middle distance, as though trying to find direction. "What is it that made that idea come to you, do you think? I mean, you've obviously not thought that way before."

"It was just a dream," she backtracked. "There's no evidence. I dreamed of another car, of two sets of skid marks in the road.

But nothing in the accident report we eventually received from the Brazilian authorities ever said anything about that. The report didn't say anything about *any* skid marks at all. According to the investigators, my father failed to negotiate a sharp turn—something that happens to many cars along that road. That's why they call it 'the Road of Death.'"

"Rodovia da Morte," he murmured. If anything, the lines between his eyes grew deeper.

"What? What are you trying to say?"

Burroughs held up his hands. "I'm not *trying* to say *anything*. I'm just wondering, that's all."

"Wondering about what?"

He took the tea mug from her, took a sip, made a face, and handed it back. "Your parents die in a mysterious accident in South America. Your brother-in-law goes to Brazil to bring their bodies back to you for burial. Twenty-odd years later, your brother-in-law disappears for over a year, and then turns up, murdered, three thousand miles from where he was supposed to be."

But Aventurine shook her head. "The car accident is only mysterious because I dream that it is. Dreams are not reality. You're just being too damned fanciful for a policeman."

His wince might have been from his adjusting his seat against the headboard, or it might have been at her words. "I might argue that your dreams are trying to tell you something. Bringing ideas to the surface that you might have missed, or that you—" he looked away— "don't want to face."

"No. I'm dreaming these paranoid things because I've spent far too long listening to Genevieve."

"Lance's great-grandmother."

Avi bit her lip. "You can stop now. You know Genevieve is not Lance's great-grandmother."

"I know nothing of the kind. I have never met the woman. I don't think. I only met Mary Wentworth." Now he met her eyes, and there was a strange sort of challenge in his expression. "I do know that she is an enormous influence on all of you. I do know that she both enthralls you and pisses you off. And I do know that if she told you now to reconsider the nature of your parents' car accident, you would do it in a flash."

The thing was—Aventurine knew Burroughs was right. She would now have to call Genevieve and ask what the old spy thought, all because he had put the idea into her head. But she was frightened of the prospect: what if it was true? What if that long-held belief that her parents had died in an unfortunate accident on a research trip for her father's next book *was all a lie?* That would mean, though, that if her dream were even vaguely close to the truth, that if someone had indeed forced their car off the road—

The idea was horrifying.

That would mean someone had wanted them dead.

Aventurine's hand was trembling, and she sloshed some tea onto the coverlet, where it made a slowly-widening stain. Burroughs took the mug away from her and set it on the bedside table. She looked at him, her mouth open.

"Go ahead," he said. "Call her. I'll leave the room if you want me to."

"It's three in the morning," Avi protested. "No one's awake at three in the morning. Not even Genevieve."

Burroughs nodded, pulling the coverlet up to her chin, and then leaning in to kiss her. It was a long kiss, not hungry, but somehow knowing. *He would have left the room to let her call Genevieve in private.* Her head was swirling.

Then he pulled away, his hands still buried in the coverlet beneath her chin. His blue eyes searched her face. "Is she the person you're covering for?" he asked. "Is she the one you've been protecting?"

How tempting it was to just say yes. Instead, she found herself letting out a short bark of a laugh. "Genevieve? She doesn't need my protection."

The briefest flash of disappointment crossed his face and was gone. Slowly, he stood up and looked around for his clothes, pulling on his boxers—she loved that he wore boxers—and then his shirt. His face was in shadow now, as only the bedside lamp gave off its small light.

"If she's not Lance's great-grandmother," he said slowly, "then who the hell is she?"

Aventurine took a deep breath and watched as he buttoned his shirt.

"She's a spy," she said.

Another dream. Aventurine was back in Lisbon, being pursued.

The alley was narrowing as it climbed uphill in Alfama. At a balconied window overhead, a raven-haired woman in a yellow dress leaned out, calling to her. *Correr! Há perigo! Salve-se!* There was terror in the voice, and as she passed, Avi saw, out of the corner of her eye, rough hands dragging the woman back into the depths of the room. There was no time to stop, for the sound of footsteps quickened behind her, grew louder. Whoever it was was gaining. *Perigo.* Danger.

Aventurine threw a panicked glance over her shoulder and could see no one. Ahead, barrels, boxes, detritus. Large enough to hide herself behind, but then she'd be trapped. Her chest ached from trying to catch a breath; her legs ached from the unaccustomed running. She let out a small sob and pushed on.

Just when the damp stone of the alleyway was closing in upon her, she saw the opening up ahead, through a crumbling archway. A figure stood there, blond-haired this time, the thin light glinting off the hair—a man. He beckoned her forward. The footsteps were closing the gap; she had no choice.

"Aventurine," he shouted, his voice strangely familiar, echoing off the bricks.

"I'm coming," she cried out. "Wait for me!"

At last, she squeezed through the gap into another tiny street where the sounds of traffic were faraway and muted. The cobbles beneath her feet glittered with damp, almost undulating like a snake. She glanced to either side but could see no one.

The arms that encircled her surprised a scream from her throat.

"Hush," the voice said. "I've got you."

When she looked down, she could make out the scars on the left hand.

Thirty

Aventurine dozed, and when she awoke again, she was alone. The bedside lamp had been turned off, and there was no sign that Burroughs had ever been there—save that the dresser was no longer blocking the door. When she dragged herself from the bed and staggered into the bath to run the shower, a knot tightening in her gut, she found that one of the towels on the bar was damp.

Well, that was the way it was going to be, then. Burroughs still couldn't trust her, and indefinite leave or no, he was still a policeman. It was good to know where she stood, right now, before she allowed herself to feel anything more for him.

She turned the water up as hot as she could bear it, scrubbing her skin until it was reddened. Then she jerked the curtain aside and stepped out onto the thin bath rug. When she turned, the words written on the mirror had reappeared in the steam.

Be back soon.

Aventurine stared at the three words, her breath caught in her throat. Her skin tingled now, and it wasn't because of the shower. She closed her eyes and tried to still her breathing, but it was no use. She felt seen.

Toweling her hair, she left the bath just as her phone, on the charger, buzzed with a text. It was none of the others; it was no one she would have expected. The text was from Ernest Swales.

Larpool Viaduct. I've made a decision.

No time. Hell, she didn't even know where Larpool Viaduct was. Hurriedly, she clicked on her maps application and looked it up. Not too far out of town, it crossed the river as part of the Cinder Track public footpath. She bookmarked the map and pulled on her clothes, gulped down a cup of the instant coffee, and left the room, locking up tight behind her.

"What's the rush?"

Burroughs was coming through the door, a take-away cup of coffee in each hand. He gave her one.

"I thought you might like a taste of the real stuff, first thing in the morning." His wry grin seemed strained, but perhaps that was just her. She took the cup gratefully. "You weren't running off on me, were you?" he asked suspiciously.

"I thought you'd run off on me," she pointed out. "I woke up and you weren't there."

She brushed past him and out onto the street. He followed.

"Where are we going?" Burroughs took a sidelong look at her face as she pulled out her phone and checked her map. "Where are *you* going?"

"Larpool Viaduct." The map told her she'd have to get to the other side of Pannet Park to access the Cinder Track. She headed off. Burroughs fell into step beside her. After a moment, she sipped from the coffee cup, and then said, "You can come if you want. But only part way."

They made their way up through town, along Flowergate, and then down again through Pannet Park. At the traffic circle, she checked her map again before they crossed in a break in the traffic and headed along Chubb Hill until they reached the stone bridge. There were steps to the left, and they ascended to the pathway, Aventurine in front. Once on the track, the trees, dead leaves rattling in the grey morning, leaned in on them. A jogger with a loping dog on a lead passed. She found here that she was stretching her stride to Burroughs's, until he laughed and shortened his. The sound of traffic was now muted.

"I'm sorry. Your excursion, not mine. Sometimes I forget," he said, slowing, "that not everyone has my legs."

"No," Avi said, glancing up at him sideways, "not everyone does." She was careful to keep a bit of distance from him, not because she didn't want to touch him, but because she wanted to touch him entirely too much. This morning, despite the errand and the anxiety it engendered, she felt full of the entire world, but could think of no way to say that; she felt as though she were *living* inside her entire body, filling all her curves and corners, down into her very fingertips. This despite the man who, all joking aside, all wild abandoned lovemaking aside, might still think her a murderer. The thought made her suddenly sad, so she pushed it away.

"What will he think when he sees that you've brought me? Swales?"

Aventurine shrugged. "No idea, and we won't find out, because you'll stay behind when I get up onto the Viaduct."

"Do you think that's wise? What do you know about this man, anyway?"

"I know that he saved my life the night you walked off on me on East Pier," she shot back. "If he'd wanted to do me harm, he needed only to have left me to go down for the third time in the North Sea." Her coffee cup was empty. She wished she'd thought this through more carefully: now she'd be carrying trash around for the rest of this hike.

Apparently Burroughs's was empty as well. He took hers and slipped it inside his own, crushing the lids down after it.

"All right, but I'm staying. Within earshot. I expect a shout if anything untoward happens."

Aventurine shot him a wry glance. "If he's going to toss me off the parapet—which I doubt, since he only has one good hand—you're going to be a bit late to save me."

Burroughs looked up beyond the trees into the filmy sky. He

twisted the coffee cups between his hands. "I really wish you wouldn't joke about this. It's not funny that someone has tried to kill us both, singularly and together. And has apparently tried to kill Lance and Paul, in the well in Sintra." *And succeeded with Shep.* But he didn't have to say that; she knew it already—oh, so well.

"I should have texted Micheline. Told her what was happening."

A couple with a pair of Yorkshire terriers on leads passed them and smiled. Avi smiled back, though she felt her face to be wooden.

"You can tell her when we get back," Burroughs said. "Or I could."

Aventurine made a face. "She'll be furious."

"Why?"

"Because she's my sister, and—" Her voice trailed off. She kept her eyes on some birds darting in the bushes on the bank beside them.

"And?"

"Because you think I'm a killer." For Micheline, everything came back to the danger he posed; but it was better that he think her a killer than he have any inkling about Paul and that night on the York walls.

He slowed. They passed beneath a road, and the traffic sounds echoed. Once away, he stopped altogether. There was more rustling in the bushes along the path, and a bird flew over them and down before landing and peering back at them warily.

"I don't anymore," he said.

"Don't?"

Burroughs seemed to be in a stare-down with the bird, which suddenly sensed some danger and flew up into the trees. "No. I don't. I think there are things you're hiding from me. I don't think you've told me the entire truth."

"I—"

"No." Burroughs held up a hand and then shook his dark hair back from his forehead. Aventurine took a sharp breath, wanting to brush that lock back with her fingers. "Don't say anything right now. Just don't." When he looked back to her, the expression in his blue eyes had warmed, softened, even, and he gazed into her face. "Sometime you might tell me, and I hope I can live with that much. But no, Aventurine. I don't think you're a killer."

Avi felt her knees go weak. She took another long breath, then pulled her gloves from her pocket and pulled them on, something to do, while she gathered her strength. "Thank God," she whispered.

After a moment, they walked on.

"What changed your mind about me?"

He made a face. "Getting knifed."

Aventurine was surprised by the shock and fear she felt, residual, not immediate. *Getting knifed.* She could imagine the feel of the ridged scar against her fingers. He could have been killed that night up on East Cliff.

She could have been killed that night down on East Pier.

Again, the question: had that been the intent? Had it been a warning? Or something else entirely?

"It could have been me," she suggested quietly, playing Devil's advocate. "I could have run after you. I could have been the one."

Burroughs laid a hand on her arm. "No. Stop it. I know it wasn't you, because I looked back when I got to the Haggerlythe. I could see you out there on the pier, Avi. *I could see you.*" He shook his head. "Yes. I turned around, and I saw you, and I—walked away." He turned away from her, looking toward the river, and then back. "You had your shoulders hunched, but you were staring up into the wind like you were daring it to get the best of you."

"It wasn't the wind." The words choked her.

"No. But I kept walking. The length of the street, and up the 199 steps. At the top, I thought I heard a cry, like a bird, or a small animal—I thought at first it might have come from the Old Town. But I could see the end of the pier before the light tower, and you weren't there. You were gone. That's when I turned back. I was in Henrietta Street when you passed with the old man. You both were sopping wet but seemed okay. I followed you back as far as the pub and saw you go in, then headed back up the steps."

"I never saw you."

"I made sure you didn't."

Aventurine looked up at him in puzzlement.

"I got the knife to the back in the churchyard at the top of the steps. I figured out later that it was you I heard, Aventurine, being pushed from the pier. And then the assailant came for me."

"The assailant." Aventurine turned and walked on. The viaduct rose up before them, and they began the ascent through the trees. "Nicola." The name tasted metallic in her mouth. Like blood.

Burroughs cast her a sideways glance. "If it looks like a duck—"

"Oh, shut up."

Thirty-one

Aventurine left Burroughs at the end of the viaduct, looking down at the houses that stretched, below, further along the Esk. A train ran below them on the Esk Valley line, rumbling on the rail. A pair of cyclists called out before passing slowly on the track. Up ahead, she could make out the bent figure of Ernest Swales, leaning against the parapet, looking back toward Whitby, and the ruins of the Abbey on East Cliff. She caught her breath, suddenly nervous, wisps of last night's dreams fluttering around her in the air.

She cast a hurried look around her for Nicola, the idea of whom now made her paranoid. Nicola, waiting for her. Atop a high place.

Aventurine cast a glance back toward Burroughs, who had now pulled out a pair of birdwatcher's binoculars, and was scanning the trees on the bank below.

There was no sign of Nicola. No sign of Micheline, either. Swales had chosen the viaduct intentionally, far enough out of town that it might have been one of the safest places to hide in plain sight. Then Aventurine caught herself. Why would Swales need to hide, in plain sight or anywhere else?

She approached slowly, her hands in her pockets. Swales turned, keeping his balance with his stick. He too had his free hand in his pocket of his green coat and wore his scally cap pulled down over his thinning hair.

"Your boyfriend's got the right idea with the spyglasses," he said.

"He's not my boyfriend," she corrected swiftly. She felt her face go hot. One-eyed or not, the old man had pretty sharp sight, since she'd left Burroughs at the end of the viaduct. She looked down at his walking stick, upon which he leaned heavily with his good hand. It wasn't as though he could have been keeping an eye out for them and then darted over here.

Swales's expression hardened, and the scar that snaked down from under his eyepatch seemed to grow whiter against his wind-burned face. "I expect you're right. I expect if he really were, he wouldn't have walked off and left you that night on the pier."

It was almost cruel the way Swales could tap into her insecurities like this. "We'd had an argument, if it's any of your business, which it isn't." Her pique made her tart. Then quickly she turned. "Hold on. Hold on a minute."

Swales tilted his head. He might have been the Ancient Mariner, fixing her with his glittering eye. He waited for her to speak.

"You saw him walk off."

"I saw him on the Haggerlythe, heading up toward Henrietta Street."

"Then—you were there the whole time."

Swales said nothing.

"That's how you were there to save me. You were there the whole time."

He nodded. "You're getting there, Aventurine."

She took a step closer. He smelled of an aftershave that stirred something in her memory, but she couldn't quite place it. Then the sense was gone, and she only smelled the salt tide on the wind. "Getting where?" she demanded. "Were you following me? Following us?"

Swales turned away again to gaze along the snaking length of the Esk below them. "Yes."

Aventurine grabbed the parapet, because she really wanted to grab the old man's arm. Maybe shake him. "Why?" Then another thought.

"Did you see who pushed me?" She stared at his inscrutable face. *Say it,* she willed him. *Say you saw her. Nicola.*

"I didn't see who it was," he said heavily. "But I saw it happen. And it's a damn good thing, or there would have been no one there to haul you out."

Aventurine caught her breath. "So, you really *were* following me."

When he turned back to her, he pulled his hand from his pocket and laid it on hers. It was surprisingly warm, but curled, as though he was unable to straighten it, the fingers bent awkwardly, the scars tight across the back of it. He was missing the tips of two fingers, she saw in shock. How had she not noticed that before?

She started shaking before she realized why.

It was the hand from the dream.

I've got you, he said, when he'd pulled her out of the sea.

Her knees wouldn't hold her. She slid down the bricks of the parapet until she was seated, slumped, on the stone base, one leg bent awkwardly beneath her. Through her dizziness, she heard running footsteps and then felt an arm around her shoulder.

"Aventurine," Burroughs said. "What is it?"

Thirty-two

"He helped me," Ernest Swales said. They were seated on a bench in a cemetery on the east side of the river, where the stones were surprisingly modern, buffed to an almost obscene shininess. Next to them was the grave of a man named Swales. Peter Swales. He held out his hands, the scars running across the back of his left one, the curled fingers indicating nerve damage, long-ago broken bones. "For some reason, his was the only telephone number I could recall. When he was contacted, he came for me."

"We thought—Mick and I—that he went to take care of bringing you and Mom home. We thought he was doing that great kindness for us, because he had those contacts and would know how to navigate in Brazil." Aventurine pressed the balls of her hands to her eyes against the incipient headache that lurked there. "We thought he was bringing you both home for your funerals." She looked up, struck by a thought. "Who is buried in your grave, then? If it's not you, who is it?"

Swales—Aventurine could not quite bring herself to use the name *Daniel Morrow*—looked away. "The ashes of someone Shep claimed from the morgue in Curicibo. Someone unknown." His smile was a mirthless grimace. "We gave some poor unclaimed stranger a proper burial, next to your mother's ashes. I hope, wherever she is, she doesn't mind."

"So, Shep knew. Shep knew it all." *The one secret he'd kept from Mick.*

But Swales shook his head. He'd taken off the scally cap, and now his scalp gleamed through his thinning grey hair. "Not before. Not before my call. He helped then."

"And he never told us. Either of us. Not even his wife."

"I was trying to protect you, Aventurine. You and Micheline. I swore him to secrecy, told him that it might be a matter of life and death for his wife. It had been for *my* wife, and it was a gamble that didn't pay off." A spasm of pain, grief, and guilt twisted his face.

Aventurine's hand was shaking as she reached out to touch, briefly, Ernest Swales's arm. Her shock was receding, perhaps her anger and confusion was, too—to be replaced by an overwhelming sense of pity, and of loss. All the years they had been without a father, she thought bitterly. Paul's entire life without a grandfather. But now she began to see a glimmer of the other side: all the years Swales had been without his daughters and his wife. A man who had been in a self-imposed exile for more than twenty years.

"You ended up here," she said, waving a vague hand around the cemetery, and the streets beyond the walls.

Swales shook his head. "Not at first. It was a long recovery, relearning how to walk, how to manage without two working hands. One eye. The—*government*—made sure I was sufficiently self-sufficient, and then gave me a new identity and sent me on my way. My cover was blown—I couldn't tell you how—and I was no longer of any use to them."

Government.

Cover.

Aventurine's head was whirling. She cast a look at Burroughs, silent, his face expressionless, his eyes alert.

"I racketed around a bit, until I lighted here," Swales continued. He looked up past the trees at the bleak sky, then out at the streets, quiet now with the secretiveness of a summer destination as winter drew on. "Not the sort of place anyone would look for me had they known I had not perished in that car accident on the other side of the world." His smile was as bleak as the world around them.

The sound of a siren, somewhere down toward the Old Town, made Aventurine jump.

"But Shep knew," she repeated after a moment. None of it made sense. How many secrets had her brother-in-law kept? How much more was there to learn?

"This part Shep knew. He was the one to make contact with my handler, at my request, once I knew who the hell I was and what had happened to me. He was the one to make sure I had a proper funeral and burial with you all. He was the one who made it all believable. So I could disappear. And not be killed." He turned his good eye on her and blinked back what might have been tears. "Though after I lost your mother, I could have died, and it would have been all the same to me."

That stung a little bit, and he must have seen it in Avi's face. "That was in the beginning. Then I began to remember you. You and Micheline, my twin daughters. How important you were in our lives, your mother's and mine. And I knew that—even though I was in hiding—that I was still in the same world as the pair of you, and I could live with that." He glanced down, then back up into her face. "I had to live with that. It's what kept you safe."

Aventurine nodded slowly. "For a while."

"Twenty years, give or take," he agreed. "But yes. Shep knew. He didn't know where I was, once he'd played his part and returned to his life. He didn't know *who* I was. I made sure to keep it that way. But he had a contact, so he kept the information about you two flowing in my direction." This time the crooked smile held an element of pride. "I read your first book when it came out, and I knew you were headed for good things. Then I read all the subsequent ones." He patted her arm. "You write well, Aventurine. Your mother would be so pleased. She was always my best and sternest editor. My harshest and most loving critic." He sniffed, then drew out a handkerchief to blow his nose.

"Do you miss that?" Avi asked, the words thick in her throat. "The writing?"

"I miss everything. I miss all that I used to be."

The silence fell between them, not quite comfortable, but not overly wary, either. Burroughs shifted and moved to lean against the trunk of a tree, not too far away that he couldn't listen to the conversation. He scanned the road beyond the cemetery gate, his eyes narrowed. Aventurine was grateful for his presence, and at the same time, grateful that he remained in the background.

"They've found out, haven't they? Whoever they are. Whoever tried to kill you. Whoever killed my mother." It was difficult to say the words. It was difficult to approach that line again, from thinking Michelle Morrow had died in an accident, to realizing that it had not been an accident at all.

"Yes."

Aventurine felt stiff and sore, from the cold and dampness of the bench in the cemetery, and probably from shock; Burroughs kept close, and beside them, Ernest Swales stumped his way along with his walking stick, surprisingly quickly. They detoured down narrow streets, keeping away from Spital Bridge, a renewed sense of urgency pushing them forward. It didn't seem as though anyone were following, but it was more than obvious now that they were dealing with professionals. They moved down into town, slipping down a side street and into a café before reaching the touristy section of East Cliff and the Old Town. Inside, they chose a table at the rear, close to the kitchen, and ordered three coffees.

"How did they find out?" Aventurine asked, looking over her shoulder at the door. Only one other person was in the dining room, drinking a cup of tea and reading a newspaper near the window at the front. "That you were still alive?"

"A picture," Swales said, and his face twisted even more, this time in disgust. "Online. Of the Little Shambles in York." The grimace grew more pronounced. "Careless, wasn't it? Some photographer took one of those artsy photos and posted it somewhere—Facebook, maybe, or Instagram, I don't know—and someone else found it. I've been holing up here, but the *government* wanted to move me or make arrangements for me to become someone else—before I died mysteriously and caused an international incident."

"Ricin in the umbrella ferrule?" Burroughs asked.

Swales shot him a look. "Something like that." He returned his gaze to Avi. "But..." His voice trailed off.

"But?" she prodded.

"I had to see you before I disappeared for good. I needed to see you, to talk to you. But I needed you to come here. I needed it to be accidental. I *meant* it to be a one-time thing."

"So, the book. *Dracula*."

Swales nodded and licked his lips. Then he waved his good hand to the waitress and pointed to their now-empty cups. She came, poured, and wandered away again.

"The book."

There was still a gap though. Something she was missing.

"How did you know about the books? How did you know where I was?"

The gaze of his one good eye was steady, the unwavering green of her own. "Genevieve."

Of course. It all came back around to Genevieve. And the government, and her contacts, and the network of people out there with whom she traded in information, like the valuable commodity that it was.

"Genevieve." She took a deep breath.

"The spy." At last, Burroughs spoke. He looked from one to the other of them, then lifted his coffee mug and downed half of it, seeming to not know or care that it was hot enough to be incendiary. "Jesus."

"Yes," said Swales. He looked abashed, or at least she thought so; it was hard to tell with only one eye and a twisted face to go on. "My contact."

For her part, Aventurine pushed the coffee away. It sloshed onto the table top. The waitress swished past, pausing long enough to wipe up the spill. "Jesus is right," Avi said. "She's been your contact all along? Your handler?"

"No. I don't have a handler. I don't work in the business anymore. I told you. My cover was blown. And I'm so badly injured now that I am basically useless." Ernest Swales's voice was bitter, but below that, now that she had been listening for a while, Aventurine was starting to recognize the cadence: the way her father spoke. She hadn't heard it, nor had she thought about it, for quite some time.

Go back, she thought, trying to lay her thoughts out in a way that made sense. *Go back.* "So, you left the copy of *Dracula* in the Victoria and Albert for me to find. You'd followed me to the fourth floor. How the hell did you know I was *there?*"

He took a deep breath, as though he knew he was about to reveal something that would infuriate her. "Your phone."

"My *phone?*"

He splayed the fingers of his good hand out on the scarred tabletop. "Have you checked your 'Find Your' feature lately? The one you used to follow Paul to York back in the summer?"

Quickly, Aventurine fumbled the cell phone from her pocket and touched it into life. She shifted screens, then pressed the app. There she found not one but two phones linked. Why hadn't she realized that the night at the festival? Her mouth dropped, and she lifted her eyes to meet her father's gaze. "She's been tracking me. All this time."

"Yes."

Aventurine *was* infuriated. She wracked her brains until she swooped in on that moment in Lincoln, at Mary Wentworth's kitchen table, when she had found Genevieve with her phone. *That long ago and she had never checked.* The realization that the old spy had been tracking her tasted like betrayal at the back of her throat. As though Genevieve hadn't trusted her. As though Genevieve viewed her as some sort of child, one she needed to keep an eye on at all times.

"This is *obscene*," she hissed. "Did she put a recording device on it, too? Has she been listening to all my private business all this time?"

Swales flexed his fingers on the table, staring down at them. "I don't think she's taken it quite that far. But Aventurine, you have to remember—she *is* a spy."

"She's ninety-four damned years old!"

"It's obviously a habit of a lifetime," Burroughs said dryly.

"You shut up," she said. He held up his hands in mock surrender.

Angrily, Aventurine grabbed the phone to disconnect it from Genevieve's but then stopped. If the old woman could use this to track her whereabouts… then surely Avi could return the favor. Unless? She quickly examined the app, to find Genevieve's phone in the house in York. But that meant nothing. That day in Mary Wentworth's apartment, they had been using a burner phone to connect to Magnus Etheridge. And if Genevieve had one burner phone, she no doubt had another. Probably an entire collection.

"Shit," she said.

"Shit is correct," Swales answered. "She's always one step ahead of us, that old girl." There was a slight tinge of respect in the words. Aventurine glared at him.

So frustrating. *So frustrating.* She thought she was getting good at this Mary Wentworth stuff, and then she came to realize just how much she was missing. Her own phone! Giving her away like that. She looked down at her cup and opted out of drinking from it: she'd had too much coffee already this morning, and she was already aware of her thoughts bouncing off the inside of her skull. *So frustrating.* She looked up again at Swales. The eyes, for God's sake. She'd been looking into them off and on for weeks and had never pegged it. "I should have known," she said.

"It's been more than twenty years."

The bells over the door jangled, and a man came in, collected two take-away cups, and left again.

"Your eyes," she said, though only the one was visible. "They're mine. They're Micheline's." She wiped a hand across her own. "And the name. Swales. I opened the copy of *Dracula* on the bus back to York, the day after you dragged me out of the water, and there it was. Your name." She laughed mirthlessly. "And the whole time it wasn't your name, was it?"

Across from her, the older man shrugged, a strangely lopsided motion. "It's a fairly common name in this village." He lifted a hand—his right, of course—and waved it vaguely around. "You saw the stone back there. I could have easily been one of the natives." He smiled ruefully beneath his eyepatch; in the overhead light, the scar on his forehead and the line from the patch's elastic seemed carved. "It's said that Bram Stoker took the name for that character from one of the gravestones up on the cliff when he was writing *Dracula*."

"But Ernest Swales is, obviously, not from around here," she pressed. "I should have known."

"I never told you that."

"No, but your voice did, and I paid next to no attention. The sound of it as you speak. I told you already. An accent of sorts. Faint. It's definitely not pure Yorkshire." Aventurine sighed. "I even wondered if it sounded vaguely Portuguese at one point, before I realized what I was actually hearing."

"You've a good ear," he repeated.

When she looked at him again, he was gazing at her with a half-smile and what might have been read as an expression of wonder. Instead of looking away, she examined his face intently: the eyepatch, the green eye, the scars, the sardonic mouth. An intelligent face, shrewd, even. The more she let her gaze rove over it—and he did not flinch from her examination—the more she recognized.

"I've missed you," she said. Her voice, despite her resolve, was unsteady.

Unlike Genevieve, he did not reject her words out of hand. After a moment, he nodded. "And I you. Both of you." He cleared his throat and looked away toward the windows at the front. A heart-rending sigh. "But I miss your mother more." His words echoed Micheline's to Paul. Swales made a small self-deprecating noise. "Every day, I wake up and it hits me again. I cannot believe that I am alive in a world where your mother is not."

It had been more than twenty years. The baldness of his grief was palpable. Aventurine felt like an intruder, but at the same time, she could not look away.

"You could have come to us. You could have told us what happened." Avi wiped her face with her hands, surprised to feel the tears. "We could have helped you through this."

But her father shook his head, his lips twisting. He patted her hand awkwardly. "You couldn't have. And I couldn't have. It was far too dangerous. My—activities—had caused the accident. My activities had caused your mother's death. I couldn't possibly have risked either of you. I hope you can understand that. What I did—killed your mother. And if I didn't *die* with her, then I would have placed you two in the line of fire. I would have put you in danger. And after your mother—" he momentarily closed his eyes and took a deep breath— "after your mother, you and Micheline are the most important things in the world to me."

Behind them in the kitchen, there was a clink of glassware being washed. The murmur of voices rose and fell, and then suddenly there was a bark of laughter. The tears were washing down Aventurine's cheeks now, unabated, until Burroughs passed her his handkerchief: the feeling of it in her hand—again—was ludicrous, and she let out a laugh which might have been borderline hysterical. Their waitress passed by on her way to the kitchen and cast Aventurine a curious glance.

"But you kept tabs on us," she hiccupped. "You knew what Mick and I were doing. You knew about Paul, and Shep, and everything."

"I have sources," he said dryly.

"You sound like Genevieve." She scrubbed her cheeks with the handkerchief; it smelled like Burroughs. She clutched it tighter between her fingers. "You sound *just* like Genevieve."

Swales smiled again, that enigmatic smile. It said so much, and so little. "Strange, isn't it?"

The door opened again, this time with a prolonged tinkle of bells: four people entered, pulling off hoods, their faces reddened. Whatever were they doing here so early? Whatever were they doing here in the near-winter? *Some people*, Swales had told her on their first meeting, *come to see the sights in summer.* It had been an invitation then, rather than a jibe, but now she lowered the handkerchief to better glare at the interlopers. Mother, father, two kids—very cranky at being forced out at this hour, it appeared. She glanced at her watch: still too early for anything other than a coffee shop to be open yet.

"You know Genevieve," she said, circling back, lowering her voice as the newcomers scraped two tables together at the front. One of them whined about the Abbey, how the grounds weren't even open at this hour. Perhaps they should just scale the wall. People did it. She'd done it. Though that seemed a lifetime ago.

"I do," he said.

"And she knows how to find things out."

"She does."

"And she's been helping you out?"

The shrug. "Sometimes she helps. Sometimes she obfuscates."

Aventurine gave an appreciative nod. *Obfuscates.* That was exactly the right word. She felt Burroughs's knee against hers under the table. He'd finished his coffee, so she pushed hers toward him. Apparently, the jitters left him alone.

"Did you suggest she contact me? To write her story?"

"I might have put a word in."

That amused crinkle at the corner of his eye. Aventurine remembered that now, with a pang.

So many questions. Each one branching out into so many others.

"How long," she asked now, dropping her voice even further and leaning forward, "had you been working for—the government?"

Ernest Swales took a long time to answer. He stared down into the remains of his cup of coffee but made no move to signal the waitress for any more. He might have been looking for the answer to the question. "Most of my adult life," he admitted at last. "Since grad school. I was recruited then."

The research trips. Aventurine remembered them vividly from the time she was small. Sometimes their mother accompanied him, sometimes not. Sometimes she and Micheline had gotten to tag along, but rarely; mostly they had stayed with friends of their parents for a couple of days, a couple of weeks. They had thought nothing of it, having remembered no other way. Wasn't everyone's father an academic who researched and published books? Didn't everyone's parents take trips to other countries a few times a year? Aventurine frowned, turning her memories over, examining their undersides. When her father was away, her mother seemed less lively, until she became incandescent at the sound of the phone ringing. And Michelle Morrow crossed off days on the calendar in the kitchen.

"She loved you so much," Aventurine murmured, closing her eyes, the better to remember.

"And I got her killed," Swales said bitterly.

As they were leaving the café, Swales turned to them, his shoulders hunched against the morning wind that tunneled down the street. "I need to see Micheline before I leave."

Aventurine nodded. "She should be here today, already. I'll let her know. What should I tell her? Should I prepare her?"

Swales squinted as he looked over his shoulder toward the swing bridge. "You know her best of anyone. Tell her what you think she needs to know. Then text me. I'll do the rest."

"And then you'll go."

"And then I'll go."

Aventurine put out an unsteady hand and let it rest on Ernest Swales's arm. His left arm, with its ruined hand. She tried to tell herself that she'd done without him for more than twenty years, and she would be fine once he had disappeared into the shadow world again. But this—losing him the second time—was more difficult than she realized it would be.

"Why?" she asked, trying to make her thoughts coherent. "You wanted to see me. You want to see Mick. Why did you wait all this time?"

Swales looked away, down toward the river, where a small boat was making its way against the tide, and then back. "Because it was all going to hell, I realized." He put his good hand over hers. "We had been so careful. All of us. And now we were on the edge of being found out."

"Found out?"

He didn't meet her eyes.

"By whom?"

The silence stretched, and she knew. Of course she knew. She had known all along.

He looked away. "Nicola is—a spy."

There it was. Out in the open.

"Agent is probably a better word. Or operative."

"So, has she been hounding all of us because of you?"

Finally, Swales cast her a look, and it was sorrowful. Or full of pity. With a slight tinge of self-loathing. "Originally? Yes. With you? I think part of it might have been curiosity, maybe envy. You said she found out about her mother—and me—by reading Bethany's hidden diaries."

Aventurine thought of the conversion in the Italian restaurant in Paddington. "I think she guessed before then—she said something once about coming across my page on Amazon. I think that set her on a search for something to confirm our—relationship—and that's when she stumbled upon her mother's diaries. It was confirmation, then, rather than discovery. Then, of course, she did the DNA test."

Surprisingly, Swales winced. "Wrong move in this line of business," he said bitterly. "Amateur. Genevieve would have a field day with that. Commander Smith, as well, had such a thing been around while he was doing his work."

Aventurine cast him a look. "You *really* sound like Genevieve when you talk like that."

Swales shrugged and poked his walking stick at the dirt. "I've known her a long time."

"You've crossed paths," Aventurine hazarded. "In your line of work."

That awkward self-deprecating smirk. "You could say that."

"So, what about Nicola?" Aventurine was still having trouble sorting the timeline out. "She didn't know you were her father—" The words still felt painful, smacking as they did up against everything she'd ever thought she'd understood about her parents' relationship. But of course, the fact that she was standing on a street corner with Swales—Morrow—was difficult to fit with her understanding of the past twenty-odd years, as well. Her head was swimming. She tried again. "She didn't know you were her father until a couple of years ago."

"And by then, she had been charged with finding me."

"Finding you? You were *dead*."

"And, as I said, safe as far as one can be, when one has been grievously injured in a car wreck, and then smuggled out of the country to recuperate somewhere far away, and to embark upon an entirely different life." He took a deep breath. "The picture—the fluke—the thing that showed that I might not be dead at all. But, Aventurine, I knew too much. Still. *Daniel Morrow knew too much.* That's why your mother and I were run off that road. That's why we were meant to die. And that's why, if we were found out, there were— operatives—out there who were charged with finishing the job."

Twenty years.

That *was* a *long game.*

Genevieve had not been kidding.

"And that's why I have to go, Aventurine. Let me know about your sister. Don't take too long."

Abruptly, Swales turned to walk on, his hands in the pockets of his coat; his shoulders were hunched, as though expecting—something. Blame? Aventurine registered once again his hitching gate, one of the many scars of an accident on one of the most dangerous roads in the world. She watched his back, which she remembered, as a child, as being much broader, much stronger. Now, he was just—a man, beaten, sad, one who had long outlived the life he had known.

He paused at the corner of Grape Lane and waited, leaning heavily now on his stick: it had been a long morning, she realized with a pang, for him. "I'm sorry," he said when they'd closed the gap. The apology hung. It could have been for anything, for everything. "Text me when you hear from your sister."

And then he was gone, lost in the maze of alleyways in the Old Town. Aventurine shook her head, trying to clear it. Unsuccessfully. He lived somewhere on East Cliff, but she had no idea where. Not that it mattered, since, once he saw Micheline, he would disappear out of their lives again. Most likely, this time, for good.

The sob caught in her throat as she scanned the early morning traffic. Aventurine felt Burroughs's hand on her arm, and she turned to him, her knees weak, and buried her face in his chest.

Thirty-three

They were making their way up the stairs to Khyber Pass when Aventurine's phone rang in her pocket. Micheline. They moved along the pavement until they were hidden from view of the road by the coffee shop.

"I'm here. I'm in a little room in a bed and breakfast on Crescent Avenue."

"Have you heard from Paul and Lance?"

"They're supposed to be here this afternoon sometime. I think they've got a room in the Old Town."

Aventurine looked up into Burroughs's face. "Listen, Mick," she said, lowering her voice. She stepped closer to Burroughs, out of the wind, perhaps out of sight of anyone looking their way. "I figured out why we're supposed to be in Whitby."

An indrawn breath. "What is it? Genevieve?"

Avi squeezed her eyes shut. "No. Listen, I can't tell you on the phone. Can we meet someplace, not your room and not mine?"

"Are you being followed?"

"I really don't know." Again, she looked around nervously. "I wouldn't be surprised."

"Nicola?"

"I wouldn't be surprised."

"Too many of us will attract attention."

"You're sounding paranoid."

"Careful. I'm sounding careful. And I'm channeling Genevieve. Or Mary Wentworth."

Burroughs's head came up sharply.

"Someday," he said slowly, "you might tell me the entire story."

"Someday."

They split up, Burroughs heading along the East Terrace and Aventurine turning onto the North Terrace a few moments later. The wind was picking up with the turn of the tide; the ice cream shop was huddled against the coming winter. The coffee window, though, was open, and Aventurine bought two, an Americano for herself and a flat white for her twin. Then she wandered toward the parking lot beside the Pavilion and down onto Cleveland Way.

Her legs were sore by the time she got to the beach huts, and she'd managed to spill some of her coffee onto the back of her hand. The tide was near full, squeezing the beach to a narrow strip beyond the safety railing. This was perfect; no one would spot them from below, anyway. She juggled both cups into one hand and checked the doorknobs on each hut as she passed: red-green-yellow-blue-red-green-yellow-blue. All locked. Until the blue one that wasn't; it had a hasp and padlock—most had keyholes flush in the wooden doors themselves—and someone had pried it off at some point. Glancing over her shoulder, she pushed the door open—there was no window in it—and slipped inside.

It was as empty as one could expect a beach hut in early December to be, though there were a few upturned crates, and evidence of clandestine use: two bottles stood guard just inside the entrance, one empty, one with cigarette butts floating in the dregs. Aventurine kicked one of the crates to the side and sat on it gingerly.

She had nearly finished her coffee when a shadow passed by the half-closed door and then paused.

"Avi?"

"Come on in. Close the door."

Aventurine flicked on her phone flashlight as Micheline slipped in and leaned against the door.

"How did you know there'd be one we could get inside?"

Aventurine made a face. "There's always one. It's a rule of beach huts." She handed Mick the remaining coffee. "You weren't followed?"

The cell phone lay on a third crate, the beam of its light pointing up into the rafters.

"I don't think so. I dawdled, looked at the waves a lot. Took some pictures."

"Nice work, Mary Wentworth."

In the odd lighting, Micheline cast her a wry glance.

"Now it's your turn to be Mary Wentworth," she said, sipping her coffee. She made a face. "Why meet like this? What's with the extra layer of secrecy?"

Aventurine leaned closer, threading her fingers together. She licked her lips. "There's no easy way to say this, Mick."

Micheline's expression was of impatience. "I've heard the worst from you," she said, her voice quavering slightly. "Just say whatever it is you have to say."

A pause. Then, again, "I know why we're supposed to be here, in Whitby."

When Micheline raised an eyebrow, the light from below gave her face a slightly macabre cast. "And that is?"

"Dad's alive. And he's here."

All right? Burroughs texted.

She sent a thumbs up.

All clear, he messaged.

They had been in the dim light of the beach hut for nearly an hour, Micheline still, her lips white. She had listened to Aventurine's explanations with only an occasional question. The battery on Avi's phone was dying, but she had the foresight to have brought a portable charger.

"But what has this got to do with Shep's death?" Micheline demanded harshly when the story had run down. "Shep helped Dad go into hiding. Now Shep's dead, and Dad's still alive." She shook her head as though to remove the spiderwebs. "I don't understand the connection. I know there has to be one, because none of this can be coincidence."

"There is a connection," Avi said. She looked down at her hands. The pages from the logbook were in her bag, but she was loath to bring them out to show her twin sister. "It's—Nicola." Now she took a deep breath. "Dad—Daniel—I don't know what to call him. He wants to see you before he disappears again. Probably forever. He wants to explain."

Micheline squeezed her head between her hands. The lighting from below made her face seem skeletal, all hollows and darkness. "What if—what if I don't want to talk to him?" Her eyes were black and glittering. "Nicola. She killed Shep, didn't she? *Didn't she?*"

Slowly, Aventurine nodded. "I—think so, Mick."

Micheline seemed to be shrinking before Aventurine's eyes. Now she pulled out a cigarette pack, shook one out, and lit it with a shaking hand. She took a long draw and then held it before her in her bony fingers, examining it like it held answers to all her questions. "I think I see her everywhere," she said, wonderingly, bitterly. "She's come to inhabit my entire life. At night, I think she lies in bed with me."

Aventurine could only imagine how that felt.

"She stole my husband from me, Aventurine, and I despise her for that." In the dimness, Micheline's eyes glittered, but she sounded as though she were far too exhausted to cry. "She stole my husband from me, and then she just—threw him away. Like he didn't matter. Like I didn't matter."

"We don't matter to her," Aventurine agreed. "She's got an objective—we don't know what it is, maybe revenge for being the outsider—and she's been messing with us, all we are and all we have in life, to gain that objective. We don't matter to her, except as some sort of curiosity. Women who conveniently share her looks, so she can slip in and out of our identities."

"We're *sisters*."

"But we're not family."

"Shep promised—in his letter—that we'd see each other again." Now, Micheline looked at the cigarette between her fingers as though confused about how it came to be there. When she took another draw from it, the skin around her lips wrinkled in a way that gave evidence to just how many she had smoked since she'd taken up the habit again. "And she took that possibility away from me. She *killed* my husband, Aventurine."

"I know." Aventurine closed her eyes, but that was a mistake. Again, she saw Shep's body, his arm flung out, inside the trunk of the car; she saw the blood. She saw the wedding band.

"She slept with my husband, and then she killed him. So, I don't want anything to do with her—unless it's to stick a knife into her stinking rotten heart. I don't want to know about her relationship to Dad, I don't want to know anything about her motivations—" she spat the word out like poison—"I just want her dead."

Aventurine was horrified. "I've never heard you say anything like this."

"I've never felt anything like this. Hatred, Aventurine. I feel *absolute hatred*."

There was no answer to this raw admission. Avi nodded again.

"Except—" and now Micheline's voice broke, the snarl becoming a sob. "I hate her. If our father has anything to do with her, I hate him. I hate what's happened to my family. But—and I hate myself for this—I *need to know*." She stood stiffly. "So, take me to him, Avi, and let's get this thing over with."

A quick text to Ernest Swales—**where? when?**—and she followed her sister back into the blustery day.

Aventurine expected Burroughs to be at the top of the pathway from the Pavilion. She didn't expect him to be with Gio.

Burroughs's smile was pleasant, though his eyes were hooded.

Gio stepped forward, but there was a hesitancy in his expression.

"I'm glad to see you, Avi," he said. "My stage crew seems to have vanished. But here you are—can you help me out with tonight's show?" He waved a hand back toward the row of hoardings along the windows. He leaned in against the wind. "You are coming tonight, aren't you? All of you?" His smile widened. "I mean, you don't still hate me, do you? That thing with Nicola—it was all a misunderstanding."

At the sound of Nicola's name, Mick stepped forward, her green eyes still blazing.

"Aventurine might not hate you, Gio, but I do." Before anyone realized her intent, she drew back and delivered a hard slap to his right cheek. He staggered but didn't fall until she pushed her way past him and continued toward the parking lot.

Aventurine shrugged. "Sorry, Gio. Not available."

Burroughs shook his head and held up his hands, then followed the pair of them as Gio slowly climbed to his feet.

Thirty-four

"I'm in Whitby."

Quite frankly, Aventurine was surprised that Genevieve had answered the phone, even more so that it had only taken a single ring to connect.

"I've told you not to go there."

"But you never told me why."

There was a long pause.

"So now you know."

"Now I know."

"I hope you realize that you're going to ruin everything. If you haven't already."

"I might be able to fix everything. Or at least bring everything to a head. Or out into the open."

"Don't be stupid, Aventurine. These are not amateurs you're up against. We've spent more than twenty years trying to keep this entire situation under wraps, and you might have just undone everything in a matter of moments." Genevieve was angry, though her voice was controlled.

"Let's try months." Aventurine was surprised at how angry she was as well. Just a while ago she would have bowed her head and backed off in the face of Genevieve's chastisement, but now she straightened. She was developing a spine. It felt good.

"Have you seen the others? Are they being as reckless as you are?" From York—if she was in York, in the gloomy house in Scarcroft Road—the sound of Genevieve's disgust was plain. To have put a plan in motion more than twenty years previously, and then to have it all in danger of crashing down, just when you thought it was safe: Aventurine could imagine the wheels in the old spy's head turning, turning. Planning how to sort out this mess people—people she trusted? No, she didn't trust anyone—had made of her operation.

Her *long game.*

Avi was still confused, but she was beginning to see glimpses. Was beginning to see the loose threads that she could tug at, to unravel the secrets. The years of secrets.

"I've seen Daniel Morrow. I've talked to Micheline. I'll see Lance and Paul when they arrive later today. And I've seen Dominic Burroughs," she added defiantly. "But no bad guys yet. We might have outsmarted them this time." Aventurine said nothing about the dresser again blocking the door. She hadn't seen the bad guys coming—the bad *woman*—this entire time, and had been surprised and ambushed at every turn.

Mary Wentworth her ass, she thought bitterly. Aventurine was obviously not cut out for this spy business, no matter how Genevieve had tried to train her. She'd never make a decent operative. What a disappointment she must be to the old spy. Aventurine just stopped herself from playing the world's tiniest violin.

"Don't use that name." Genevieve's voice was sharp. "Daniel Morrow is dead. He died in a tragic car accident with his wife. Your mother."

Aventurine threw up a hand, though she knew the old woman could not see. "Fine. We will, as you say, *play it your way.* But yes, I have seen Ernest Swales. Who is very much not dead."

"He's the undead." Genevieve laughed mirthlessly.

"No, you've got your characters mixed up."

But the old woman ignored her.

"Is he there with you now?"

"No. We split up. Went our separate ways."

"That's best."

"But you know I'm going to see him again. You know that. Because he's the one who brought me here."

Nothing from the other end.

"He's the one, Genevieve, who sent me *Dracula.*"

The sharp intake of breath was almost gratifying. "Damn him," Genevieve hissed. "Damn him. Why would he risk everything like that?"

"Because, like you, what he reads into this whole situation is that it's about to collapse. He thinks there's only a limited time before he's discovered. Possibly killed. For real this time. And he wanted to see me. See us." Aventurine thought of their childhood, of Mick's being the favorite, the one who had been named after their mother. The miracle baby. The surprise. The child who now felt beyond betrayed by her father.

And she was going to bring them together. Aventurine hoped it would reconcile them, rather than blow them further apart.

Thirty-five

"She was just a child, twenty years ago," Aventurine said. She still couldn't see the part Nicola had played; at the time of the accident, she had to have been only in her early teens, if that. The timeline made no sense.

Micheline leaned back on her heels, as far from Ernest Swales as possible. Her arms were crossed, her thin face nearly cadaverous. Resuming smoking had caused fine lines to form around her mouth. She looked as though she wanted a cigarette now.

"Did you know she was your daughter?" Mick asked at last. Her voice held a note of raw fury and pain.

"I didn't know she existed," Swales protested. "Your mother and I: we'd argued about my—*traveling*—we'd hit a rough patch and separated." He grimaced now, looking out to sea. They were along the footpath to Robinhood's Bay, and the wind buffeted them. They were well away from town, and even the Abbey ruins were no longer visible, once they had passed the holiday park. "The thing with Bethany—was nothing. A one-night stand. I felt dirty, and guilty, because I *was* dirty and guilty." He wiped his good hand along his bearded jaw. "Bethany didn't know anything about my family. We had no further contact. I had not known that Bethany had had a child."

"You never told Mom."

Swales shook his head. "I couldn't. I don't know if you can understand this. The thing about your mother is that she had such faith in me. Such faith that I was a good man. So I never told her what I was and had been all our lives together. I never told her what I had done, once we got over that rough patch, because I didn't want to risk our relationship, our lives together. And I didn't want her to believe any less of me." He swallowed and looked down. "I kept pushing that one night away, further and further away, until I had convinced myself that it had never happened. For years I did that. For the rest of our married life I did that."

Aventurine chewed her lip; Micheline squeezed her hand convulsively until her knuckles ached. She could feel the waves of anger rolling off her sister. All of this was confusing, infuriating— despite having known, on some level, from the first time she'd seen the photograph of Nicola in Henry Hallsey's hand. Henry didn't know about this, Nicola had said. Aventurine found herself sincerely hoping that he would live the remainder of his life never finding out. It would be bad enough for him to lose a daughter, but to lose all faith in his beloved wife as well? Perhaps even his faith in the world as a whole.

But at least, at last, it was confirmation. Aventurine leaned her forehead into Micheline's shoulder for just a moment. As soon as Micheline had told her that Nicola was a *cousin, half-sister, or grandmother*—Aventurine had had the sinking feeling in her chest, had felt as though their entire lives had been built on quicksand.

Nicola was their father's daughter. The thought echoed.

"It wasn't until recently I found out that she—had also been recruited. Because of who she was."

Aventurine's head shot up. Beside her, Micheline was very still. Ernest Swales did not look at either of them.

"By the other side."

"But—"

Eyes burning, Micheline stood and took a few steps toward the cliff edge and then turned again. "She was coming for you. The whole time. Through Shep. *Through my husband.*" Her teeth were bared. "She was coming *for you.*"

Aventurine's brain felt sluggish. She couldn't quite understand. Micheline's fury was building; had Ernest Swales been closer to the edge of the cliff, no doubt Micheline would have hurled him headlong into the sea.

"She was playing a long game," Swales agreed.

Genevieve's words.

"My husband was trying to help. All that time ago. Trying to help you."

"Yes."

"And then that one thing he did for you—way back then—came back more than two decades later *to get him killed.*"

"Yes." Swales's voice was as bleak as the clifftop on which they stood.

"I think I'm going to be sick," Micheline said. And indeed, she had gone even paler than usual, and her hands were shaking. She turned away again quickly, looking out over the ocean. Aventurine eyed the distance between her sister and the edge warily. Mick wasn't the suicidal kind: if she was, she would have done it in those deep, dark days after Shep's disappearance. But still, each of the revelations about their parents, about their half-sister, about Shep's unwinding fate, was a blow, each more difficult to withstand than the last. Each towing its own kind of grief in its wake.

Helplessly, Aventurine put out a hand to her twin.

Micheline jerked away. "No. Don't. I don't want anybody to touch me." Her voice was high and brittle. She might have been glass. She might shatter.

Aventurine threw the only lifeline left. "Not even Paul?"

Micheline turned, the expression on her ghostly face slowly collapsing in on itself. She raised her hands slightly but then sank down in the dying grass. The sobs that wrenched their way from deep inside her were agonized. She knelt, leaning into her shaking arms, her keening sounding very like the gulls which circled overhead.

Aventurine knelt beside her, hands on knees, not touching. Helpless.

"But—" Aventurine tried again. She desperately wanted to take Mick into her arms, to comfort her, to let her know that, although things were not all right and possibly would never be all right again, at least they were not all *wrong*. Micheline had now sat back up on her heels, staring outward, tightly compacted around the bright, hard knot of her grief and anger.

"Say it," Swales urged. Roughly. As though he, too, were close to tears.

"Your own daughter—is the one charged with finishing the job. With finishing you. Your own daughter."

He nodded. "Nicola. Yes."

You hate me, don't you? Gio had pleaded, back on the West Cliff. But he had no idea, she marveled, to what depths hatred could go. Nicola: to discover that your entire existence was not what you had thought; to discover that your biological father had had nothing to do with you your whole life; to discover that there was a way to seek vengeance. To feel that there was a need for this kind of vengeance, and the feeling knew no bounds. This was hatred, an all-consuming hatred, and this was the furnace that drove the engine that was Nicola. Aventurine gasped with the horrified wonder of it.

And Micheline, who had professed a profound hatred of Nicola. Aventurine put out a hand but could not bring herself to touch her twin. Could not bring herself to be rejected.

Avi glanced around hurriedly, but no one else was on the Cleveland Way—and she could see for miles, back toward Whitby, forward toward Robinhood's Bay. The bluff on which they huddled commanded a view of the cliff, the sea, the fields undulating inland. Nicola would not be able to surprise them; they would see her coming.

But—if they did see her coming, what could they do? Aventurine glanced around for an escape route. Genevieve would surely have one. Surely, Swales—Morrow—who had orchestrated this meeting and chosen the location, would have one as well. Boat? Car? How far away was the closest road?

The problem, of course, was that any escape route could also be a way for someone to get to them.

Nicola had always seemed to act alone. A lone she-wolf.

"I don't know whether she was handed this particular job *because* she's my daughter," Swales continued. "Whether she took it on before she *knew* she was my daughter—or whether she took it on *because* she knew she was my daughter." He was back to looking out to sea, though Aventurine was not sure he was really looking; still, his thoughts were traveling along the same routes hers were. "As you've probably figured out by now, I've spent most of my time over the past several years trying to avoid her side." His tone was bitter.

"And you're no longer safe here," Aventurine said. "In Whitby."

He glanced over at her from under his grey brows. Brow. "I'm not safe anywhere." His mouth worked.

Her knees were aching, her jeans becoming damp from the ground. "No, I get it. You're probably not." Aventurine licked her lips, risked a hand now to Mick's shoulder. Her sister did not respond, not even to shrug her off. Avi didn't know whether this was forward motion or retreat. "I'm fairly certain that when I was here last, she was here, too."

He nodded. "You think she was the one who pushed you off East Pier."

"I'm sure of it." Again, Aventurine looked around. The cliffs and fields were still empty and bare. Somewhere far off a dog barked, and another one answered. "You know I was down on the pier with a friend."

"Your policeman."

It was too cold to blush. Avi touched her free hand to her face anyway. "He left, and almost immediately, I was pushed. It was as though she was waiting for me to be alone before she acted. Then, with me in the sea, Nicola followed Burroughs back to the 199 Steps and ran a knife into his back."

Swales too looked around, his expression calculating. "I told you that I had heard of that attack on the grapevine—there wasn't much about it in the news. I didn't realize that he was your friend. I should have expected that." He grimaced, returning his gaze to the pair of them, still kneeling at the cliff edge.

"Even before that, the car Burroughs and I had been driving had been sabotaged—and we ended up in a hedgerow, thanks to his defensive driving training, rather than plastered across the grill of a panel truck."

"You think Nicola was responsible for that, too?"

Aventurine frowned. She shook her head to clear it, but it was no use. "Logically, she probably would be, but logistically, it gets more iffy."

"What do you mean?"

"She had been in Milan a couple of days before. Lance had seen her. He thought it might have been me. He sent a picture." Quickly, she searched her pockets for her phone and showed him, thanking heaven once again for her foresight in backing everything up in the cloud.

Was that another spasm of pain passing over Swales's face? It disappeared far too quickly for Avi to be able to tell. "I'm always surprised at how much she looks like you two," he murmured. "It's incredible."

"So, if she was in Italy, she couldn't have been in Hay-on-Wye sabotaging Burroughs's car."

Swales handed back the phone. He looked down at Micheline and did not approach. "A lot can happen in a couple of days," he countered. "It takes two hours to fly from Milan to London. It takes three hours to drive from London to Hay."

"No," Aventurine protested. "Literally a flying trip?"

"You don't know what she was doing in Milan, really, do you?"

"Other than spying on Lance and Paul?"

Swales looked at her and shook his head in mild disappointment. It was the same sort of look she had seen from Genevieve, whenever she had said or done something the old spy considered to be especially obtuse.

"What's her interest in Lance and Paul?" he asked.

Slowly, Micheline struggled to her feet. If her face had seemed cadaverous before, it was now a death mask.

"She tried to kill them in Portugal," Mick ground out, her eyes blazing at their father. "In Sintra. She caused an accident at the Initiation Well. Fortunately, Lance's sprained wrist was the only result—though other people were taken to the hospital."

Swales nodded and gulped. "I'd—heard about that. It wasn't an accident, then."

He didn't look as though he believed it was. Micheline's glare burned brighter, and her lips thinned, pressing together.

"For someone who is causing this kind of havoc," Swales said slowly, glancing between them, "she's being rather haphazard about it."

"She's tried to kill me, Burroughs, Lance, and Paul."

"Unless she hasn't," Mick said. She held Swales's eyes. "Tried to kill them. Because she knows how to kill. Shep—" she caught her breath. "Shep's murder proves that."

Aventurine knew immediately what she meant. And that she was right. If Nicola had really wanted them dead, they would be. All the other attempts had been rather hit-or-miss. As though the result really didn't matter. "I thought—these things might be warnings. But I couldn't figure out what the warnings were for."

"They were for me."

"You—"

Shifting uncomfortably, Swales drew his own phone from his pocket. After thumbing through it for a second, he handed it to her.

A photo of Paul and Lance in what was recognizably Milan, drinking coffee at an outside table, a waiter dressed in black with a long white apron carrying a tray in the background.

"*What is this?*" Micheline was leaning in to look.

"This was sent to me through—channels," Swales said uncomfortably. "It appeared online, among a selection of pictures promoting books by N. B. Hallsey."

"It's them. It's Lance and Paul. In Milan." Aventurine looked up, feeling her eyes widen. Her hands, suddenly, were shaking. "She took a picture—it was online, attached to her professional name—why?"

Again, the grimace. Swales shifted again, as though in pain; Aventurine wondered fleetingly what he might be feeling as a residual of the accident all that time ago. "Because she meant it to get around to me, wherever I was hiding in the world."

"I don't follow," Avi said.

"I do," Micheline said.

"There have been others. Mostly of you, Aventurine. Once or twice of you, Micheline." He flipped through the photos until he came to one of Avi seated at a white-covered table, a half-finished salad before her. The Italian restaurant in Paddington. Nicola must have taken it before she'd done her flit.

"I'm still not getting it." Aventurine's head was beginning to pound. "On her author page?"

"She wants me to know how close she is to people—people I love." He looked up, his one good eye haunted. "Have you ever read *The Spy Who Came in from the Cold?* by John le Carré?"

Aventurine shook her head. Micheline did as well.

"The Brits get the Russian spy to come over to them—out of the cold, in the parlance—by letting him know they have his daughter."

Aventurine lifted her head. "Nicola. She's trying to get you to turn?"

"Not quite that." But Swales's expression did not change. "She's trying to flush me out of hiding."

"By letting you know how close she is. To me, and to Mick. And to Paul."

She reached for Micheline's hand again, and this time there was no resistance. She squeezed. The one thing they shared: their son.

All this time Aventurine's fear had been that the police—Dominic Burroughs—would find out what Paul had done, that awful night up on the York walls. When her fear should have been about Nicola. His half-aunt. Who was taunting Ernest Swales—Daniel Morrow. *We've killed your wife. We've killed your son-in-law. We can get your daughters. We can get your grandson.* She stared in horror at Swales. Morrow. Who was her father, come back to life.

"And when I come out of hiding," he said slowly, "she'll eliminate me."

"Eliminate you?"

Swales looked around again at the deserted landscape, obviously still very uncomfortable.

"I told you. Daniel Morrow knows too much."

"Daniel Morrow has been dead for more than twenty years."

"Shep Genthner was dead for more than a year," Micheline reminded them, her voice dripping with bitterness.

"And this is a long game." Of all the things Genevieve had told them, this, it turned out, was the most truthful.

"This is what I was afraid of, why I hadn't tried to contact you for all these years. I got your mother killed. I couldn't risk the both of you, too." Swales's voice lowered. "Once I knew she existed—I didn't realize Nicola would be the one to come for me this way. I never thought she'd go to such an extent, just to flush me out. That's why I've got to go."

"Today?"

He nodded. "I've caused too much destruction. Too much grief and pain. I can't risk causing any more."

"But Paul?" Aventurine demanded. And Lance, too, since they'd thrown their lots together. "You haven't met your grandson."

"And it's best I don't, don't you think?" Now Swales's voice held an awkward wistfulness. "He's lived all his life thinking I'm dead. Probably it's best to leave it that way." He sighed. "It would be easier for him if I remain a myth, rather than become a reality."

Micheline squared her shoulders. "Yes. It's best. Paul is the person I care about most in the world, now that you've managed to get my husband killed."

Swales looked even more stricken, if that were possible. "I know. And I will never be able to tell you how sorry I am."

Mick looked away. "Save it. Save it and just go."

Two people and two dogs appeared, scaling a rise to the east. Swales immediately became more formal, though it was unlikely they could hear from that far away. "It's time for us to split up anyway. We've been together long enough, and if anyone asks those people, for example, we'll be remembered. It will be remarked upon." He smiled, holding out a hand. Awkwardly, Aventurine shook it, resisting the urge to throw her arms around this ghost.

"You can't just leave," she hissed.

"It's been good to meet you," Swales said loudly. "I hope the rest of your travels are pleasant."

"There's so much—"

"I know. Thanks for letting me see those pictures. They're very beautiful."

With that, he readjusted the cap on his head, and, leaning on his stick, limped his way on the path. He paused briefly to pet the dogs and then disappeared over the rise.

"He can't just go—" Avi repeated, aghast, staring at her sister.

"Let him," Micheline said. Though her voice was not much more than a murmur, her fury was still obvious to Avi's ear. "Let him go. We're better off without him anywhere near our lives. Look what it's got us. Look what I've lost because of him."

They let the couple with the dogs pass, and then Aventurine took Micheline's resistant arm, to follow them back toward Whitby. Nicola would not be coming from that direction; Burroughs was stationed at the trailhead and would have messaged had he seen anyone.

Nicola. Her endgame was the death of Daniel Morrow. Her father. Their father. Because he knew too much, he had said ambiguously.

But more than that, because of the grievance against him—against all of them—that went way back to the discovery that had disordered her world.

Thirty-six

"**B**ecause of him, Because of our *father.*"

There was nothing else to say to this. It was true. Convoluted, but true.

"He blames himself for Mom's death," Aventurine attempted.

"He should." Micheline spat, then threw her cigarette to the path and crushed it underfoot. She bent to pick up the butt and put it in her pocket. "*Spies.*" She spat again.

Micheline said it as though *spying* was a game, like darts or snooker. A game that Daniel Morrow had been playing. A game that Genevieve Smithson was still playing. A game that risked everything—*for everyone else.* Through which they cruised unscathed.

Except. That Daniel Morrow had not emerged unscathed. Aventurine looked along the cliff toward the ruins of the Abbey, which pointed accusingly to the gunmetal sky. She could still hear the pain and despair in Ernest Swales's voice as he spoke of his wife, dead more than twenty years. Then too were his physical injuries, the scars on his face and hands, his missing eye, the limp that hindered his walk. And since his convalescence—wherever that had been, however long that had taken—he had not worked for the government. And for however long, he had been hidden—holed up here, in Whitby, among other places.

And Genevieve?

Who knew what scars, physical and emotional, that old woman carried. Who knew how she had learned to live with them for nearly eighty years.

"I'd like to imagine that our father was working for what he envisioned as the common good," Aventurine said slowly. "I'd like to imagine that he believed he was working against evil. Otherwise, I can't bear it. I can't bear any of it."

"But—your husband wasn't collateral damage."

"No."

"Mine was trying to help. Trying to help Daniel Morrow. And then, look what it got him. Look what it got me. And Paul."

Micheline's fury and grief were raw, open to the unforgiving sea air. It was difficult to listen to. They walked on, and Aventurine watched in impotent sympathy as Micheline drew out another cigarette, her hands still shaking, only now so hard that it took two matches to light up.

"Mick. Stop. Shep was trying to help you. Us. If Daniel Morrow had not been our father, would he have flown down to Brazil to retrieve Mom and Dad's remains?" The memory of the confusion of the days after the news had come to them gave her a sharp pain in her ribcage. "You know he wouldn't have. You know he did that for you."

"Don't you dare lay this at my door." Micheline's teeth were bared.

Aventurine threw up her hands. "That's not what I'm trying to do, Mick. You know that's not what I'm trying to do." She looked back down at the water to their right. She couldn't see the base of the cliff below the path: was the tide flowing in or out? "You know Shep found our father and helped get him out of the country, to safety."

Micheline took a long drag on another cigarette, her eyes narrowed. "I *don't* know. I don't know anything about anyone or anything anymore. That's my problem. All I know is that my husband is dead. Knifed in the back, left in the trunk of a car like so much trash." She pressed her free hand against her mouth to stifle a sob. "After he'd been seduced by a woman pretending to be me. I can't think of anything else. I can't get beyond that."

Aventurine covered her own face with her hands. *Gio had been seduced by a woman pretending to be her. And Burroughs—Dominic— had been knifed in the back.*

They were coming along behind the Abbey Brewery now, and Aventurine could see Burroughs, seated on one of the park benches, not looking very comfortable at all. He rose to his feet when he saw them approaching. A dog, off its leash, loped up to him, and, as she watched, he bent down to rub its ears. Something in her chest constricted. She could have lost him, before she'd had a chance to really know him. Would she have felt the same level of rage as Mick, had Nicola succeeded?

"We have to figure this out, Micheline," Aventurine pressed. "We have to think about what to tell Paul. We have to decide what to do about our father. Ernest Swales. Daniel Morrow."

"No, Aventurine," Mick snarled. "We have to figure out what to do about Nicola."

The way she said the name was ugly. Aventurine had never heard her sister sound—nor look—so dangerous.

Part IV:

Cataclysm

Thirty-seven

Aventurine woke from her exhausted doze to find the hotel room empty once again. And dark. She hit the button on her watch: nearly five-thirty. She felt achy and disoriented. Still an hour and a half before she had to meet Mick, Paul, and Lance for dinner, over in the Old Town.

No Burroughs. But she had expected that: on the pillow beside hers was still the note he had written out for her on the clifftop and had handed to her, having waited instead. *Called to Lincoln. Back soon.* She had tucked it away but now rolled over to turn on the bedside lamp and look the note over again hungrily. A promise, in his cramped and squared-off handwriting. A note to her, this time, rather than about her, in that little notebook of his. She missed his presence; even when he was silent, she felt him near. Aventurine sighed. She was getting it bad; she knew the signs.

She washed her face and combed her hair, trying to shake her mood. *Stay safe,* she had directed Micheline, who had refused to come back with her, preferring to head off toward the Crescent and her own guest house. *Don't do anything stupid.* But Aventurine still felt the niggling unease in the back of her thoughts: she had never seen Micheline in the desperate rage she had shown this afternoon. There was something chilling about it. But—they could hash it out over dinner, the four of them, trying to figure out what to do about

Nicola. Together. How to prevent Micheline from becoming some lone wolf bent on a personal vengeance. Paul might know what to say, how to appeal to his mother's emotions, right her ship. Or Lance, with his calm practicality. Together they might be able to come to some intelligent course of action. And, barring that, they could carry it all back to Genevieve in York and lay it in the center of her spider's web. She would know what to do, in a way that would punish Nicola without Micheline being implicated.

They just needed to temper Mick's fury.

There was no use waiting around here; Avi could walk. She grabbed her things, swinging her jacket around her shoulders, then moved the dresser and let herself out. She locked the door behind her and checked it twice to be sure; but of course that didn't matter. Nicola had gained entrance before, basically at will, and she could do it again. If she appeared. Aventurine threw up a little prayer that their subterfuge, leaving Lisbon separately and arriving in Whitby separately, had bought them some time: after all, Nicola couldn't follow all of them; she would have had to make a choice. And with any luck, Nicola would not arrive in Whitby until they'd all had an opportunity to disappear again. They just needed to stay one step ahead of her until they formulated a plan.

But they didn't even know what she wanted with them, if it wasn't Daniel Morrow.

Unless she didn't know he had gone into deep cover. Deeper cover.

Something skittered at the back of Aventurine's mind, like a mouse in the corner of a darkened room. She shook her head, trying to shake it free, worried that, in the light, it would disappear entirely.

Aventurine took the stairs to the lobby. She was crossing to the front doors when the desk clerk flagged her down.

"I've got a message for you," she called. "Miss Morrow?"

Aventurine turned back, puzzled. She thanked the clerk, then moved away from her curious eyes to open the envelope with her name on it. Who delivered messages when they could just text?

I've got our sister. I'm sure you can figure out where. Come alone.

The ink was brilliant green, and mocking.

Our sister.

Nicola had caught up with them.

Aventurine dashed across the road between a car and a lorry; someone honked at her, but she ignored it. Through the Whalebone Arch toward the steps down to Khyber Pass. In the darkness, the Abbey loomed over East Cliff; down at the waterside, lights shimmered and moved in the light rain. The afternoon's wind seemed to be building this evening to a gale, with the tide. Aventurine could hear waves from below West Cliff. Both piers crawled out into the water like curling black serpents; she could see nothing moving along them. Avi fumbled in her bag for her phone, thinking *Genevieve, Genevieve, Genevieve.* The steps were slick, and, when her foot came out from under her, she grabbed instinctively for the rail. The phone slipped from her hand. In horror she watched it, as if in slow motion, tumble through the air until it smashed onto the stair and bounced its way down.

She righted herself and sucked in a sob. At the bottom she found the phone, the glass smashed. When she attempted to power it up, the screen remained stubbornly black. She shoved it into her bag and hurried across to the abandoned coffee shop and the final set of stairs. Once down onto Pier Road, deserted in only the way the main street in a summer resort could be, she broke into a run toward the swing bridge. It wasn't long before her chest burned and her legs ached, but she pushed on, against the rain and wind, her lips tasting of salt that might have been from the sea, or it might have been from tears.

Micheline.

Mick.

Her sister. Her twin. Her other half. The mother of her son.

At the bridge she had to pause, doubled over, hands on knees. Panting loudly.

"Here," someone said, slowing beside her at the rail. "All right?"

She straightened but couldn't speak. She hoped the lights on the bridge wouldn't show her tears for what they were. She waved the man off with a weak smile and moved on quickly before he could inquire further.

Run, she told herself. *Run.*

Mick.

There were few people out in the wind and the rain; along Church Street she passed a pub or two, their lights looking bereft against the encroaching winter night. Each time Aventurine had to pause, leaning against the old stonework of the buildings along the street, she was conscious of wasting valuable time. Nicola had Micheline. Nicola had killed Micheline's husband. Nicola had probably been behind Lance and Paul's fall at the Initiation Well. Nicola had tried to kill Burroughs and Avi, together and singly. Anything could be happening out there in the burgeoning storm, and none of it good, she was sure of it. Micheline was in danger. Micheline even now could be injured, or dead—but her heart rejected that idea: she would *know.* Aventurine was certain Mick was still alive—but how much longer? How much time did she have? Her face and hair were streaming now, but Aventurine was barely aware of the cold or her wet clothing. There was only one thought in her mind. She pushed away from the wall and dodged around the foot of the 199 Steps to Henrietta Street.

At the Haggerlythe, she found herself staggering down the hill toward the end of the pier and slowed. It was difficult to see down onto East Pier with the dark, the rain which now slashed at her face in the angry wind. The brick barriers appeared only as a darker darkness; the red glow from the light tower at the far end seemed to mock her. If Nicola were out there with Mick, they would see her before she saw them. Her jacket was dark, as were her jeans; she pulled her hood up, to hide her hair, and forced herself to move carefully, to muffle her footsteps, though she could barely hear herself think over the crashing of the tide against the stonework. She forced down the rising terror at the sound, at the memory, and stepped out onto the pier itself.

Mick, she thought as hard as she could, wishing for a telepathic connection. *Micheline. I'm coming.*

Aventurine reached the first barrier and paused, huddling next to it, trying to hear something other than the surf. It was impossible. She peered around the end, trying to make out anything beyond it: shadow, movement. Nothing. Keeping low, she scurried along the base of it, leaning into the brickwork against the wind.

It was dangerous out here, she knew it, and was growing ever more so by every moment as the storm intensified. She desperately hoped Nicola and Micheline were sure-footed or sheltered by the last wave barrier out there. Still, the red light gleamed, like a reflection of the fires of hell. Aventurine bent as low as she dared and moved further out along the stone pier until she reached the next barrier. She could see neither of the other women along its length. Again, she leaned against it, listening, moving outward. If the pair of them had crossed the footbridge and were out on the extension, she'd have to follow them, she couldn't not—but the thought absolutely terrified her. Still, she had to get to her twin. She had to rescue her. Or, God help her, die trying. She put both hands against the end of the barrier, looking out at the last curve before the lighthouse and the footbridge.

They were nowhere in sight.

Had Aventurine guessed wrong? *I'm sure you can figure out where,* Nicola had written in her note. Aventurine had guessed the place where Nicola had tried to kill her before—but what if she was missing something? What if, even now, Nicola was terrorizing Mick somewhere else and, in jumping to this particular conclusion, Aventurine had ruined all chances of finding her twin? The sobs of fear and frustration were racking her, and she gripped the wall more tightly, the wind buffeting her. A sudden wave broke over the side and soaked her shoes.

Then she distinctly heard the voice.

"*Shit.*"

Aventurine turned and faced Nicola. Who was alone. And who, this time, held a gun.

Thirty-eight

A gun? Here? Aventurine was trapped at the end of the pier.
"What do you want with me?" she shouted. A moment of panic. "Where's Micheline? Where's my sister?"

In the red glow from the lens of the light at the end of the pier, Nicola's face showed more animal than human.

"*I'm* your sister. Did you forget?" The smile was smug, and ugly. So was the shrug. "I have no idea where Micheline is. She hasn't shown up here yet."

"*Yet?*"

Again, the shrug, but the gun, its barrel like a black staring eye, remained steady. "I only need one of you. And you got here first."

Aventurine let go of the brickwork with one hand, took a small step. Nicola raised the gun and smiled again. Her teeth shown whitely.

"And I'm sure you know what I want. If you haven't figured it out yet, Aventurine, you're even more idiotic than I gave you credit for." Nicola used her free hand to wipe the wet hair from her face. "I want Daniel Morrow," she said. "I want *our father.*"

Another wave broke and wet Avi further, this time to her ankles. There was a howl of wind, which died back as suddenly as it had sounded. "I don't know where he is," Aventurine protested. "He said he was leaving Whitby." She glanced over her shoulder; no help would come from that end, because no sane person would be out here in this rising storm. No one who wasn't so idiotic as to fall for this ruse of Nicola's, as she had done.

This time it was Nicola who took a step closer, the gun unnervingly steady in the wind.

"I'm gratified to know that your loyalty to Micheline would bring you out here for her. I'm trusting that her loyalty to you will bring her here soon as well. And I bet Daniel Morrow is still here somewhere— he wouldn't leave before you all do. He is probably still following you about. And he'll come for you, both of you. As he's done before." She grimaced, and again her teeth showed in the odd red lighting. "As he's always done."

There was a bitterness there, a fury. The sound of a resentful, abandoned child, carried forward into adulthood. This was not just professional, it would seem. For Nicola, her mission had long ago turned personal. As perhaps her handlers had known it would.

"He didn't know about you," Aventurine protested, scanning the dark pier toward the Haggerlythe, willing Micheline to stay away. "None of us knew about you. And Micheline and I have been without a father for more than twenty years."

"Don't give me that bullshit," Nicola snarled. Another step.

There was nowhere for Aventurine to go, no way to escape. The storm surf was building, the pounding against the base of the pier becoming louder and more frequent, the waves splashing up to soak them both.

"Nicola!"

Micheline, suddenly—appearing from behind the shelter of the first barrier. She was fighting her way toward them, against the wind.

"Mick!" Aventurine screamed against the storm, her voice shrill and hoarse to her own ears. "Mick, go back! Stay back!" Her view was momentarily obstructed by a splash of spray as yet another wave crashed against the pier. "Mick, she has a gun!"

"I don't care! She killed Shep!"

"Yes," Nicola said. "I did. I found him. I got what I needed from him. And I killed him."

Her casual tone was shocking, as she meant it to be. The words brought Micheline to a skidding halt, and again her face curled into the expression of absolute hatred that Avi would never have believed possible had she not seen it.

"You killed him," Mick screamed in fury. "And you left him in that car like—like—so much trash!"

"Your precious Shep," Nicola laughed contemptuously. "The love of your life. The man who slept with *me*."

Each word was like a blow to Micheline; she shrank back into the wind as though unable to bear the beating.

"He *was* so much trash, wasn't he?" Nicola continued. "A man who couldn't remain true to his wife. Who couldn't be loyal." Her smile was spiteful. "Because if he could betray you for me, who else do you suppose he was sleeping with? How many other women? How about Aventurine, here?"

"Never," Aventurine spat. She took a step, but then Nicola raised her gun hand and eyed down the barrel at Mick. A threat Avi couldn't face; she stepped back again.

"No," Micheline said. "No. You tricked him. He would never have done that had he known it was you."

"You don't know that," Nicola returned complacently. "And now you can never be sure. You'll go through the rest of your life wondering. Always wondering. Who else did Shep sleep with? For the rest of your life, Micheline."

"Stop it!" Aventurine shouted. She couldn't bear the agonized expression on her twin's face. "Nicola, stop." Wasn't it enough that she'd taken Shep away physically? Did she have to take him away emotionally as well? This cruel streak in Nicola was shocking and horrifying. How had their father engendered such a monster? How had Bethany and Henry Hallsey raised such a one?

But Nicola ignored her, still gazing along the barrel of the gun at Micheline. Her voice, raised above the wind, was savage. "He wasn't even a good lay, Mick."

"Nicola, I'll kill you—I swear I'll kill you!" Micheline's words contained all the grief, all the fury, all the need to avenge her husband's loss. Her husband's murder. They were echoed by the fury of the building storm. She leaned into the wind, her arms raised, her mouth open in a howl, and started across the expanse between them.

"No, Mick!" Avi cried again. "That's what she wants!"

Then, Paul. His arms came around Micheline from behind, and he dragged her back, into the lee of the barrier.

"Mom," he shouted. "No!"

The moment of distraction was all Nicola needed. She lunged, got an arm around Aventurine's throat, and pressed the cold metal of the gun up against her temple. "You're right," she laughed. "That's exactly what she wants. One of you will do as well as the other." When Avi grabbed at her arm, trying to free herself from the unyielding grasp, Nicola jerked back with her elbow, and Aventurine heard the snick of the safety unlocking. "Try me, sister," Nicola hissed into Aventurine's ear. There was a threat, but also some weird satisfaction in her voice. "*Sister.* We'll see how long it takes Daniel Morrow to come to your rescue this time."

It almost sounded as though she hoped he wouldn't.

"Aventurine!" Micheline cried, struggling against Paul's hold. She sounded despairing, like one of the Whitby gulls.

Again, Aventurine felt—and heard—Nicola's laughter...

"Hey! Paul," Nicola called. "Good to meet you. I'm your aunt! The one who's not your mother!"

Paul's face twisted in fury.

Nicola jerked Aventurine backwards, further away from the lee of the brick barrier wall. The stones underfoot were slick, and as each wave crashed into the pier, it threw water up and over them. Aventurine could taste the salt on her lips. When Nicola stopped abruptly, Aventurine nearly fell. She grabbed at Nicola's sleeve again, but Nicola tightened her arm against her windpipe until Avi gasped for air and stars whirled in front of her eyes.

Micheline tried to wrest herself from her son's grip. Paul held on. Lance had appeared behind him, his chest heaving from running. In the light from the tower, Aventurine could see the shimmer of Lance's dark face as he took in the scene in all its dangerous impossibilities. He looked terrified, and torn, as he pushed past to place himself between Paul and Micheline, and Nicola and Aventurine.

"Don't come any nearer," Nicola shouted. She jerked her arm back against Aventurine's throat, painfully, and the gun pressed coldly into the skin at Avi's temple.

"What do you want, Nicola?" Mick shouted now. "Tell me what you want."

"I want our father," Nicola hurled back. "Call him and tell him he comes down here or Aventurine dies, a bullet through her skull, and her body tossed into the sea."

For a moment, the other three froze.

The storm was building. Another wave broke, this time washing up and over Avi's shins. They would not be able to stand against the storm tide for much longer. Aventurine thought, panicking, that if Nicola didn't kill her, the waves would kill them both. Kill them all.

But—was that Dominic Burroughs, nearly bent double, running along the wet stones from the Haggerlythe? He zigzagged as he came, as though to make himself less of an easy target, should Nicola spot him and decide to fire.

"Our father?" Micheline repeated.

Stall, Mick, Aventurine prayed. Truly, had they ever shared anything vaguely resembling telepathy, now would be a good time to practice it. *Stall, Mick.* She could see Burroughs now edging closer, sticking close to the barrier, and soon, surely, Nicola would, too. But any time Mick could eke out was more time before Nicola's finger pulled back on that trigger. As long as there was half a second more time, escape was still a possibility.

She didn't want to die like this.

She didn't want to die at all.

Aventurine wondered what Shep had been thinking, in that moment before Nicola had stabbed him. Did he know she was about to kill him? Did he see his wife in his imagination, or his son? Did he plead with her for one more chance?

Her eyes blurred with the rain and the salt spray. *Dominic.* She could see him inching along beside the brick wall. Dominic, whom Nicola had already tried to kill once. Or perhaps twice.

Aventurine willed him to meet her gaze. *Look at me.*

Then again, *I don't want to die.*

"Call our father," Nicola shouted, intent upon her purpose. If anything, her arm across Aventurine's throat had tightened, cutting off most of her air. "It's your only chance to save your twin."

"Aventurine!" Micheline's voice was agonized, but she pulled her phone from her coat pocket and punched in a number.

Burroughs was nearly to Mick and Paul.

"Your boyfriend's here," Nicola sing-songed into her ear. "Isn't that just the sweetest thing?"

And then, as though fashionably late to this farce of a party: a figure hunched against the rain and wind and surf, pulling himself along with his stick. It was obviously hard going, with his left leg dragging. Ernest Swales. Daniel Morrow. He must have known they were out there. He must have been following one of them. Any of them.

Nicola saw him then. "Good girl, Micheline. Here he comes." Again, the triumphant, bitter laugh in Aventurine's ear. "I knew he'd come," Nicola snarled. "I knew he'd come for one of you."

Aventurine thought of kicking backwards, maybe knocking Nicola down before she could get off a shot, but they were so close to the edge of the pier, so close to the raging surf. They could both go over, and there was no guarantee either of them would be able to fight their way back to shore. Avi blinked against another soaking, a wave hurling itself over the stonework. Death by drowning. Death by having her brains blown away.

Dominic.

Aventurine didn't realize she had spoken the name aloud until she heard Nicola's bitter laugh again.

"I should have slept with that one, shouldn't I have, Aventurine?" she asked. "Or stayed to make sure he was truly dead, that night on the East Cliff."

Aventurine struggled.

"Don't," Nicola advised. The gun barrel pressed a little harder.

They were all there, on the storm-swept pier. Genevieve might have tried to move all the chess pieces, but it was Nicola who had succeeded, finally, in getting them all where she wanted them. She had played a long game to get to Daniel Morrow, and now, finally, she had succeeded.

"Nicola," he called, limping forward, unsteady against the wind. "Let her go. I'm coming. I'm the one you want."

Burroughs put out a hand to grip his arm, but Morrow shrugged it off. He stepped forward, out of the lee of the barrier, Burroughs close behind.

"Burroughs," Nicola shouted. "Dominic. Stay where you are, or I'll put a bullet through my sister's brain. You wouldn't want that, would you?"

Burroughs stopped. In the weird light, Aventurine thought she read agony on his face, but then the expression was gone. Maybe she had imagined it. The stars whirled behind her eyes now. Again, she considered her own death—her own disappearing from consciousness, from life. The possibility of never feeling Dominic Burroughs's arms around her again, of never hearing him laugh sardonically at something she'd said. Of never looking into those eyes, which, she had learned, were not icy in the slightest. Despite herself, Aventurine let out a sob.

Nicola let out a disgusted hiss.

"Let her go," Daniel Morrow ordered again. He took another step forward. He touched Micheline's shoulder on the way past, where she was still struggling, vainly, with Paul. "Let Aventurine go, Nicola. I'm coming." He held out his empty hand; a wave washed over the stones, and he staggered, leaning heavily into his stick, but managed to stay upright.

"At last. We meet. *Father*," Nicola shrieked against the wind. "Bastard! I should shoot you where you stand. Moscow wouldn't mind."

"Then what?" Aventurine had found her voice, raspy though it was. "You'll have eliminated your target. Then what? We're all here, Nicola. *All of us.* Will you kill us all? You don't have enough bullets in that gun."

"Shut up," Nicola shouted, her own voice strident. She jabbed the muzzle once more into the side of Avi's head. "I'll take him, and I'll take you. That'll be enough. Just shut up."

The arm around Aventurine's throat was taut, like a steel band, but she thought she felt the faintest of shudders.

"Aventurine!" Micheline still pulled against Paul's arms. "Do what she says! Just do what she says!"

"Don't do anything stupid, Aventurine," Dominic called. He took a step.

"Don't risk your lover's life, Dominic," Nicola taunted. Then, "Come on, Dad. Step out where I can get a clear shot."

Daniel Morrow took one dragging step forward, then another. The rain dripped down his eyepatch and across his scarred cheek. "Let her go, Nicola." He moved the stick forward, followed it awkwardly.

A glimmer of hope. Might he use it as a weapon, once he got close enough?

"Not until you're here. We'll wait." Another wash of water, and she staggered slightly, the arm at Aventurine's throat pulling. "All these years they've been looking for you, and I'm the one who's going to bring you down." Nicola sounded pleased. Proud. Again, the person who needed to do the most harm to all of them. "It took ages to play your daughters and your grandson, just to get you to show yourself— but here we are. And now I'm going to kill you."

The wet and cold were working their way inside: Avi's clothes and hair were soaked, her skin icy. The noise of the surf was deafening. Such had to have been the scene Bram Stoker had imagined when the *Demeter* ran between the piers and aground on the now invisible Tate

Hill Beach, with a crew of dead men, and an unmentionable evil in the hold. But they weren't dead, Aventurine reminded herself fiercely, and they far out-numbered the evil. There was a chance. There was hope. Maybe not for her—she let out another sob but then bit her lip—but the others would be safe. Micheline, and Paul, and Lance. And Dominic. The people she cared for most in the world.

"Dominic," she whispered again.

Nicola laughed.

Another wave, another crash, another soaking. Aventurine's knees were weak. Behind her, Nicola held firm. How much longer could they hold on? One rogue wave, and they'd both go over. Even now, another wave drenched Daniel Morrow, who leaned heavily into his stick. Not long before he'd be close enough. Not long now. It was only a matter of time before—what?

"What are you going to do once you kill him?" Aventurine demanded hoarsely. "He'll be dead, but you'll be trapped. You're outnumbered, Nicola. You're done."

"Oh, I wouldn't worry about that. I've got out of worse." Aventurine felt the shrug. "I'll just take another of you hostage, to get back to town. Then none of you will ever find me." The self-satisfied tone had crept into her voice again. "And I'll be out there, Aventurine. None of you will ever know where. I'll be out there, peering over your shoulders. Your lives will be hell."

"You won't be safe out there, Nicola. You won't be safe unless you disappear entirely." Another step closer for Daniel. "Maybe your friends in Moscow will have you. Maybe they'll decide you've served your purpose, and you'll get a Bulgarian umbrella to the thigh."

Nicola was having none of it. "You're close enough now. Ditch the walking stick."

Daniel Morrow let the stick fall to the stones, where it clanked and rolled away a few feet.

"Kick it away," Nicola ordered.

Daniel held up his hands. "I can't. I can't walk without it. If you want me, you're going to have to shoot me from there."

They were like a tableau, Aventurine thought dizzily. She and Nicola at the end of the pier, Micheline, Paul, and Lance entwined at the end of the barrier wall, Burroughs off to the side, and Daniel Morrow, leaning forward on the treacherous footing, fighting the elements. The surf crashing all around them. Cataclysm.

In the moment Nicola turned the gun away from her temple, Aventurine used the last of her strength to elbow her in the stomach. A shot fired close to her ear, deafening her, and she dropped to the stones, trying to gauge how far from the edge she was.

"Aventurine, stay down!"

Another shot, and in the confusion, she thought she recognized the voice, and her chest constricted. She lifted her eyes in time for the red of the light to pick out Gio's hurtling form. *Gio?* A shout, a scream, and then only the sound of the surf, crashing against the pier.

Thirty-nine

G*io?*

Aventurine lay still, feeling the freezing stone beneath her cheek.

She was alive.

Avi heard shouting, and then Micheline was atop her, sobbing. Sobbing. Slowly, Aventurine struggled to her knees, where her twin, soaked to the skin and with her face glimmering wetly, stroked her hair.

"You're alive, Aventurine," she gasped. Mick leaned forward, pressed her forehead to Avi's. "You're alive."

For the first time that she could remember, she turned from Micheline as Dominic Burroughs dropped to his knees beside her. His eyes glittered, his face pale in the eerie light.

"Aventurine," he said. His voice was thick. But welcome. So welcome.

"I'm alive," she said to him.

"Thank God," he said, and crushed her to his chest.

Forty

In the morning the lifeboat was still working the waterfront, but it was no longer picturesque to Aventurine. Now that she knew who it was looking for, the morbidity of it shook her to the core.

They had been interviewed by officers from Ryedale and Whitby and had been told to stay available for a team from Harrogate.

"Will we have to talk to people from—MI5?" Micheline asked, her voice shaking. She held a mug of chocolate in both hands, and was huddled inside her coat, but she still looked gaunt and cold.

Burroughs said nothing.

Daniel Morrow, who had joined them in the restaurant once the police had gone away, looked down into his tumbler, where the whisky glowed amber. "I won't say no. I won't say no to— elements—of the US government taking an interest. But I think that might happen, if it does happen, in the next couple of weeks, as the uproar dies back here." He slugged back the remainder of his drink. "For now, I think, we all just keep to the story of the lover's quarrel and its tragic ending. We don't know anything. *We just don't know.*"

Still, Burroughs said nothing. He met Aventurine's eye and held her gaze, steadily; was she mistaken, or had the blue become ice again? He knew more, from an investigator's experience, than he was letting on, she knew. His indefinite leave, she also knew, had become an official suspension until his part in the night's events had been cleared up. *Common practice,* he'd said.

"I've been honest," he said at last, "about what I saw. Anything else is just hearsay." He cleared his throat. "But I'm fairly certain that—the higher echelons—will be clamping down on much further available public information."

Now Aventurine looked around at the group huddled at the big table. This time of day, the place was well-lit, impersonal, all glass and metal. Strangely, she was happy about that; she did not want to be hidden in a corner any longer. She did not want to be cozy and secretive. She needed everything out in the open.

"Meanwhile," she said slowly, "what do I say to Henry Hallsey?"

After everyone had gone, Aventurine tried to call Genevieve on Burroughs's phone.

Straight to voicemail.

Bone-weary, after the long, long night, she let Burroughs undress her in the darkened room. Then she lay down, drawing the duvet up around her chin.

"The dresser," she said, not knowing anymore why it would be necessary. He did not question. He merely drew it up against the door. Aventurine was grateful for that, even as she was grateful for the length of him, sliding into the bed beside her and tucking her into his shoulder. She let her hand rest on his hip bone, buried her face in his chest. "I could have lost this," she murmured.

He caught his breath, then kissed the top of her head, lingeringly.

She dozed and was only vaguely aware of him climbing from the bed.

This time when she dreamed, her mother turned to her: the curve of her cheek, the kindness in her eyes. Aventurine felt the momentary shock of recognition.

"I've missed you," she whispered. "We both have."

Her mother smiled gently, and Avi thought she felt the touch of a hand on her face, a flutter of sensation. "I've been here," the familiar voice said. Familiar, but sounding so far away. "I've watched you."

"And—Nicola?"

"I wish I'd known," Michelle Morrow said. "We might have saved her."

Forty-one

He was dressed and seated at the table, scribbling in his little notebook, when she finally rolled over.

"What are you doing?" she asked. The bed felt wide and empty without him, but the lonely feeling was quickly replaced by impatience when he snapped the notebook closed and dropped a hand on it. She sat up and pulled the covers up under her arms.

"Nothing."

"That's your official policeman notebook, so it's not nothing."

He looked away. "Aventurine, I'm on leave. I'm probably not going to ever be able to work as an *official policeman* again. I've crossed too many lines."

There was something in his voice she didn't recognize. Confusion? Despair?

"Because of me." Aventurine felt as though she were probing a kind of wound.

"And I still don't know the whole story."

Was it always going to be this way between them?

Her clothes were folded atop the dresser. She reached for them, struggled into them, the impatience growing. "You know what, Dominic?" she demanded, buckling her belt and reaching for her red Converse, which were still damp. "This I don't need. Either you take me as I am, with what I have available to give you, or you head off down the line, back to Lincoln or wherever."

"Aventurine—"

"No," she said. She bent to tie one sneaker, and then the other. "Just no, Dominic. I had the hit-or-miss thing with Gio, where we never committed to anything. Never committed to each other. And I convinced myself that that was okay, that it was what I wanted. But I'm older now. And I know my value. I'm not going to be your lover when you forget your mistrust for just a moment. You need to know that there are some things which are not mine to give you. I'm doing everything I can, but if it's not enough—"

"Avi—"

Jacket next. Also still damp. Then she picked up her purse and slung it over her shoulder. "I'm going out, and I'm going to walk around town for a while. Maybe go down to the beach. I'm going to think. I'm going to feel the cold on my face and the wind in my hair, and I'm going to remember that I am alive and that I am valuable. That my time is valuable. You stay here and decide what I'm worth to you, because when I get back, I expect an honest answer."

Aventurine dragged the dresser away from the door, enough to get out. She left him seated at the desk and registered at the last moment that his shirt was buttoned crookedly, and his feet were bare. His blue gaze followed her until she closed the door behind her.

Outside, it was sleeting, the ice clicking on the street, on cars. Aventurine jammed her hat down onto her head and turned along the promenade, letting the wind off the water slash at her. She drew her shoulders back and stared at the sea, which had nearly taken her—nearly taken them all—last night. Somewhere out there were Nicola and Gio. She caught her breath. The water dared her to give up, to flee. But she had remained free of its clutches last night, and it would not win over her this afternoon.

Instead, she glanced up at the sky. She loved it, she supposed, all roiling and grey-scale. It, at least, was honest, without deception or subterfuge. The sky said inclement weather; the tiny slivers of ice thrown down by the bilious clouds were gathering at the edge of the pavement, a white sheen building against the brown and dead grass. The world was on edge, between fall and winter, and she welcomed that edge. It reflected her back to herself.

There were shadows that lived in winter, Aventurine knew, trudging toward the way down to the Pavilion. Across the Promenade, the buildings leaned toward the street, hulking, almost threatening. She supposed they had to be like that, standing guard, shielding the town from much of the wind off the sea.

Her shadow was long. In the west, a stripe of orange sky between the clouds and the spit of land that might have been Sandsend: sunset, after a particularly gloomy day. The sleet stung her skin. The streetlights would be coming on soon.

As Aventurine drew closer to the Pavilion, she turned into the lot and started downhill along the drive, her thighs protesting. In the window, she found that the posters for Gio Constantine had been removed, and that rekindled her odd grief. There would never be another poster for a show by Gio; it was as though a pillar of her life had been removed, and she was listing slightly. She paused and stared at the empty window, taking in the smudges where the tape had been pulled away. Gio had been a constant in her life for close to ten years, though a distant one for most of that time. Still, she had grown accustomed to his presence, and the thought of his no longer being in the world was surprisingly painful. Aventurine put a hand to her lips and blew the empty window a kiss. *Goodbye.*

She might have whispered the word, but even if she had, it would have been blown away by the wind.

Aventurine turned slowly and took the path down to the beach. In the near distance she could see the incongruous colors of the beach huts, and a single silhouette walking away toward Sandsend, leaving a darker trail of footprints in the wet sand. A cold walk, along the water in the sleet, but then she reminded herself that that was what she was doing and kept trudging down the hill toward the sand.

Down here she crossed the strip of beach toward the waves. Much calmer than last night: they seemed sullen today, the ocean slightly more grey than the clouds that rode the sky above it. The tide was nearly dead low and would be turning soon; the desultory waves, barely more than a white lace of sea foam as they tried to lap at her feet and failed, whispered resentfully to themselves. Aventurine blew out a breath, and the film hung over her head for a moment before swirling in the wind and disappearing. That was what it was like, she thought, life. A swirl—beautiful, if you were lucky—and then gone.

Michelle. Shep. Nicola. Gio.

Gone.

Others as well, but those were the ones who swirled before her and disappeared.

Michelle. Shep. Nicola. Gio.

She turned and headed down the beach.

As she approached the ramp leading back up to the Pavilion, Burroughs pushed away from the rail and turned to face her, his hands in his pockets, pushing back the tails of his coat. The wind ruffled the hair against his forehead.

"I'm here," he said.

Forty-two

They walked along without touching.

"Aventurine," Burroughs said at last, clearing his throat. There was an odd note to his voice. A thickness, a hesitance.

Avi came to a stop. Her hands clenched at her sides as she turned to face him. And waited.

"You need to know this."

Her stomach turned over, and she quickly thought to herself: *Micheline. Paul. Lance.* And then *Daniel.* But she had seen them all earlier, all safe. Gio was gone. Nicola was gone. But the others were safe. *Safe.*

Genevieve.

She licked her lips nervously. "Tell me."

I'm an old woman, Aventurine.

"Lance's great-grandmother." Burroughs's eyes narrowed, perhaps against the wind, perhaps because he understood the lie but would not be questioning it. "Genevieve. Smithson."

Aventurine closed her eyes, her chest constricting.

Old women die.

"She's—" Burroughs paused, as though having difficulty. "She's—been arrested."

It didn't register. For a long moment, she could only stare at him, trying to understand the words from his lips.

Genevieve was *not* dead.

"Arrested?" she gasped.

His blue gaze was level. It contained a wealth of understanding that surprised her. "Yes. For the death of Neil Barrett."

Aventurine put out a hand, but there was nothing to steady herself against. "Neil," she whispered.

It was a shock. That Genevieve would do this. And yet—not. She was an old woman, and she was throwing herself in front of a train. For Paul. For all of them. She had to wrest her attention back to Burroughs's words.

"It looks as though she's gone to the station in York and turned herself in to the senior investigating officer. It also looks as though the charge is probably going to be manslaughter, as her story has elements of self-defense to it."

"Manslaughter," Aventurine repeated stupidly. Her tongue felt thick in her mouth. "Self-defense?"

Burroughs nodded, watching her expression closely. "Yes. I've not got all the details, being on leave and all, but it sounds like he attacked her on her nightly walk, and she hit him with a walking stick, sending him over the wall." He cocked his head, still gazing on her face. "I haven't seen her confession, but apparently she made such a habit of walking the walls that there are plenty of people who will vouch for her, and the walking stick."

"But she was—arrested?"

"Pending ongoing investigation, of course. I guess her conscience finally got the best of her after all these months, and she turned herself in."

"Is she—in jail?"

"No. She's been released on bail. She's ninety years old—"

"Ninety-four," Aventurine corrected him automatically.

"Ninety-four, then." Burroughs took the correction in stride. "The York authorities don't believe she's a flight risk."

The urge to give into hysterical laughter was almost too much to bear. Aventurine turned away and covered her cold face with her hands.

Burroughs misunderstood her reaction. He put a hand on her arm. "I'm sorry, Aventurine. I didn't know it would affect you this much." When she didn't answer, he took her hands into his own. After a moment, she leaned into his shoulder, breathing in the scent of him. "I was thinking it might be best if you broke the news to Lance, as you know him that much better than I. I had no idea this would upset you so."

"I've just—known her for a while," Aventurine choked out. "I had no idea she would ever do such a thing." Let Burroughs take that for whatever he wanted. "I've got to tell Lance. We've got to go to her." The more she thought, the more she realized that signs that Genevieve might make this particular move were there all along. The old woman had had a soft spot for Paul ever since they'd met: teaching him to cook, talking to him about things he'd never said to either Aventurine or Micheline. At the last, she was doing this to protect him.

At the last.

Ninety-four.

Sirens were going off in the back of her mind.

Burroughs leaned back and looked down into her face. Then he kissed her forehead. "I'm sorry, Aventurine. And—I'm sorry I ever doubted you."

Again, she was forced to swallow the hysterical laughter. "You couldn't have known," she murmured, closing her eyes.

"But you told me," he insisted. "You told me that you didn't kill him."

"If it looks like a duck—"

"Oh, shut up about the damned duck," he chuckled. "Oh, my darling woman, shut up about that damned duck."

Part V:

End Game

Forty-three

"Are you sure this is all right?" Burroughs asked, not for the first time, as they alighted on the platform in York. "All of us? Showing up together? It might be too much for her. It might be a bit of a shock to an old woman's system."

"She expects us," Lance said. "All of us. She told me to text her once we knew what time we'd be in Scarcroft Road."

Something in his voice made Aventurine glance over sharply. His expression gave nothing away.

"And did you? What was her reply?" Aventurine fished around in her pocket for her paper ticket, since she could not use her phone for a digital one at the barrier.

Lance looked away. "She hasn't answered yet."

Paul snorted. "She's probably making a cake for our arrival."

But when they turned into Scarcroft Road, Aventurine could see that the heavy curtains were drawn, and the light was on next to the door, as though they weren't expected until after dark. Something about the cold darkness of the house made her doubly conscious of winter. Or of that night in July, when she and Lance had found the door unlocked, the occupant missing. She hurried on ahead, bounded up the pair of stone steps, and let the heavy knocker fall. It thunked metallically, hollowly. She knew, even before the others clustered around her on the pavement below, that there would be no answer. She knocked again, but without hope.

"Text her again, Lance," Micheline urged. "Or call her. Let her know we're here."

Lance dutifully pulled out his phone.

Aventurine, holding her breath, turned back to the door and turned the knob. *Turned the knob.* The door, and its myriad of locks, was unlocked.

"Burroughs," she said urgently over her shoulder. "Dominic?"

Without waiting for him, she pushed forward. There was mail on the carpet just inside, and the door crushed it against the wall.

"Don't go any further, Aventurine," Burroughs ordered. "The rest of you stay outside. Someone call the police."

"She might be ill," Aventurine protested over her shoulder. "She might be injured." Then, "Genevieve?" she called, and listened for an answer, any answer. No light showed under the door to the kitchen at the far end of the hallway. *"Genevieve?"* Evading Burroughs's outstretched hand, she swung around the newel post and dashed up the stairs. "You look in the downstairs rooms."

From the landing, she could see the light from the door of the old woman's bedroom, opened a tiny crack. "Genevieve!" she shouted again, louder, panic rising. There was no answer. The first floor sounded hollow and empty.

Aventurine's footsteps dragged now as she approached the door. She could hear the others on the stairs behind her. With a shaking hand, she took hold of the knob and pushed.

Genevieve lay back on the pillows of the bed, her eyes closed, her lined hands holding the edge of the duvet at her chest. The chest which did not rise and fall with her breath.

The room was strangely cold.

"Genevieve?" Aventurine said again, her voice small, lost. She knew that there would be no answer.

The others would reach the room momentarily. She stumbled toward the bed but stopped short of touching the old spy. Instead, she took in everything. The neat hair, the waxy skin, the tiny veins in the closed eyelids. The chest which did not rise and fall.

Slowly, Aventurine reached out a trembling hand to touch the old woman's fingers. They were cold. So cold.

Slowly. Slowly. Aventurine leaned forward and kissed Genevieve's cheek, something she would never have dared do in life.

A book lay on the bedside table, and Aventurine, in shock, only half-registered it. When she put out a hand to steady herself, she felt the worn edges of the jacket under her fingertips, and she clutched at them convulsively. The ringing in her ears was growing louder.

"What is it?" Burroughs appeared in the doorway.

Clutching the book to her chest, she looked up at him. "She's dead," she said, confusion making her voice rise almost in a question. "Call 999. Genevieve's dead." She took a step backward, stumbled, righted herself.

"Don't move," Burroughs ordered. "Don't touch anything."

He brushed past her, already drawing his phone from his pocket. Shaking, Aventurine looked down at the all-too-familiar cover in her hands: her own book. She dropped it from her numb fingers and watched it tumble away. It came to rest open and face-down on the carpet. A folded piece of paper, yellowed, had fallen out.

Stiffly she stooped to retrieve it. Thick paper, it crackled slightly as she unfolded it. A document. Avi blinked, blinked again. A birth certificate.

Daniel Moreau.

Mother's maiden name: Genevieve Smithson.

Father's name: Honoré Moreau.

The pain came between her ribs, sharp, a stab. Aventurine staggered slightly, reaching a blind hand out for the doorframe. She could hear Burroughs finishing the call, then moving toward her, but she did not turn her head. She did not move her eyes from the faded print in the serried boxes of the birth certificate.

Daniel Moreau.

Again the pain.

Daniel Morrow.

Acknowledgments

Many, many thanks have to go to the following, for helping to make *Aventurine at Sea* come to life:

To Deirdre Wait, who not only has dreamed up the gorgeously atmospheric covers for Aventurine to wear, but was instrumental in pushing her—and me—beyond the first book. Believe me, no one (including me) would ever have known what happened to Shep without her. While we're at it, let's throw Eddie Vincent and Cynthia Brackett-Vincent into the mix, because I'm a better writer and a better human for having these people in my life.

To the orthopedists at Maine General Hospital, especially Doctor Ian Patten, who turned me into the Bionic Woman after I blew out my knee on the Whitby train, and made further adventures, and further research, possible.

To my brother Christopher Britting, who died way too young, but who had a habit of naming cats after famous Russian spies.

To Teri Brown, Heidi Conroy, Lynne Doble, Karen Ward, Donna Fox, and Jean Govoni, because researching in Lisbon and Sintra would not have been any fun without you all. Special thanks to Heidi, my all-time favorite librarian, with whom I descended into the *Poço Iniciático da Quinta da Regaleira*, without falling down the circular staircase into the bowels of the earth. Next stop, ladies—Venice!

To the members of the Writers' Workshop class, who put up with me and my scenes, hoping I'd mention them on this page. Hello, Weird Kids! What would I do without you?

To Olivia Knapp and Adeline Niles, who got me thinking about the kind of apocalypse Phil Rickman tended to tie his books up with (*Candlenight* comes to mind). Part IV of this story is for you. Oh, and thanks to the enormously missed Phil Rickman for writing all those books. Aventurine went to Hay-on-Wye because of Merrily Watkins, actually, and to Llanthony Priory because of Prof Levin.

To Oysterband, who are waving us a long, long goodbye, and who have been a mainstay of my musical life for too many years to count. I can't imagine writing stories to any other soundtrack. The theme song of *Aventurine at Sea* absolutely has to be "Over the Water," unless it's "Sail on By." Or is it "Roll Away"? Ian Telfer, John Jones, Alan Prosser, Al Scott, Adrian Oxaal, Sean Randle (as well as former members and friends Dil Davies, Ray "Chopper" Cooper, Lee, Pete Flood, and of course, June Tabor, and the sorely missed Rowan Godel): I owe you a lot. And I'll miss you terribly. Also, thanks, Alan, for calling me "tenacious" at the New Forest Folk Festival; that made the summer, wrenching this story into shape, bearable. And Tim Porter! Tim, the sound engineer who tells me how to fix vacuum cleaners and sump pumps from 3200 miles away.

To Ian Blake, as always, for caffeination, adventures small and large, pints at the purple splendo(u)r of the Sussex Arms, all the Sunday Zoom meetings, and all those afternoons of research help. You have been a Very Important Friend since that soft day in Southwark. Thank you for taking me seriously. Don't forget the coaster!

And of course, to Rebecca Bearden Welsh and Brenda Sparks Prescott, because, as always, *these things are Simply Not Done.*

About the Author

Anne Britting Oleson lives and writes in a small town in Central Maine. A frequent traveler to the UK, she has published eight novels including *The Springs* (March 2023), and the Aventurine Morrow Thrillers, *Aventurine and the Reckoning* (January 2022), *Aventurine on the Bailgate* (September 2023), *Aventurine on the Border* (June 2024), and *Aventurine at Sea* (July 2025), as well as four poetry chapbooks. She has three children, seven grandchildren, and two cats. Follow Books by Anne Britting Oleson on Facebook and @annebrittingoleson on Instagram for the latest news.

If you enjoyed this book,
please consider writing a review
and sharing it with other readers.

Many of our authors are happy to participate in
Book Club and Reader Group discussions.
For more information, contact us at info@encirclepub.com.

Thank you,
Encircle Publications

For news about more exciting new fiction, join us at:

Facebook: www.facebook.com/encirclepub

Instagram: www.instagram.com/encirclepublications

Sign up for the Encircle Publications newsletter:
eepurl.com/cs8taP

* 9 7 8 1 6 4 5 9 9 5 8 7 6 *